THE FEAR OF LETTING GO

Fairhope, Book 4

SARRA CANNON

Dead River Books

For Casey
Whether by blood or by choice,
some people are a part of our families,
and our hearts, forever.
So glad my brother chose you.

CHAPTER 1
JENNA

The music is loud tonight, just the way I like it.

"Can I get another beer down here?"

I slide my empty bottle across the counter toward Knox. He nods and pulls a cold one from the cooler beneath the bar.

"Keep 'em coming," I say.

Next to me, my best friend Leigh Anne laughs. "You're like a bottomless pit," she says. "How can you eat almost an entire pizza and still have room for a six-pack of beer?"

I shrug and grab a handful of peanuts from the bowl in front of me. "It's a gift," I say. I don't mention that it's probably a product of being hungry most of my life, never entirely sure where my next meal might be coming from. When I was growing up, when someone put food in front of you, you ate as much of it as your stomach could fit.

It's a rare Saturday off work for me, and with school out for spring break, most of the college crowd is ready to party. It's good to see so many people out at Rob's tonight. Since

Knox took over, helping his uncle and his cousin Jo get the business back on its feet, they've been growing into the best hangout in Fairhope.

"We should dance," I say. I grab Leigh Anne's hand and drag her protesting ass onto the dusty dance floor.

"You know, I always took you as more of a rock and roll kind of girl," she says, shouting over the music.

"Me? No way. I'm a country girl, through and through." I take her hands in mine and twirl her around. Between school and my job at the restaurant, I've been working entirely too hard lately. I need a little bit of fun in my life, and dancing is just what the doctor ordered.

The small dance floor is crowded with sweaty bodies, and I pull her right into the middle of them. All I want to do right now is dance until I feel sweat trickle down the back of my neck. For just a little while, I'd like to forget about my ghosts and let go.

An old George Strait song comes on, and I loop my arm in Leigh Anne's and pull her around. She finally gives in and smiles.

Half an hour later, we stroll back to the bar, our hearts racing and our eyes shining.

I down the rest of my beer, which isn't quite so cold anymore, and ask for another. "That wasn't so bad now, was it?"

Leigh Anne shakes her head and laughs. "Everything's fun when you're around."

"Damn straight," I say, knocking the bottle on the counter twice for emphasis. "I haven't had a weekend off in ages."

"I haven't either. Not here in Fairhope, anyway." Leigh

Anne has been traveling up to Boston most weekends lately, getting ready for her upcoming testimony against a famous movie star who raped her a couple years back when she was in school there. "It's nice to be home for a change."

I squeeze her hand. "How have things been going up there?"

She shrugs. "As good as can be expected," she says. "Some of the media has died down for a while, but I know it's just going to start back up as soon as the trial begins in a couple months."

"Assholes," I say. "They don't care about the people involved. They just want a good story, however they have to spin it."

"It's only going to get worse," she says. "I'm scared to death."

"It's going to be fine," I tell her. I know how difficult it was for her to stand up and tell the truth about what happened. "No matter what happens, in the end you can know you told your side of the story."

"Yes, but I'd also like for Burke Redfield to spend the next ten years rotting in some jail cell instead of making multi-million dollar movies."

"He will," I say. "Five different women testifying about what he did to them? There's no way that bastard is walking free. I promise you."

Only, I know I can't promise anything. With the money and influence a guy like Burke has behind him, there's no telling what will happen come May. She knows it and I know it, and nothing I can say is going to take that fear away from her.

Which is why we both could use a little let-loose time in our lives.

"Either way, I'll be right there behind you every step of the way," I say. "I just have to figure out where I'm going to stay while the trial is going on. I need something cheap and from what I'm learning so far on the internet, Boston doesn't really do cheap."

She laughs. "That's true, but don't worry about it," she says. "I told you Penny and Preston's family is already making arrangements for everyone."

Preston. Dammit. Why does the sound of his name always send tingles down my spine? I can barely be in the same room with him these days without getting a hot flash. And Preston Wright is not the kind of guy I need to be getting all hot and bothered about. In fact, he's exactly the kind of guy I need to stay twenty feet away from at all times.

"I know, but it doesn't feel right to take charity from them."

"It's not charity," she says. "They want to help. Besides, it will be great to have everyone together in one place, away from the media circus. They're looking into renting a couple of neighboring houses in a nice gated community. No press access. If you stay in some hotel, we'll barely see each other."

I nod and plant a big kiss on her forehead. "I'll do whatever you want, sweet-cheeks. Just say the word."

"Don't go kissing my woman in public," Knox says, sliding another beer toward me. He leans over the counter and pulls Leigh Anne into a whopper of a kiss. The kind that makes your knees go weak.

The kind I haven't had in entirely too long.

"I can't help it if she's in love with me," I tease.

"I love you both," Leigh Anne says, but her eyes are locked on Knox's.

God, I want what they have someday. How exactly does one find a love like theirs? I guess they say it happens when you least expect it, but I have never expected it. Not a single day in my whole life have I ever really believed someone like me could ever have something like that. Where I come from, true love is nothing more than a fairy tale. And fairy tales are dangerous.

I take another sip of my beer, letting the cold rush of it go straight to my head. My eyes roam across the crowd, and I'm feeling that itch again. I don't need true love. All I need is someone good enough to get me through the night.

CHAPTER 2
PRESTON

I suppress another yawn. Amici's is the most romantic restaurant in town—and the most expensive—but tonight I can barely keep my eyes open in the dim light of all these candles. The soft music in the background isn't helping.

And it's only eight-thirty.

It will be a miracle if I survive this date.

"Like I was saying, there's just something so incredibly magical about the sunset down there," Iris says. "Have you been?"

I shake my head and take a quick sip of my water. I wish I could just pour the whole thing on my head, ice and all. "I'm sorry, where were you talking about again?"

Iris smiles. "Aruba," she says. "I went with my family on vacation last summer, and I was just saying how much I enjoyed it. As long as you don't wander too far off from the resort, it's breathtaking down there. I was asking if you've even been?"

"Oh, no. I haven't been to Aruba," I say. I look around for the waiter. Where the hell is he with our food, anyway? I feel like I've been sitting here for three hours.

"You really should go sometime," she says, resting her chin on one delicate hand. She flutters her eyelashes at me, and I wonder if she's having a good time or if she's as bored as I am. "Do you have a favorite beach?"

"I like Fairhope's beaches," I say. And it's true. I've been on dozens of family vacations over the years, visiting beaches from Montego Bay to Ibiza, but to me, there's nothing quite like home.

Iris apparently disagrees. She scrunches her nose and shakes her head. "Fairhope is nice, but I don't like the water on the Atlantic," she says. "I'm talking about real luxury vacations where you stay in private suites with a personal concierge and a swimming pool all to yourself. Clear blue water as far as the eye can see. There's nothing like that here in Fairhope."

She gazes at me, her eyes twinkling in the candlelight that flickers between us on the table. I know that look and something deep in the pit of my stomach turns sour.

"You know what would be a riot?" She pulls her arms up close to her body and raises her eyebrows in excitement, as if she truly just now had this amazing idea and hadn't been intentionally steering the conversation to this exact sugges- tion. "We should go for spring break. Just drop everything and head to Aruba for a week. Wouldn't that be amazing? Let's be spontaneous."

For emphasis, she reaches across the table and strokes my hand.

"I bet we could have a lot of fun in Aruba, don't you

think? Just the two of us?" she asks. Then, she casually adds, "Do you think you could borrow your dad's jet for a night or two?"

Just once, I would love to be surprised.

I sigh and pull my hand away. Normally, her proposal might be tempting. A beautiful beach with a gorgeous girl? That should be a no-brainer. But I am getting sick and tired of people always looking at me like I'm some money tree. Does this girl even like me as a person? She barely knows me. This is our first date and already she's planning week-long vacations to luxury resorts. With my father's jet, no less.

"That sounds amazing, but I can't leave town right now," I say, leaning back in my chair. "My twin sister's baby is due soon, and I wouldn't miss that for the world."

Iris swallows and sits up. "Oh, I thought Penny's baby wasn't due until next month," she says, doing her best to hide her obvious disappointment. "I completely understand, though. Maybe this summer."

"Maybe," I say, knowing full well there will be no Aruba vacation with this girl. There will never even be a second date. I wish for once a date had actually wanted to get to know me as a person rather than skipping right to the topic of how to spend my father's money. I try to change the subject. "You're majoring in Communications? That sounds interesting."

"Interesting? I hate it," she says. The waiter sets a plate of steaming lobster linguine in front of her and she pauses and thanks him. The lobster is the most expensive thing on the menu. "My dad pretty much told me that if I wanted him to pay my tuition while I was down here, I better get a respectable degree. Honestly, though, I have no intention of

8

going to graduate school like he wants me to. I've been thinking about taking a few years off after graduation and maybe going to Europe for a while. That is, if I don't have a good reason to stick around Fairhope a little bit longer."

Her eyes linger on me a beat too long before she glances down at her pasta.

I study her for a second. She's beautiful. Long dark hair. Long eyelashes. A slamming body. She comes from a wealthy family over in Mobile, and I know my parents would approve of her in an instant. So what's my damn problem?

I twirl a fresh noodle on my fork, watching it spin in circles. That's all I've been doing for the past twenty-one years. Spinning in circles, living the same life day after day. And yes, I realize how ridiculous that sounds coming from a guy like me. After all, I was born into the wealthiest family in the state of Georgia. I have access to a private yacht, a family jet, a huge estate with tennis courts and swimming pools. Everything I could ever want is right at my fingertips.

So why am I feeling restless? I don't want to take any of it for granted. I know how lucky I am to have the things I have. But at the same time, something is missing. Something big.

And I'm not going to find it sitting across from me tonight at dinner.

I glance up and she smiles, but it looks forced and I feel guilty. "I'm sorry I'm not great company tonight," I say. "I think maybe I'm coming down with something. I haven't been feeling right all day, to be honest."

Her shoulders fall and she sets her fork down. "It's okay," she says. "If you want to get out of here, I'll totally understand. Maybe we can do this again some other time?"

"Finish your dinner," I say, not wanting to be a complete jerk and ask for a to-go box. "Tell me again about that beach in Aruba."

§⋆

I DROP IRIS OFF AT HER APARTMENT BY NINE-THIRTY. That has to be some kind of record for the fastest I've ever gotten out of a date, and I know I should head back to my place or maybe see what Penny and Mason are up to. But instead, I find myself driving to Rob's. I tell myself I'm only going there because I want to catch up with Leigh Anne and see how things are going with the trial preparations, but I know there's more to it than that.

I'm hoping Jenna might be there tonight.

I'd overheard them talking the other day, saying they both had the weekend off from work over at the restaurant, and even though I told myself it was none of my business, I immediately regretted already having a date set up with Iris.

Had I really expected this date to be any different from the dozens of others I'd gone on since I broke things off with Bailey? She and I had been going out, off and on, for almost four years. I finally cut ties with her around Christmas, knowing I was only holding her back from finding someone who would really appreciate her. Someone who would fall head over heels in love with her. Which is exactly what happened, as it turns out.

But I'd be lying to myself if I said I didn't have an ulterior motive in wanting to be single for a while.

So why haven't I gotten up the nerve to ask Jenna out? I would have much rather been out with her tonight instead of yet another girl who cares more about my money and my name than she does about me.

But there's something about Jenna that makes me nervous for the first time in as long as I can remember.

Probably because there is a very real possibility that if I ask her out, she'll laugh and say hell no. Out of all the girls I know, she's the only one who might actually like me less because of my money.

Still, as I park my car and walk into Rob's, I can't help but search for her among the crowd. I stand by the door, my eyes scanning the bar and then the dance floor.

I catch sight of a wisp of blond hair and a pale, creamy shoulder. The dark ink of a tattoo peeks out from the top of her shirt as she moves. Her eyes are closed and she's completely in the moment, not caring what anyone else in this room thinks of her. What would it feel like to be so free?

"You just gonna stand there by the door or are you gonna come on in and buy a drink," Knox shouts, and I realize he's talking to me.

I smile and nod, reluctantly pulling my eyes away from the dance floor. Leigh Anne is sitting down at the other end of the bar, and I walk over to her. She's got a glass of water in front of her, but I don't miss the fact that there's a half-empty beer bottle sitting next to it. I leave an empty stool between us and sit down.

"What can I get for you?" Knox asks.

"I'll take a Jack and coke," I say. "Anything to erase the memory of yet another bad date."

Leigh Anne pats my shoulder. "I thought you were going out with Iris tonight?" she says. "She seems so sweet."

"Sweet and practically ready to elope in Aruba," I say. "I

feel like it's getting to the point where I can count the minutes until my dates start talking about how to spend my father's money."

"Oh, poor little rich boy and his hard life." Jenna reaches for her beer and laughs. She's out of breath from dancing and sits down hard on the stool beside me. "I can't imagine what a hardship that must be," she says, raising an eyebrow. "All the pretty girls clamoring for your attention, hoping you'll whisk them away to some exotic resort and make mad love to them all week. Poor you."

"Trust me, it gets old," I say, already feeling stupid for complaining about it. I probably sound like a spoiled child.

"Oh, I don't doubt it," she says. "Yet you keep right on trying, don't you?"

"What's that supposed to mean?"

"Ignore her," Leigh Anne says. "She's working on her sixth beer at this point."

Jenna laughs. "I think I'm done after this one," she says. "What other trouble you think we can get ourselves into tonight?"

My stomach does a weird flip. Man, I could think of about a hundred things I'd like to get into with her right now.

"Don't look at me like that, Preston Wright," she says. "I wasn't talking to you."

"What? I wasn't looking," I say.

Knox sets my drink in front of me, and I practically down it in one gulp. Liquid courage, so they say. Maybe one more of these and I'll finally get up the nerve to ask Jenna out.

"Well, don't look at me," Leigh Anne says, standing. "I

promised Mom I'd go to church with them in the morning, and I have got to get home and study for a couple hours before I go to bed. All this travel has put me way behind."

"You're going to church with your parents?" Jenna asks. "I don't see how you can be so nice to them after the way they've treated you."

Leigh Anne gives a sad smile. "I know, but they're trying. That's got to count for something, right?"

My heart aches for her, and I hate that I've been a part of her sadness. Leigh Anne and I dated all through high school. We were one of those perfect golden couples everyone expected to get married and have babies. Long story short, I cheated with Bailey, one of Leigh Anne's best friends, and Leigh Anne left for Boston the following fall.

Just goes to show she's one of the nicest, most forgiving people in the world for not still hating me after what I did to her.

If I could take it back, I'd do it in a heartbeat.

"Girl, you are a way better person than I could ever be," Jenna says. "You're such a marshmallow. If I were you, I would have told my mother what I thought of her a long damn time ago."

Leigh Anne turns her head to the side. "Come on, it's my mom," she says. "Yes, she's a bitch, but she's blood, you know? You can't turn your back on family."

Knox pulls Leigh Anne into a kiss, but I notice a strange expression on Jenna's face as she turns away. I want to ask her about it, but it scares me a little. I've never seen her look that sad before. Her eyes fill with tears and she looks away for a moment.

"I'm going to head out. I'll talk to you guys later." Leigh

Anne gives Jenna a quick hug. "Don't drive home, okay? Get a cab or have Knox or Preston take you home."

"Yes ma'am." Jenna raises her beer in a salute, all signs of sadness quickly wiped away. "Maybe I should get going, too. There's not a single guy in here worth sleeping with."

"I beg to differ," Leigh Anne says as she gives Knox a wink and heads for the door.

Jenna rolls her eyes. "Save it for your private time," she says with a laugh. She starts to stand, but I put my hand on hers and her eyes widen.

"Don't go," I say. "Come on, have one more drink with me. I'll call my driver to come take us both home later."

"Your driver? What? He's just going to drop everything on a Saturday night to come pick you up and drive you home from the bar?" she says. She sounds amused, and she sits back down.

"That's his job," I say.

"Exciting life," she says. "Can you imagine what it must be like for him? I mean, let's fast forward a couple hours and say it's midnight on a Saturday night. What do you think he's doing?"

I shrug. "I guess I never thought about it."

"Do you think he's just sitting around his house with his uniform on, waiting by the phone? Hoping you'll call? No. He's probably been sitting in his recliner, watching some TV, snacking on some chips or whatever," she says. "Then, just when he's sure no one's going to need him, he strips down to his t-shirt and boxers and climbs into bed, all snuggly and warm. And then, dammit, the phone rings. Or maybe it's a text? The young master summons him to the bar downtown for a ride home. He has to get his ass up out of bed, throw on his work clothes and try to look presentable, all because the rich boy couldn't bring himself to pay for a cab."

"Hey, that's not really fair," I say, hurt. "It's not like he's a slave. He gets paid good money to get out of bed and drive me around."

The moment the words leave my mouth, I realize how incredibly snobby I sound. How childish and annoyingly privileged.

"Your dad pays him to drive him to work and important business meetings," she says. "You're just taking advantage of the situation."

"He really doesn't mind."

"How do you know?" she says. "Did you ever ask him?"

"No," I say.

"Then you don't know," she says. "Hell, I don't know, either. Maybe he loves getting out of bed to be at your beck and call. If it were me, though, I would hate it. I'd show up and smile and take you where you needed to go. But I would hate it."

I love the way she's not afraid to tell me what she really thinks. She's never scared to speak her mind or bring me down a peg if I deserve it. To be honest, I never really thought about Jameson's feelings on the matter. And lately, I've been calling him a lot later than midnight.

"Well, damn, now I felt like an asshole for the second time tonight."

"Don't look so beat up," Jenna says. "I'm not trying to bring you down. I'm just saying I have some experience with this, and maybe you shouldn't be so casual about waking someone out of their beds in the middle of the night to drive you all around Fairhope."

"You do?" I ask. This is new. "What kind of experience?"

She looks away, like I've caught on to some secret information she didn't mean for me to have. "Oh, that? It's nothing, really. Just that my momma used to work for a rich family back where I grew up," she says.

"And where's that?" I know almost nothing about where Jenna comes from or who her family is. She doesn't talk about them much. Or at all.

"Nowhere you want to be," she says. She takes another long sip of her beer and sets the empty bottle down on the bar. "Okay, if we're going to stick around for a little while, you're going to dance with me."

My jaw drops open, and I hold my hands up. "No way," I say. "I am not a dancer."

"Everyone's a dancer," she says. "Now stop being a pussy and come show me your moves."

The moment her hand closes over mine, my heart begins to race. I let her lead me toward the dance floor and pray like hell for a slow song.

CHAPTER 3
JENNA

Dancing with Preston is exactly the opposite of what I should be doing. I should be staying as far away from this rich boy as I can, but God, there's just something about him that I cannot seem to resist. And resisting someone this hot is not my strong point. Especially when I've been drinking.

Typical Jenna.

Whatever is going to get me in the most trouble at any given moment is what I usually end up doing.

And Preston Wright is trouble with a capital T.

Not only is he my best friend's ex—and a cheater at that —but he's the son of the wealthiest, most influential couple in Fairhope, if not the entire state of Georgia. What business does a girl like me have with a guy like that?

But as the music plays on, I dare to move a little bit closer.

His eyes are locked on my face and when my hips grind against his, he moves his hands up to the waist of my jeans.

My entire body lights up like a Christmas tree. One that's on fire.

I am terrified to raise my eyes to his, because I have a feeling I know what I'm going to see there. Desire. Something more dangerous than fire or volcanoes or diving headfirst into a pot of boiling water. To a guy like him, I am a forbidden fruit. I'm exactly the kind of girl his parents will hate, because I'm exactly the opposite of all those other girls he's been going out with.

It's the only reason he wants me.

I know full well the most there would ever be between us would be a month or two of hot, sweaty sex. The kind that leaves your knees weak and your heart thumping, simply because you know it won't last.

Usually, I'm ready to sign up for that kind of action from a handsome guy. No strings attached and all that. But Preston is different. He's part of my social circle, no matter how hard I've tried to avoid being mixed up with the rich kids. I still don't understand how the hell that happened, but here I am, friends with the elite crowd in Fairhope.

Friends to lovers might work out in the movies, but my life has never been a fairytale. I'm all too aware of the realities of what it means to get in bed with a guy who has money. Lord knows, I watched my momma fall for that dream, and I'm not about to start repeating her mistakes.

I'd end up with a heart full of sorrow and he'd go on his merry way, feeling good about his month in the slums, like he'd been on some grand rebellious adventure. Then, of course, he'd go right back to those rich girls with their fancy clothes and fancy tastes.

Aruba? I wouldn't even know what to do with myself at a

five-star resort in Aruba. My whole life, I've never once stepped foot out of the state of Georgia.

I turn around, wiggling out of his hold on me, but after a few moments, he pulls me in again, his fingertips dancing dangerously along the edge of my waistband, brushing against bare skin. He presses his body close to mine, and I can feel the warmth of his breath on my neck and shoulder. I tell myself not to lean in to him, but I can't help it. He feels so damn good.

My heart races and I'm so aware of my lips and my tingling skin, the heat of his body against mine, that I can hardly breathe.

I turn to face him and as my eyes meet his, it's electric. Magnetic.

Trouble.

I swallow and put my hands on top of his, scared to touch him anywhere more intimate. Afraid I won't be able to stop myself.

"You're going to get a bad reputation," I say.

A smile slides across his lips slowly, like a secret. "Why is that?"

"You ditched your pretty date early and now you're dancing with me like you want something," I say. "Small town. People talk."

He doesn't take his eyes off mine for an instant and the energy between us sizzles. "Let them talk."

The song changes and slows. Preston slides his hands from my hips to my back and my arms naturally rise to circle his neck. I force my eyes away from his and lean against his chest instead. Why did I think that was somehow safer?

My cheek rests against the solid muscle of his chest. I

listen to the pounding of his heart, feel the warm grip of his hands.

Over the past few months, I've noticed the long looks that last a beat too long and the way he comes to sit by me any time there's a spot free. I've found my thoughts drifting to him when I least expect it and my pulse racing the moment he walks into a room. But until this moment, we've never touched or come so close to making a mistake we'll both regret.

I close my eyes and imagine his bare chest, slicked with sweat. His hands finding their way to the most secret parts of my body. I bet he knows just how to use those hands. And I bet I could teach this sheltered boy a trick or two of my own.

I practically groan at the possibilities, knowing this can't happen. Even one night would be too much.

I take a deep breath and pull away, forcing a laugh. "Come on, cowboy, let's grab one last drink," I say. "This song is too slow."

He frowns but follows me back to our seats at the bar.

I know I have to lighten the mood or we'll be goners.

"Knox, can we get another couple drinks down here, please?" I shout, leaning over against the worn wooden bar.

"Sure thing," he calls back.

I scoot my stool back and sit down, putting a little breathing room between Preston and me. He still has that hooded look to his eyes, sizing me up like I am piece of fruit he's ready to devour. I ignore the heat that zings through my body.

"I am so glad it's almost spring break," I say. "It's been nice on the beach now that the weather's warmed up a little."

"Are you planning on going anywhere?" he asks. "Back home?"

I make a face. "Definitely not," I say. "Never again if I can avoid it."

"Where is home, by the way? I don't think you've ever really talked about it much."

"I don't ever really think about it much," I say. A big lie, if there ever was one. "I'm sticking around here. Probably going to pull some extra shifts at Brantley's and try to spend as much of my free time on the beach as possible. You? Aruba, I presume?"

He rolls his eyes and laughs. "I'm staying here, too. Dad has some things lined up for me at the office. Meetings and paperwork. Saturday I'm throwing my annual spring break bash on the yacht, though, if you want to swing by."

"I think I'll pass on that," I say. "I'm surprised you aren't getting away. I thought all the rich guys spent their vacations at luxury resorts getting drunk and sexing the ladies."

"As nice as that sounds, I'm not going anywhere until Penny's baby comes," he says. "I would die if I missed holding that little girl the day she was born."

Another rush of warmth flows through me. Is there anything sweeter than a man who can't wait to hold a baby for the first time?

"Hard to believe it's almost time," I say. "Won't be long now. I got a pretty fancy schmancy invite to her baby shower in a couple weeks. Much to your mother's delight I'm sure."

Preston's mother hates me, which is understandable after that tiny little matter of me helping Penny pawn a priceless diamond tennis bracelet last Fall. She'll probably never forgive me for introducing her precious little girl to the world of pawn shops. I hate to think what she'd do if she knew Preston was up here drinking with me right now.

"Yeah, Mom is going all out, as usual," he says. "Penny protested, saying she'd much rather everyone make donations to the local children's hospital instead of buying her gifts, but I guess women just love buying little bows and ribbons and pretty pink girly things."

"It's in our genetic code to want to buy things for babies," I say. "Besides, it's your mother's first grandchild. She's going to spoil that child, whether Penny likes it or not."

He laughs. "You've got a point there," he says. "I'm just glad they're taking it so well, especially since Penny and Mason decided not to get married until after the baby comes."

"I'm sure that's killing your mother."

"You have no idea," Preston mutters. "And you changed the subject, by the way. I really would love it if you'd come by the party Saturday."

"It's not exactly my scene, Preston," I say.

"Why not?"

I stare at him. Is he honestly that clueless? "Where do I even start?" I lean back against the bar. "Frat boys taking turns doing cannonballs off the side of the boat? Half-naked girls in the hot tub? Caviar and champagne flowing like water? No thank you."

He shakes his head. "It's really not like that. We have a good time at those parties. It's more down-to-earth than that."

"I bet," I say, wondering if he thinks that's what down-to-earth looks like. A party on a five million dollar boat? "I'm sure there will be no shortage of babes lined up to meet the handsome single billionaire, accidentally pressing their fake boobs against your bare arm, hoping for a tour of your private cabin."

I take a sip of my beer. I know I'm not being fair to him. I'm about to admit I've had one beer too many when my butt begins to vibrate. I hop up from the stool and pull my cell phone out of my back pocket, hoping maybe it's Leigh Anne telling me she changed her mind and wants to watch a movie.

Instead, it's my brother's name flashing across the screen. My smile fades, and my stomach lurches. This is the fifth time he's tried to call in the past week. I hit 'ignore' and stuff the phone back into my pocket.

"Who was that?" Preston asks.

"Nobody," I mumble, unable to keep the sadness and regret out of my voice. Definitely one too many if I can't even mask that ancient pain.

His eyes narrow. "Everything alright?"

"Yep," I say, tearing the label off my beer bottle and avoiding his gaze. I begin folding the paper into the shape of a tiny frog. "I think maybe I should head home, though. It's getting late and I have to work tomorrow."

"It's not even midnight," he says. "You want to come back to my place and hang out for a while? We could grab some donuts and play some video games."

I can't help but smile. Someone's been paying attention to my weakness for donuts after a night of drinking. "Thanks, but I think you and I both know that's a bad idea."

"We do?" He raises an eyebrow.

"You may not be smart enough to realize it yet, but I've got us both covered on this one," I say with a laugh. I lift a hand toward Knox and he turns my way. "Would you mind calling me a cab?"

"Wait," Preston says. "Don't do that. Just stay for one more dance."

I shake my head, my smile gone. He needs to understand that this cannot go where he's hoping it will go. "One slow dance is too many for me."

He clears his throat and runs a finger along the rim of his still-full glass. "You sure? Because I was thinking it was nowhere near enough."

My heart tightens in my chest and my mouth goes dry. Damn, I would love to just grab him right now and kiss the hell out of him. Take him home and see what kind of trouble we could really get into when the lights were out.

"I'm sure," I say, a little too breathless to make it believable. I force myself to look away and nod at Knox. He reaches for the bar's phone and starts dialing. "You don't want to get mixed up with a girl like me," I tell Preston before I down the last of my beer. I stand and lean in close, my cheek brushing against his. "Besides, I would wreck you."

He groans as I step around him and head for the door. I don't look back, but I have a feeling his mouth is hanging wide open.

As I step out into the warm spring air, I wonder if he has any idea it's really the other way around.

CHAPTER 4
PRESTON

"There's my precious boy."

My mother rises from the table and walks over to plant a kiss on my cheek. She still talks to me like I'm ten years old.

"Hi, Mom," I say. I give her a hug and walk over to my seat by the pool. "Sorry I'm late."

I was barely able to drag my tired ass out of bed this morning. After I left the bar last night, I couldn't get Jenna out of my mind. I tossed and turned for hours before I finally got up and watched a movie. I passed out on the couch around five in the morning.

But Sunday brunch is a tradition for my family, and my mother would have my head if I missed it.

"How was your date last night?" Penny asks. She's got a plate full of healthy food in front of her. Egg-white omelets and fresh fruit. She's been obsessive about taking care of herself these past few months with the baby on the way.

"Not worth talking about," I say.

"I'm telling you, no girl could possibly compare to Piper Hendricks," my mother says. "You just won't believe how that little girl has grown into the most beautiful young woman. I was just talking to her mother last week and she was telling me all about Piper's work with the animals down at the shelter. She's in school to be a Veterinarian, you know. Smart and beautiful."

I try not to groan. Under the table, Penny pats my hand. She understands better than anyone else the torture that comes from our mother's match-making. And it's only gotten worse for me since Penny and Mason ran off together last fall. It's as if our mother has realized I am her last hope of a respectable marriage, and she's going to find the perfect girl for me, or die trying.

"I'm sure she's lovely, Mom," I say. I don't want to get into another argument about it now. Let her try to hook me up with whoever she wants, but for now, I am done going out with girls who match my mother's idea of perfect. They always turn out to be incredibly boring and predictable.

"She is. But of course, you'll get to see for yourself soon enough."

I narrow my eyes at her as Flora pours me a glass of juice and sets a plate of pancakes and bacon in front of me. "Thank you Flora," I say. "What do you mean I'll see for myself?"

My mother wiggles in her seat, as if she's been dying to share this news with me. "We've just booked a family vacation to Paris for this summer," she says. "One month in the most beautiful hotel in the city. It's going to be amazing."

"Wait, when is this?" Penny asks. She puts her hand

protectively on her pregnant belly and exchanges a look with Mason.

Mom swallows and raises both eyebrows. "End of July, sweetheart," she says. "And I don't want to hear any excuses from you about not wanting to travel with a baby. I did it all the time when you and Preston were babies. It will be good for you to get out of the house. New mothers are in danger of falling into depression sitting around in their houses for months after their babies are born, not living their normal lives."

"We're not going to Paris with a three-month-old baby," Penny says.

"Don't you worry about it for one second. I've already made arrangements for a nanny to come with us. She'll take care of everything, I promise. All you have to do is get the plane. You can spend the whole time in the hotel suite, if you want to."

Penny glances at me. The story of our lives could be told in meaningful glances exchanged around our parents. We learned early how to read each other's thoughts with nothing more than a simple raise of an eyebrow.

"Let's not worry about it now," I say, knowing that if I don't put an end to this conversation soon, Penny and Mason will be out the door before I can say Paris three times fast. "I'm sure it'll work itself out."

Which is code for, there's no way in hell Penny is going to Paris. I don't particularly want to go either, truth be told. Being in a foreign country with my parents for a full month of my summer sounds like hell.

"Well, I only mentioned it because the Hendricks' are coming with us," Mom says, beaming. Her full attention is back on me. "You have to remember Piper, right? She and her parents visited several times when you were little. They live over in Houston. Her father's the heart surgeon?"

It's honestly not ringing a bell, but now the whole purpose behind a trip to Paris is incredibly clear to me. Could my mother be any more transparent? She and Mrs. Hendricks probably spent a few hours on the phone planning the future wedding of their two remarkable children. They probably already have all kinds of romantic dates set up for Piper and me in Paris this summer. I envision trips to the Eiffel Tower where our parents mysteriously get caught in traffic and can't make it, leaving Piper and I alone at the top, destined to fall in love.

I suddenly feel so exhausted I can hardly keep my eyes open.

Luckily, Dad arrives at that moment and conversation turns to his work and what's been going on this past week in the stock market. Of course, even work talk has been a source of tension at our brunches lately. Last year, Mason's father—my father's former CFO—was arrested for embezzling millions of dollars from the Wright Corporation. A lot of my father's time these past few months has been devoted to cleaning up messes Mr. Trent left behind. But with Mason now a part of our family, and he and Penny expecting a baby in a month, it's best for Dad to keep his complaints to himself.

I'm relieved when everyone has finished eating and my parents excuse themselves to go play a round of golf at the club.

"The weather is so beautiful this time of year," my mother says. "Don't you just love spring in Georgia?"

I stand and kiss her again on the cheek. "Have a good time," I say.

"Sure you don't want to come with us?" Dad asks, clapping a hand on my shoulder. "The Johnson's will be out on the course today. I'd love for you to make some connections with them before the school year's out."

Dad is always thinking about making connections. I wonder if he ever does anything just for pleasure, or if business is the only thing on his mind twenty-four-seven?

"Maybe some other time," I say.

"Okay, but it's never too early to start making your presence known at some of these business social events," he says. "Won't be long before you're filling my shoes out there."

I nod and hold my tongue. This is another thing my father never fails to remind me of when we're together lately. I still have a full year of undergrad left, but he's already grooming me for taking over the company.

When they're gone, Penny pats the chair next to her again. "Sit down, if you have a few minutes to talk," she says. "I feel like I hardly see you anymore."

"I know, I'm sorry," I say. "Between school and working at the office now a couple days a week, I feel like I don't have enough time to just goof off and have fun."

I pull the metal chair out and turn it to face the pool.

"Want something to drink?" Mason asks. "I feel like I need a vodka after that conversation."

I laugh as he gets up and heads to the bar in the living room. "No thanks. I had more than enough last night," I say. I turn my attention to my sister. "How are you feeling these days?"

"Tired," she says. "I can't sleep. It's hard to find a position that's comfortable these days, and I feel like I'm up every hour to pee."

I smile as she rubs her belly. "You look radiant," I say.

She rolls her eyes, but smiles. "So last night's date was a dud?"

"Same as always," I say. Mason comes back to the table with a vodka and orange juice for himself and an ice water for Penny. "I'm just so tired of feeling like I'm having the same damn conversations on every date."

Penny sighs. "What was it last night? Wanting to go sailing on the yacht? Build a house together on the beach and raise three-point-five children together?"

"Private jet to Aruba," I say. "About an hour into the date, she casually suggests how beautiful it must be there this time of year and how we should be spontaneous and go for spring break, just the two of us."

Mason laughs. "Yeah, as if she hadn't planned on bringing that up," he says.

"Exactly." It feels good to get some sympathy from Mason and Penny, at least. They've both been there, so they understand what it's like when all anyone cares about is what you can do for them. "Then Mom has to start in on this Piper chick. I'm only twenty-one and everyone's ready to see me settled, as if it's some kind of game to them."

"Pin the bride on the billionaire," Penny says with a laugh.

"It's not funny," I say. "I'm so over it. You guys are the lucky ones, not caring what anyone else thinks or says. I would like to have just one relationship where it wasn't always all about money or the future. What's a guy gotta do to just have a little fun every once in a while?"

"You could always take off on some grand adventure," Mason says, rubbing Penny's back.

"Mom and Dad might not recover from another one of us going awol for a month or two," I say. "But it's tempting, let me tell you."

"What you need to do is stop dating the same kinds of girls," Penny says. "You need to find someone more down-to-earth who doesn't give a shit about how much money you have. Someone you can just have fun with, no strings attached."

Jenna's face flashes in my mind. The way her body felt pressed up against mine on the dance floor last night makes me bite down on the inside of my lip.

"Preston Wright, you dirty dog," Penny says, slapping my leg. "You've already got someone in mind, don't you?"

"I don't know what you mean," I say.

"Liar," Mason says. "And I already know who it is. You should go for it, man. The way you two have been exchanging looks the past few months even has me hot and bothered."

Penny smacks him on the arm.

"Hey, what's that for? Lord knows I'm not getting any from you these days, preggo."

"I do not need to hear about your sex life," I say with a laugh.

Penny sticks her bottom lip out in a pout. "Come on, no secrets," she says to me. "Who is it?"

My stomach tightens. I haven't ever said it out loud to anyone, but there's no denying the tension between us whenever we're around each other. After last night, I'm ready to do whatever it takes to get her to go out with me.

"Jenna," I say, almost embarrassed to admit my crush to my sister. "I know what you're going to say. She's too close of a friend and it'll just get complicated, but—"

"I think she's perfect for you," Penny says. "She's the only girl I can think of who won't put up with your shit, but who will definitely be up for a good time. And Jenna does not care one bit about your money, I can tell you that. She'd be the last person in the world to suggest a private jet to Aruba."

I try to hide my smile, but I happen to think Penny's right. Jenna is the perfect cure for every bad date I've been on since Bailey and I broke up. I just hope I can convince her to take a chance and go out with me.

CHAPTER 5
JENNA

I step into the quad and lift my face to the sun. It's finally starting to warm up, and I love this time of year. The cherry blossoms all along the quad have just started to bloom and their cheery pink and white blossoms fill me with happiness.

I can hardly believe there's only one more day of classes before spring break. Where has this year gone? I had planned to really slow down and enjoy my senior year, but it's passing by in the blink of an eye. In just a couple short months, I'll be standing on this grass, graduating with honors.

The thought almost makes me laugh. Who would have ever guessed Jenna Lewis would make it through college, much less with honors? I'm so proud of myself, but I'm also terrified about the future. My adviser keeps asking me to stop by her office so we can talk about job opportunities and fill out some applications, but the truth is, I'm dreading the whole process. I've already looked through most of the current openings in Fairhope and there's not a lot out there. I'm sure I could find something better if I widen my search, but I don't want to leave Fairhope.

Over the past year, I've made some of the best friends of my life. The thought of leaving now and having to start all over makes me so sad. What if I never find friends like these again?

But I certainly don't want to graduate and keep working at Brantley's as a waitress the rest of my life.

I decide not to think about this week. It's my last ever spring break, and I'm determined to enjoy myself.

I wish Leigh Anne was going to be in town the whole week, but Monday, she and Knox are flying up to Boston for a couple days to go through some of the final preparations for her testimony at trial. I'll be so glad for her when this whole thing is over. The trial starts the same week of our graduation here at Fairhope Coastal, but I promised her I would get to Boston as soon as I can after the ceremony is over. I want to be there when the jury reads their guilty verdict and puts that asshole away for a very long time.

"Lost in thought?"

Someone moves up behind me and tugs on one of my pigtails. I swing around and see Preston Wright standing there, a big grin on his face like we were ten-year-olds on the playground.

"Hey." I haven't seen him since we danced at Rob's last weekend, and my heart flutters at the sight of him. "You done with classes for the day?"

"Just finished," he says. "You?"

"Same."

"I don't suppose you've given any extra thought to my invitation," he says.

I start walking toward the parking lot again and he follows. "I already told you it wasn't really my kind of thing," I say. "But have fun."

"We always do," he says. "But it won't be as much fun without you there."

I don't have anything to say to that. I'm sure his family's yacht is gorgeous, but I can't picture myself on it.

"What are you doing later this week?" he asks. He clears his throat, and I realize he's nervous. "I was thinking if you had a night off work, maybe we could hang out."

I stop walking and turn to him. We're standing underneath a beautiful cherry tree with white buds just starting to bloom. "Are you asking me out on a date?"

His mouth drops open slightly and he hesitates, as if trying to read me. I give him my best poker face.

"It doesn't have to be a date, exactly," he says. "Just two friends spending time together. It could be fun."

I bite back a smile and start walking again. "Well, in that case, I'm afraid I don't have a lot of free time coming up this week."

"Wait," he says, touching my shoulder. "What if I said it was a date? Would that change your answer?"

"The answer is no, Preston," I say. I reach my beat up old truck and unlock the door. "Just because we had one dance the other night does not mean I want to start going out with you."

He stares at my truck, frowning. "What happened to your car?"

"It died a slow and painful death," I say. "I found this on Craig's list for a steal last week, though."

"Is it safe?"

I stare at my truck. It isn't much to look at, but it runs good. It took almost every dime I'd saved up to afford it, but that's another thing golden boy here would never understand. "Yes, it's safe," I say. "Probably a lot safer than that sporty little black thing you drive sometimes."

I climb into the truck and shut the door. He's still standing out there, so I roll the window down. No automatic windows on this old thing, though, so it takes me a second to hand crank it. "Look, I think it's very sweet that you want to spend time with me, but I'm not the girl for you. Trust me on this one."

"I think I'm capable of deciding that for myself," he says. He smiles and he's so damn charming, I want to say yes. "Besides, I'm not asking you to elope or anything. Think about it, okay?"

I nod, my heart beating a lot faster than I wish it was at the thought of spending time with him. "I'll see you around," I say.

I rev the engine and he backs away to stand on the sidewalk. It takes all my willpower not to jump out of the truck and tell him I've changed my mind, but I don't do relationships.

And I have a sneaking suspicion that with a guy like Preston, one night would simply not be enough.

CHAPTER 6
JENNA

I drag myself in to work at ten the next morning. The first order of business is starting up some coffee.

"Late night?" my manager, Maria, asks, one eyebrow raised.

"Not intentionally," I grumble. I feel like I've been run over by a mack truck.

I made it home at a decent hour last night, climbing straight into bed after I got home from work at midnight. But no matter how hard I tried, I could not get to sleep. Preston haunted me like the ghost of boyfriends-never-to-be-in-a-million-years. Every time I closed my eyes, I imagined what it would be like to have him there in bed beside me, on top of me, behind me.

Oh God, make it stop.

I'd eventually crawled out of bed, uncorked my bottle of tequila, and watched old reruns of Buffy.

Now, Spike was more my kind of guy. A bad boy on the wrong side of death.

I finally passed out somewhere in the vicinity of four a.m.

Thank God Brantley's isn't open for breakfast or I might have had to call in sick.

I woke up at nine-thirty this morning with a tequila hangover and a crick in my neck. I barely had time to shower and throw my hair in pigtails before heading in. Part of me is a little surprised Maria hasn't told me to turn back around and get my ass together before coming back.

Lord knows I cannot afford to lose this job.

See? Preston is already dangerously close to screwing up my life and we haven't even kissed yet.

Correction, will never kiss.

And yet, as I pour my first cup of steaming hot coffee, I wonder if he was thinking of me, too, or if asking me out was just a bout of temporary insanity.

"Mind if I grab a quick cigarette before I start my shift?" I ask.

"Your shift's already started, hon, but go on ahead," Maria says. "You still got forty minutes until we open."

"Thank you."

I load my coffee with sugar and cream and head out back to the picnic bench that has become like my second home. I know I really should stop smoking, but I can't seem to help it. When you work in a restaurant, taking a smoke break is just about the only break you're going to get. And I work a lot.

"Good morning," Leigh Anne sings as she walks up, looking pristine as usual.

"Morning, dear," I say. "Hey, I thought you were going shopping today with your mom?"

"Maria saved me. Said she needed an extra hand," she says. She slings her purse onto the table and climbs to sit next to me, our feet resting on the bench. "I was dreading spending the day with my mother. I was just trying to be nice, you know? Show that I'm making an effort."

"Are they?" I ask. "Making an effort, I mean?"

She shrugs. "They think they are."

I roll my eyes and take another sip of coffee. I made it really strong, and it tastes delicious. "One of these days, you really ought to tell your mother exactly what you think of her."

Leigh Anne laughs. "I don't think she'd really hear me even if I did."

"Doesn't mean you shouldn't say it. For yourself if not for her," I say.

She nods and puts her hand in mine. "You're pretty smart, you know that?"

I shake my head and throw my cigarette to the ground. "I've been feeling pretty stupid lately, to tell you the truth."

"I don't supposed that feeling has anything to do with a certain someone you were seen slow dancing with last weekend at the bar?"

I cringe and drop my head into my hands. Small towns are the worst. "What, did Knox tell you about that?"

"He told me the two of you were getting awfully cozy there for a while. He said for a minute there, he thought you guys might even leave together."

I take a deep breath, letting the air fill my lungs until it almost hurts to keep holding it in. "Would you hate me if I told you I thought about?" No use lying to Leigh Anne about my feelings. In fact, if there's anyone who could convince me to stay far away from Preston, it's the woman sitting next to me. She knows what it's like to have your heart crushed by him.

"I could never hate you," she says.

"I should never have entertained the idea. Not for a second. Especially knowing how he treated you. Besides, I would never date a friend's ex. I don't know what I was thinking."

"You were thinking he's the hottest guy in town. Or I think that's how you put it once upon a time." She bumps my shoulder and laughs. My cheeks are probably beet red. "There are a lot of amazing things about Preston. He's kind of hard to resist. Believe me, I've been there."

My stomach aches.

"He asked me out," I say softly. I pick at the week-old red nail polish on my short nails, watching as one big flake drops to the pavement.

"I'm not suprirsed," she says. "I have to admit, I've seen the way he looks at you sometimes. I kind of knew this was coming."

I swallow and sit up. "What do you mean?"

She shrugs. "I don't know. Just sometimes when we're all together, I'll look over and catch him staring at you, the hint of a smile on his face and something much more serious in his eyes. He likes you, Jenna. I just haven't been able to tell if it was more of a romance thing or a sex thing. Until Knox told me about last weekend, I didn't think you were even interested."

I shake my head. "I didn't think I was either," I say. "How long have you been noticing this?"

"Since before Christmas," she says. "Before he broke things off with Bailey."

"But he's been going on all these dates with other girls," I say. "If he likes me, why didn't he ask me out sooner?"

"Probably because of me," she says. "Or because you're always taking him down a peg. Maybe he's been afraid to ask you out."

I laugh.

Leigh Anne gets quiet, and I know what's coming. I'm tempted to head her off at the pass and change the subject before she gets a chance to say anything, but part of me needs to hear what she's going to say.

"What did you tell him?"

My stomach knots up. "I told him no. He isn't the type of guy I'm going to end up with, and you and I both know it," I say. "And fooling around with a guy like that would only lead to trouble. So what's the point?"

"But you like him?"

I want this conversation to be over. I should have left that damn bar last weekend when Leigh Anne did. I never would have had the memory of his touch on my bare skin.

"I don't know what I feel," I say. "Everything I think and feel about him is tied up with what family he comes from and what he's done to my friends. How am I supposed to wade through all that crap to find the truth?"

She laughs. "I guess the only way to wade through it is to strip all that other junk away and see if there's anything left."

"And how do I do that?"

"If you think there's something there between you, maybe you should give him a chance," she says. "Get to know him a little better and see if there's something more between the two of you that doesn't involve his past or his money."

I turn to look at her, shocked. "You can't seriously be telling me you think I should go out with him? What about the way he treated you back in high school?"

This was the last thing I expected her to suggest, and I'm not sure I can wrap my head around it.

"He made a mistake. He broke my heart. I'm over it," she says. "If he hadn't cheated on me back then, maybe I would never have met Knox. It's impossible to turn back time and try to figure out the what-ifs. All we can know for certain is that where we are right now, in this very moment, is a result of the exact path we took on the way here. One small change and everything might be different. Yes, there are things I wish had never happened, but at the same time, I can't imagine life without Knox. I have to believe it all happens for a reason and that somehow, I'm right where I'm meant to be."

I shake my head and step down from the picnic table. "Now look who's the smart one," I say with a smile.

"I've been doing a lot of thinking lately about forgive-ness," she says. "Holding on to pain is a tough thing. Some-times holding onto it is worse than what caused it in the first place. With Preston, we were just kids. Yes, he cheat on me, but I know in my heart he didn't do it to hurt me. He just wasn't thinking about me at all. And I know he regrets it now, anyway. What's the use in holding on to that kind of pain? There simply isn't room for it."

There are tears in her eyes, and I know she's thinking about Burke. That's one bastard none of us will ever forgive, and what he did to her caused the kind of pain she might never be able to let go of. Not completely.

I have no idea what to say to her to make it better, so I take her hand and pull her into a hug.

We hold each other for a long moment before she pulls away and wipes a few stray tears from her cheek. "All I'm saying is I think Preston's a good guy at heart," she says. "And I really want you to be happy. I'm not saying this to be judgmental at all, but a string of one-night-stands can only make you happy for so long."

"For one night, to be exact," I say with an exaggerated wink.

Leigh Anne giggles and shoves me backward. "You know what I mean."

"I do," I say. "But long term relationships scare the crap out of me. Especially when it comes to rich dudes who have been known to cheat. Trust me on this one."

She narrows her eyes at me. "I hate it when you say stuff like that."

"Like what?"

"Make some vague reference to your past when you have no intention of sharing the whole story," she says. "One of these days, I'm going to beat it out of you."

"Are you ladies going to stand out here all day gabbing? Or do you think you might be able to find the time to come set up my restaurant before the guests get here?" Maria says. She doesn't stay to hear our answer.

"We'll talk later," Leigh Anne says. "I just wanted you to know that I would be okay with it if you wanted to go out with Preston."

"Thanks," I say. "But I plan on staying far away from him."

"Famous last words," she says.

"Dun dun dun," I add.

We're laughing as we pull open the back door to Brantley's and head inside for our shift.

CHAPTER 7
PRESTON

A sleek black truck pulls into the parking lot of the marina and a bunch of people pile out of the back. Two guys grab a blue cooler and head my way. Three girls I recognize from school follow closely behind, and a friend of mine from high school climbs out of the driver's seat. He waves up at me as he leads the group onto the boat.

"Preston, my man," he says, lifting his hand and slapping it into mine. He claps me on the back just a little too hard. "What's up? Thanks for the invite. Wouldn't be spring break without the traditional Wright blow-out."

"Hey Aidan," I say.

He moves past me and quickly introduces the other five as they come on board. They are all students at Fairhope Coastal who decided to stick around for the break, but I haven't seen them at one of my parties before. One of the girls, Mandie, winks when I shake her hand. She's wearing a pair of very short cut-off jean shorts and a red bikini top that is about three sizes too small. She crosses in front of one of her other friends to stand beside me, her bare skin brushing against my arm.

I take a step to the side.

"For those of you who haven't been here before, the whole place is fair game except for the state rooms on the lower floor," I say. "Those are family suites and off-limits for now. Oh, and keys?"

Aidan nods and reaches in his pocket for the keys to his truck. He slaps them into my hand, and I toss them into a bowl on the railing behind me. It's my main rule of partying on my family's yacht. If you're going to drink, you're not going to drive.

"Have fun," I say. "Wilson is mixing drinks at the bar on the main deck. Just follow the sound of the music."

I hired a local DJ to play some music, and I wouldn't doubt if you could hear it all the way to the public beach from here.

The group heads toward the front of the boat, but Maddie hangs back.

"You coming?"

"In a minute," I say. I've been playing the good host, welcoming people onto the boat, but the truth is, I'm just standing up here hoping I'll see Jenna's old truck pull into the parking lot. I sent her a few texts reminding her about the party, but she hasn't responded. I know she won't show, but I can't help but want to see her.

"I've been looking forward to this all week," Mandie says. She maneuvers so close to me, I have to force myself not to move away. I'm already dangerously close to the edge of the ship. "Your parties are legendary."

I force a smile. This is a game I'm used to, and while I have been known to enjoy it in the past, today I'm having a hard time pretending to care.

Mandie doesn't seem to notice. "If you have some time, I'd love a private tour of those rooms you were talking about downstairs," she says, one eyebrow raised. She actually licks her lips.

"I'll keep that in mind," I say, almost laughing as Mandie presses her breasts against my arm. Maybe Jenna was right along. Maybe these parties are kind of lame and predictable. I grab the bowl of keys and hand them to Mandie. "Think you can do me a huge favor?"

She smiles. "Anything for you," she says.

"Make sure no one drives home if they've been drinking."

I turn and start walking down the steps toward the dock.

"Wait," she calls. "Where are you going?"

I smile and turn back toward her. "I have something I need to do," I say. "Go get a drink. Have some fun. I'll be back later."

But I have no intention of coming back.

IF SHE WON'T COME TO ME, I'LL GO TO HER. I GRAB A SIX-pack of beer from the gas station on the corner and drive over to Jenna's apartment complex, my heart racing.

As I climb the stairs to her apartment, my hands grow sweaty around the cardboard handle. This seemed like a good idea ten minutes ago, but now I'm nervous as hell. What if she's ignoring my texts because she genuinely doesn't want to spend time with me? As much of an asshole as it makes me sound, I've never had to chase a girl I liked before. I am usually the one being chased.

I take a deep breath and knock on her door.

No one answers, so I knock again, disappointment hanging heavy in my stomach.

After the third knock, a door opens, but not Jenna's. Leigh Anne walks out of the apartment two doors down and stops cold. I had completely forgotten they lived so close to each other.

I clear my throat, my cheeks warm. I feel like a child who's been caught doing something naughty.

"Preston?" she asks, suppressing a smile. She glances at Jenna's door and then her eyes dip to the beer in my hand. "What are you doing here? I thought you had your big party today?"

"I did," I say. I run a hand through my hair. I can't think of any good excuse for why I'm standing here that doesn't make it obvious how hard I'm crushing on Jenna. I don't say anything.

"Jenna's not home," she says. "She's pulling a double shift today at Brantley's. She probably won't get off until close to midnight. Want me to tell her you stopped by?"

"Sure," I say. I shuffle my feet, and lift the beer up. "Guess I'll just go home and drink this alone, then."

"What happened to the party?"

"It's still going," I say. "I just didn't feel like being there anymore."

She tilts her head to the side, her eyes narrowed. "Wait, you left your annual spring break blowout yacht party, the one you once called 'epic', to come to Jenna's apartment and drink a six-pack of beer?"

I wish she would just drop it because with every word, I feel more and more like an idiot.

"Wow, you've got it so much worse than I imagined." She smiles and leans against the railing.

I sigh. Leigh Anne always could see straight through me. "The truth is, I was standing there watching a replay of the same party I've had for the past three years," I say. "Only this time, my two best friends are at their house getting ready for their new baby to arrive, and suddenly it didn't seem as fun as it used to be."

She waits, as if she already knows there's more to it than that.

"And yes, okay, I can't stop thinking about Jenna. It feels weird talking to you about it, though, considering our history." This whole situation is just awkward as hell.

"It is a little weird, isn't it?" she says, wrinkling her nose. "But I'm not blind, Preston. I've known you had a thing for her since Christmas."

My eyes snap to hers. "You have?"

She shrugs. "I'm more observant than I used to be. Especially when it comes to my ex-boyfriend having a thing for my best friend."

I close my eyes and shake my head. Damn. "I know, I'm sorry. I really—"

"Wait," she says, stopping me. "Before you say anything else, I think it's important to get this out. When I left town, there was definitely this feeling things weren't finished between us," she says. "You hurt me, but when I first came home last summer, it seemed like you still had some feelings for me."

"We're being totally honest?" I ask.

She nods. "I don't see any reason to hold back now."

"Yeah, I definitely still had feelings for you," I say, my throat constricting. "I probably always will in some way, but that doesn't mean I'm not happy to see you with Knox. I'm glad you guys found each other."

"I know," she says. "I want you to be happy, too."

My heart feels tight, like someone is squeezing me from the inside. "After I found out what happened to you in Boston, I spent a lot of time thinking about how things might have been different if I hadn't cheated on you. If you'd never left."

A sad smile plays on her lips. "I just had a similar conversation with Jenna," she says.

"You did?" I'm almost scared to hear more.

"You can't blame yourself for what happened," she says. "Burke Redfield is the only one who's responsible for what he did to me, Preston. I know you guys all just want to be there for me and try to go back and fix whatever might have gone wrong, but what's done is done. All we can do now is try to move on with our lives and make the most of it. Besides, if I had stayed and we'd worked things out between us, do you think we'd really be happy?"

"I imagine I'd be ring shopping right about now," I say. Wasn't that how I'd always imagined it? Proposing the summer before our senior year in college?

"And then we'd be planning a wedding, living out our lives exactly the way our parents always wanted," she says. "Never once really considering whether it was what we wanted or not." She touches my hand. "Don't let it eat you up, Preston. Everything works out the way it's supposed to in the end. You deserve to be happy just as much as I do."

I nod. I know she's happy with Knox and that she wouldn't trade that for anything, it just sucks she had to go through what she did to get here.

"And yes, it's weird to think about another one of my best friends dating you," she says with a laugh. "But this is different. I think you guys might be perfect for each other. If you cheat on her or hurt her in any way, though, I will come after you."

"Understood," I say, lifting my hands in surrender.

She squeezes my arm and walks past me.

I watch her get about half-way down the stairs before I call out to her. "Leigh Anne?"

"Yes?" she spins, holding on to the railing.

"Do you think I even have a shot with her?"

She glances over my shoulder at Jenna's door and smiles. "She's giving you a hard time, huh?"

To say the least. "Maybe she's not interested," I say. "I'm not used to having to fight so hard."

"Keep fighting," she says. She starts back down the stairs and at the very bottom, she looks back up at me. "Oh, and Preston? There's a party tomorrow night out at Knox's. It's a small little get-together. Just a few friends. Penny will be there, and so will Jenna. You know, if you want to swing by."

I smile and bite the inside of my lip. 'Thanks, Leigh," I say.

"No problem," she says. "But if Jenna asks, I have no idea how you found out about it."

I laugh and watch as she gets into her car and drives away.

CHAPTER 8
JENNA

I down the rest of my hotdog and fold my paper plate into a nice little airplane. I send it sailing toward the fire, watching the paper shrivel up and flash a brilliant white before it turns to ash.

It's just chilly enough outside tonight for a bonfire, and I'm sad knowing it will probably be the last one until Fall. The realization that it may be my last one with this group forever only amplifies the sadness. Where will I be after graduation? It's on my mind entirely too much lately, and I wish I had an answer.

I look around at all my friends and simply cannot imagine my life without them. They've become the family I never had growing up. A stable support group that I know would do anything to help me if I asked. Penny and Mason sit across from me, a full plate of food resting precariously on her stretched belly. Leigh Anne is sitting on Knox's lap drinking a beer, the fire making her long blond hair flash gold in the light. Jo, Knox's cousin, is the only loner like me.

I've never seen her with a guy, but the way she stares longingly at the other couples sometimes leads me to believe she wouldn't mind being paired up.

As for me, I'm in no rush to become part of a couple.

I like the stability of good friendships, but when love becomes part of the equation, life gets complicated fast. I watched my mother drown in her relationships, never really able to pull her head above water. I don't want to be like her. In fact, most of my choices in life are guided by her mistakes. I think of my mother's choices, and then try to do exactly the opposite.

My brother hasn't stopped calling, and I'm scared to know the reason why he's being so diligent this time. He either needs money and thinks I have some to give, or something has gone terribly wrong back home. Either way, I don't want to be a part of it.

Headlights shine on the trees around us as someone pulls up the winding dirt road to Knox's lake house. My heartbeat races, knowing there's no one else it could possibly be. I hadn't realized Preston was coming tonight, but the moment I see him walk around the corner of the house, my mouth goes dry and my cheeks flush. Suddenly, the fire feels entirely too hot and uncomfortable.

"There you are," Penny says. "I was wondering if you were going to make it over here tonight."

He stares directly at me as he says, "I wouldn't have missed it."

"How did the big party go yesterday?" she asks as he joins us around the fire. "I can't believe I missed my first spring break blowout. You'll have to tell us all about it."

"It wasn't the same without you guys there," he says.

He leaves it at that, but I know the truth. Leigh Anne told me he left the party early and showed up at my place with a six pack. I avoid his eyes, not wanting him to know that I know. I've already spent too many hours today thinking about what might have happened if I had been home. Would I have turned him away? How many times can I possibly say no before the tension between us boils over and I can't resist him anymore?

But saying yes and letting him into my life as anything more than a casual friend would be like standing up and walking straight into the fire, letting it consume me like that plate. A flash of hot, white light, and then nothing left.

When I dare to look up, I find his eyes on me. He lifts the corner of his mouth into a small smile that I try my damnedest not to return. Why does he have to be so gorgeous? So completely irresistible? I wonder what it would be like to have that mouth on me.

As if to cool the heat building in my nether regions, a large, juicy drop of rain plops onto my nose. I look up and several more raindrops fall onto my forehead and into my hair. Two seconds later, thunder rumbles and the bottom drops out of the sky. Leigh Anne squeals and grabs Knox's hand. Mason and Preston help Penny out of her seat and together, we all make a run for the covered porch on the backside of the cabin. We're drenched by the time we make it, and we all stand there laughing as the fire turns to smoke and ash.

"You really know how to make an entrance, don't you buddy?" Knox says, punching Preston playfully on the shoulder.

"Look at this rain," Jo says. "It came out of nowhere."

"I knew it was supposed to storm later this week, but it was supposed to be clear tonight," Leigh Anne adds.

"Spring in the South," I say. "You just never know what to expect."

"What should we do?" Penny asks. "Got any board games or anything inside? I'm not ready to go home."

"You don't want to be driving in this anyway," Preston says.

"True," Knox says. "Come on in, let's see what we can find."

We all leave our shoes and wet socks on the porch and pile into the cabin. I gasp as I see the inside for the first time in several months. We usually just hang out by the lake when we come here, since a good portion of the cabin was destroyed in a fire many years ago. But wow, Knox has really been working hard to restore the old place. I'm completely awestruck at the level of detail he's put into the restoration.

"Knox, this place looks unbelievable," I say. I run my hand across the smooth cherry banister of the staircase. An intricate rose pattern is carved into the post at the bottom of the stairs. "Did you do all this by hand?"

"Yes," he says, smiling. "Do you like it?"

"It's absolutely gorgeous," I say. "I can't believe you've done all this in just a few short months."

"He's been thinking about trying his hand at flipping houses," Leigh Anne says. "Penny is helping him figure out the details of the business side of things, and we've been going around on weekends looking for a good starter property."

"Flipping houses?" Preston asks. "What does that entail?"

"Mostly it's just finding a property that has a lot of potential, but needs a lot of work. Then I'd go in and fix it up myself in my spare time, hoping to turn around and sell it for a good profit."

"That sounds really cool," Preston says. "I'm impressed."

"Now that Dad's bar is back in the black and business is picking up, you should have a lot more time on your hands if you want it," Jo says.

"I still plan on working at the bar, too," Knox says. "So don't go hiring my replacement just yet."

Jo elbows me. "I've been trying to talk your buddy Colton into coming to work for us. We could really use the extra help now that things are going better for us. He'd make a hell of a lot more money at Rob's than he does over at Brantley's, I'm sure," she says. "He doesn't seem to want to budge, though. Word is he's got the hots for one of the servers over there, if you happen to know anything about that."

I blush and look down at my bare feet on the smooth wooden floors. I glance up at Preston and his jawline is tense. Is he jealous?

It's no secret Colton and I had some fun together once upon a time, but I wouldn't say he has the hots for me. Not enough to turn down a better job.

"I'll talk to him if you want," I say. "I'm sure he has some other reason for not wanting to jump ship. Trust me, there's nothing going on between us."

I don't even know why I felt the need to say it, but Preston looks so jealous, I wanted to reassure him I wasn't seeing someone else. Which, considering the fact that I just turned him down, is completely ridiculous. Why do I care if he thinks I'm seeing someone?

But the knots in my stomach tell me I do care.

"Either way, we are going to need to hire someone soon, if you hear of anyone looking," Jo says.

"Look what I found," Leigh Anne calls from the living room. She's holding up a box for the game Twister.

Everyone groans, but joins in. Penny plants herself on the couch and plays referee while the rest of us make fools of ourselves, tangling our bodies into ridiculous positions. We laugh and play for hours, my body lighting up any time I find my hand touching Preston's or my body pressed against his. By the third game, I'm exhausted and my cheeks hurt from smiling so much.

I find my way to the kitchen to get a glass of water, and when I come back, I lean against the wall in the corner, watching them and thinking just how lucky I am to have found them all.

And just how much I'm going to miss them when the time comes.

CHAPTER 9
PRESTON

I've been trying to get Jenna alone all night, but any time I sit next to her or strike up a conversation, she creates some excuse to get up or talk to someone else. I wonder if my terrible attempt at asking her out has completely pushed her away at this point.

Defeated, I say my goodbyes and decide to head back to my place. I plan to take a very cold shower and drink some very strong bourbon.

The rain has stopped, but my Escalade slips and slides over the fresh mud like it has a mind of its own. I'm about five hundred yards from the paved road when the wheels slide to the left and begin to spin aimlessly.

I put the vehicle in reverse and press hard on the gas, but the damn thing only sinks deeper into the mud.

I try everything I can think of from turning the wheel to going forward or back, but after a couple minutes I have to face the fact that I am stuck. I slam my hands against the steering wheel and pull out my cell phone, but I have no service out here in the woods. Dammit. This is just not my freaking night.

I climb out of the car and survey the damage, but let's face, I have no idea how to get myself out of this mess. My only choice is to walk the half mile back to Knox's house and ask for a lift back into town. After just a few steps, my shoes and jeans are coated with mud.

I'm half afraid the stuff is going to swallow me whole before I can get to Knox's cabin when headlights come around the corner.

Jenna's truck sails past me, stops, and then slowly backs up. She rolls her window down and her eyes dip to my muddy jeans.

"Car trouble?" she asks.

"I got stuck," I say, pointing back up the road toward my car.

"What? Surely you can't be saying my beat up old Ford is safer out here than your fancy ride," she teases, her eyes glimmering in the dim light.

The irony is not lost on me, but I'd rather debate it from the cab of her truck.

"Can I get a ride into town?"

"Sure," she says, laughing. "Hop in."

I walk around the front of the truck, cursing as my shoe literally disappears into the mud. I try to lift my foot, but the shoe stays right where it is. I have to bend over and stick my hand deep into the sludge to retrieve it, so now my hand and arm are covered too.

Jenna's laughing as I climb into the truck.

"You should see yourself," she says.

I try to act angry that she isn't taking pity on me, but her laughter is contagious. "Next you'll make some joke about me being a stick in the mud," I say. "I'm sure I'll never live this down."

"Probably not," she says. She bites her bottom lip and damn, she looks so good, I can't stop staring at her.

Tension builds in the air between us. She looks away first, readjusting herself on the seat and clearing her throat.

"Where are you headed?" she asks as she pulls onto the main road. "Back to your apartment? Or back to your parents' to pick up one of your spare cars?"

She tries not to smile, but I can see she's incredibly amused.

"It's still early," I say hopefully, not quite ready to give up on the idea of us. "I'd be up for hanging out some more if you aren't too tired."

"Early?" she asks. "It's midnight."

"It's spring break," I say. "Where's your sense of adventure?"

I really don't want this to end with her dropping me at my apartment in ten minutes and speeding off. I know that if she would just give me a chance, there could be so much more between us.

She glances over at me and licks her lips nervously. Her hands grip the steering wheel so tightly, I can see her knuckles turning white. Do I really make her that uncomfortable?

"Is that some kind of a dare?"

"Maybe."

"Why do you want to hang out so much?" she asks. "You've got a bajillion friends in this town."

"I want you," I say, which makes her squirm in her seat. "We're friends, right?"

She lets the air out of her lungs in a long whoosh. "We are friends," she says.

Yes, but I want more. Why is that so hard to say? Why am I so scared to just put myself out there with her? When we're alone together, there's tension and desire, but she's either denying it or I'm reading her completely wrong.

"You really don't think there's something here?" I ask, my heart thumping against my ribs.

She bites her lower lip, and even in the darkness of the truck, she's so beautiful it takes my breath away. God, what I wouldn't give to touch her. I want to be so much more than friends, and she damn well knows it.

"What exactly are you saying, Preston Wright?"

"I'm saying I want to hang out with you, Jenna Lewis," I say back. "What's so scary about that?"

She shrugs and leans back against the seat, finally loosening her grip on the steering wheel. "It's not the hanging out that scares me."

"What is it then?"

She doesn't answer. She just keeps her eyes locked on the road, the smile gone from her face. We've both been dancing around this attraction for way too long, and I know I'm running out of chances with her.

"I can't stop thinking about you," I say, laying my cards on the table. "I'm sorry if that seems scary to you, but it's the truth. You haunt me. I can't sleep for thinking about you, Jenna. You're different from any other woman I've ever known, and I know there's something more between us. I think you feel it, too. I've resisted it for about as long as I can, and if you don't at least give me a chance, I may never sleep again."

She laughs and this time, there's no hiding the wide smile that lights up her entire face.

"Come on," I say. "One night. If you don't have a good time, we chalk it up to bad timing or whatever. But at least give me this one chance."

"Well, I would hate to be responsible for the town's golden boy dying from insomnia," she says. She takes a long breath in and out. "Okay, one night. Just as friends. All I was planning to do was go open up a couple beers and veg out in front of the TV, anyway. What do you want to do?"

"I'm up for anything," I say. "What do you want to do?"

She shakes her head. "Now, see, I thought maybe you had some grand plan already worked out," she says.

I swallow. She's going to make me work for every inch. "We could head to the Marina," I say. "The yacht is docked and we could hang out there for a while. We have tons of movies or we could shoot some pool. Whatever you want."

"I've avoided that yacht for a reason, in case you haven't noticed."

"We could go back to my place," I say, wishing I had taken more time to think this through or plan something fun.

"I have a better idea." She parks the car and looks over, mischief gleaming in her eyes. "Want to get high?"

I nearly choke on my words. "What? Jenna, I don't—"

"Stop," she says with a laugh. "That's not what I meant so don't have a heart attack on me."

She points out the front window and raises an eyebrow.

Confused, I lean forward and look out the window,

noticing our surroundings for the first time. We're parked at the edge of town by the old Fairhope water tower.

Understanding sinks in, and my eyes widen.

"Wait, you don't mean..."

"Yes, I do mean," she says with a smile. "You're not chicken are you?"

"At first, I thought you—"

"I don't do drugs, Preston," she says. "I would have thought you'd have realized that about me by now."

I can't even feel relief at the no-drugs comment because now my heart is pounding from the thought of having to climb this water tower. How high up is she wanting to go?

"Is it even safe to go up there?"

"Perfectly," she says, opening the door of her truck. "As long as you don't fall off."

CHAPTER 10
PRESTON

"Don't tell me you're really too scared to do this," she says. She reaches into the back of her truck and grabs two beers. She shoves them in the back pockets of her jeans. "After all that talk of wanting to hang out with me, you're going to let a little thing like a fear of heights get in your way?"

I swallow a thick lump of fear and get out of the truck. "Hang out, yes. Climb an old water tower and fall to my death? Not so much."

She laughs and grabs my hand. The simple, spontaneous touch sends a shot of adrenaline straight through me.

"I won't let you fall," she says.

"That's very sweet," I say. "But considering I probably outweigh you by a hundred pounds, I don't think you can keep me from falling."

She stops and turns to face me, but doesn't let go of my hand. "If you're really that scared, I'm not going to force you to go. You're welcome to sit down here by yourself for a while, if you want. I'm going to go up and enjoy the view."

I take a deep breath and look at the metal rungs of an old ladder running up the side of the tower. It's so high, my palms sweat just thinking about it.

"I don't know," I say. I want to spend time with her, but I have always had a hard time with heights, and this is extreme. "Why don't we just put the tailgate down on the truck and hang out here? Or drive over to the beach?"

She shakes her head. "You're all talk, aren't you?"

"What's that supposed to mean?"

"The other night when you came into that bar, you were telling everyone how tired you are of your life. The same dates. The same parties. Always doing the same things over and over without any real sense of adventure," she says. She looks up at the water tower. "Well, here I am, offering you a little adventure, and you're too scared to even give it a try."

I inhale, my eyes locked on her face and that mischievous look in her eyes. She's testing me.

"There has to be something else we can do that doesn't involve climbing thirty stories on a water tower that's been out of commission for fifty years," I say with a nervous laugh. "This is dangerous."

"Maybe I'm dangerous, too," she says in a low, sexy tone, her eyes narrowed. She's biting her lower lip and oh god, she's killing me with that look.

I groan and clear my throat. "You know exactly what you're doing to me right now, don't you?" I look at the first few rungs of the ladder and my heartbeat races. Of all the things she decides to test me with, this is the one thing that would make me hesitate, and I have a feeling she knew that before she even brought me here.

"You say you want something different? This is your chance to mix it up a little," she says. "Let's see what you're made of, golden boy."

Jenna steps closer to the ladder and puts one hand on the metal bar.

I turn around, run a hand through my hair. Crap, can I do this? "There aren't even any safety precautions," I say. "Look at this, it's just a bunch of thin little bars going up the side. One misplaced foot and it's goodbye forever."

"That's the way a lot of things in life are," she says. She's already five or six rungs up. "Doesn't mean it isn't worth taking the risk."

I laugh and shake my head. "Shit," I mumble.

"You complain about your life, but the truth is, you intentionally live inside your safe little bubble, never daring to step outside of it," she says. "Face your fears. Push yourself to the limits. It's the best way to know you're really alive."

With that, she turns and starts climbing so fast, she's twenty feet up before I even have a chance to breathe.

I lean against the hood of her truck, my hands clammy and cold.

This is insane. I should just let her go up and come back down. Let her make her point. Preston's too scared to change. Fine. It's not worth risking my life to go up there.

Right?

I turn and look up at her. She's halfway there with no sign of slowing down. She also hasn't looked back once to see if I'm following her.

But at least she hasn't fallen. How many times has she done this before?

I'm amazed at her fearlessness. How can she just take off without even giving it a second thought?

I lean my head back and let out a nervous breath. Crap, I can't let her go up there without me. Maybe she's right. Maybe it is time to challenge myself. Do something different and daring.

I swallow and take three deep breaths in and out. I walk to the bottom of the water tower and wrap one shaky hand around the bar. My chest rises and falls with each nervous breath. I close my eyes, knowing it's best not to look up and see how far it is to climb. It's best to just do it and not think at all.

"Come on, Preston," Jenna calls down. "You can do this. I promise you, there's a major reward for you if you make it up here."

I look up, despite my better judgment, and see her already at the top, holding on to the railing and leaning over.

I pray to God the reward is finally knowing what her lips taste like.

That would be worth climbing up and down this thing a hundred times.

I step back from the tower and pull my jacket and sweater off. I'm so nervous, I'm sweating in all these clothes. I strip down to my black tshirt and psych myself up. If Jenna can do this, I can do this.

I step to the ladder and just start climbing. I try not to think about how high up I am or how far I still have to go. I just climb, thinking of Jenna's face and what it would be like to kiss her and hold her in my arms.

I put one hand above the other, carefully making sure my foot is firmly planted on the ladder before I try to push myself up another step. The higher up I go, the sweatier my palms become. I wipe them on my jeans and cling to the side, having to take a break to catch my breath.

I make the terrible mistake of looking down to see how far I've gone. I am disoriented, and for one horrifying moment, I'm afraid I'm going to fall.

Fear catches in my throat, cutting off my breath. I pull in close to the ladder and lean my head against the cold metal.

"I can't do this," I shout.

"Yes, you can," she says. "You're already more than half-way. The hardest part was taking that first step, trust me. All you have to do is not give up."

I force air into my lungs and find the courage to keep moving.

Jenna keeps talking as I climb.

"You are so much stronger than your fears," she says. "How many chances have you gotten to really prove your own strength? To show that you are more than just Tripp Wright's son? More than the money in your bank account or the car that you drive? This is your chance. Just keep climbing. You're doing amazing."

I focus on the sound of her voice. I climb and push through the fear that threatens to paralyze me.

And when I hit the top of the water tower and step onto the platform, the pride and excitement and relief that washes through me is better than any drug. I can't stop smiling.

"I cannot believe I just did that," I say. "Holy shit."

My hands are numb, but I force a fist into the air and

shout.

"Wooohoooo."

"Woohoo," she yells, leaning over the railing. "You did it."

Jenna raises her hand to give me a high-five, but I pull her into my arms and spin her around on the platform. I expect her to pull away and make some excuse about this being too complicated, but she throws her arms around me and buries her face in my neck. I hold onto her for a long moment, and when she does finally pull away, we are both out of breath. Our faces so close, I can't concentrate on anything but her lips.

"Hey, I think you said something about a reward," I say, my hands drawing the bottom of her shirt into fists as the back of my fingers brush the bare skin at her waist.

For a moment, I think she is going to lean in and let me kiss her. Her eyes meet mine and her nails dig into the back of my neck, drawing me closer. But before I drop my lips to hers, she turns my head to the side and backs away.

I draw in a breath and stare out. My lips part, and I can hardly believe the beauty that greets me.

The wide ocean expands as far as the eye can see in either direction. The moon is huge and full, its light shining on the water, highlighting each crested wave. The sky above is endless, dotted with millions of bright stars that cover us like a blanket. I have never felt so open. So free.

So completely insignificant.

"I told you it would be worth it," she whispers.

Without taking my eyes off the night sky, I reach for her hand and lace my fingers with hers.

She was right.

Being up here with her is worth every terrifying moment.

CHAPTER 11

JENNA

I take the beers from my pockets and set them down on the platform. I've been up here more than a dozen times, but the view always takes my breath away.

I take the top off one and hand it to Preston, but he shakes his head.

"I think you've earned it," I say. I knew he was scared to climb up here, but I don't think the extent of his fear was clear to me until he was halfway up, clinging to the ladder for dear life. I feel a little guilty for pushing him so hard.

"Okay, one," he says, taking the beer and downing half of it in one gulp.

I laugh and open one for myself. I sit down , threading my legs through the railing and leaning my arms and head against the middle rung.

"I love it up here," I say. "It's so beautifully lonely, you know?"

"It's beautiful," he says. He sits next to me, but doesn't dare to dangle his legs over the side like I have. "There's no freaking way I would ever come up here alone. They might never find my body at the bottom of this old thing."

I laugh and shake my head. "I shouldn't have teased you. I didn't realize how scared you really were."

He shrugs and takes another sip of his beer. "You were right. I need to push myself more. It's easy to get stuck in the same old routine," he says. "You didn't seem scared at all. Do you come here a lot?"

"Every once in a while. I usually leave my phone in the truck, so it's just me and the wind," I say. "No one to bother me or interrupt my thoughts."

"What do you think about?"

I smile and look out at the ocean and the sky full of stars. "I usually come because I want to think about my future. Where I'm headed. Where I want to be someday," I say. "But usually I end up thinking way too much about my past."

"You don't like to talk about it much, do you?"

"Very observant," I say, a hint of sarcasm in my tone. I know it's a sore spot with my friends, but they know better than to push the issue. Most of the time.

"I think about my future a lot, too," he says. He must have decided now wasn't a good time to push me, either, and I'm glad he didn't ask more about my past.

"What's there to think about?" I ask. "I don't want to be rude, but isn't your future all cinched up? It seems obvious your father is grooming you to take over the company someday. I'm surprised there's not already an arranged marriage to go along with it."

He laughs. "My relationship with Leigh Anne was the closest thing to it," he says. "Everyone, including my parents

—okay, especially my parents—wanted us to get married someday."

"I bet her parents wanted it even more," I say, thinking about the ridiculous things Leigh Anne's mom has said to her in the past. That woman has the emotional intelligence of a dollar bill.

"You're probably right," he says. "I screwed it up big time, though."

"Why did you cheat?" I ask, my heart beating a little faster than I want it to. We're on shaky ground here, talking about past relationships.

"I don't know," he says. He rests his arms on the railing and stares out, his eyes dark. "I was a stupid kid who had no idea what real consequences were. My parents always jumped in to clean up any mess I made, so I never thought about how being with Bailey might really hurt Leigh Anne. Bailey kept coming on to me and Leigh Anne and I were arguing a lot about school. She wanted to go to Boston, but I wanted her to stay in Fairhope. I think part of me knew if she left, things were over between us, anyway. So one night, Bailey and I were the last two on the yacht after a big party, and it just sort of happened. I know it makes me sound like an asshole, but I was just having fun. Things with Leigh Anne had gotten complicated and there were all these expectations for us. But with Bailey, it was simple. At least at first."

"We all make dumb mistakes when we're teenagers," I say. God knows I made a lot of them. Worse ones than cheating, that's for sure.

Silence stretches out between us, and I listen to the waves crashing against the shore below. The tide is coming in, and in the distance, the white peaks of the larger waves roll forward and disappear.

"You were right, though," he says after a while.

"About what?"

"About my future being all cinched up," he says. He finishes his beer and sets the bottle down behind him. As he moves, his leg brushes against mine and he leaves it there, his warmth pressing against me. "My parents have had it all figured out since I was a little boy. I was always supposed to go to school here in Fairhope so I could do an apprenticeship at the company, double-major in business and economics, and take over some of the smaller duties after graduation. We haven't talked about dates, but when he's satisfied I have a good grasp on how things are run, Dad will retire and leave it all to me. I'm supposed to settle down here in Fairhope with my own house here in town, pick a wife and have a couple kids just like they did. Mom and Dad will keep their fingers in every aspect of the business, and I'll be their little dutiful little puppet, playing out their game exactly as I've been programmed."

"You don't sound too happy about that."

"How could I possibly complain about an empire being handed to me? I don't even have to earn it. I just have to say yes, and it's mine," he says. "I'd be an idiot to walk away from that life, right?"

"I can't even begin to answer that question for you." I'd never once thought about whether Preston wanted to follow in his father's footsteps. "I guess I just assumed it was what you wanted."

"Everyone does," he says. "No one ever thinks to ask me if it's what I want, because of course it's what I want. Who wouldn't want a multi-billion dollar corporation handed to them?"

"Not me," I say with a laugh. I set my empty beer beside his. "I can't even wrap my head around the concept of a billion anything, and I certainly wouldn't want the responsibility that comes with it."

"Some days I feel exactly the same way," he says. "I look at Penny and Mason and see how happy they are now, and I wonder if I would be happier if I just walked away from it all. Built a simpler life without the headaches and pressure."

"Trust me, being poor is no picnic," I say. "I know Penny and Mason have made a lot of changes, but that doesn't mean there are no more headaches just because they stopped driving fancy cars. If you think for one minute having less money in your bank account—or no money for that matter—makes life easier, you're even more clueless than I thought you were. I'm not trying to dismiss what you're going through, but until you've been in a position where you have no idea if you're still going to have a place to live next week, you have no idea what it's like to be without money."

"Is that how you grew up?"

I shrug, a knot in my stomach tightening. I don't want to talk about how I grew up. "Let's just say there have been times in my life where I had to go a few days without food," I say.

"I can't even imagine that," he says softly.

"Then we're even," I say. "Because I can't imagine having a billion dollars and owning five different cars."

He laughs. "I only have two cars."

"Oh, only two?" I say. I cut my eyes toward him and

nudge him with my elbow. "Listen, if you don't want to take over your father's business, then don't."

"It's not that simple."

"Who says?" I turn toward him. "Life is all about choices. We go left or we go right, simple as that."

"You make it sound so easy," he says. "First of all, my father would kill me. Or keel over from a broken heart."

He sounds so sad, I want to touch him. Let him know that I understand more than he thinks. But I'm scared, and unlike him, not up for facing my fears tonight.

"I learned the hard way that we can't hold ourselves responsible for our parents' happiness. You have to live your life and be true to yourself," I say, knowing it really isn't that simple for a guy like him. He can't just pack up and leave Fairhope. People would come looking for him. No one gave a shit where I went, so long as I was gone.

Part of me wants to tell him this, but a bigger part of me hopes he never finds out about my past or where I came from. It's easier to keep the conversation on Preston and his choices than to start thinking about mine.

"Here we are, all alone where no one in the world can hear us. Tell me what you really want, Preston Wright, son of a billionaire. Let's just pretend for a few minutes that there are no consequences to your actions. It's just you and the universe and anything you want is right there for the taking. What would you do with your future? What's your ideal path?"

He rests his chin against the metal railing and stares out at the waves for a long moment. "I don't know," he says finally.

"You mean to tell me you spend all this so-called time

thinking about your future, and yet you have no idea what you would do if you weren't held down by your parents' expectations?"

He pulls back. "I know it sounds stupid, but the truth is that I never get past the expectations part of it," he says, as if realizing it for the first time. "I try to think about my future, and the only thing I can see is this big wall in front of me, like I have no options. No freedom."

"Do you realize the irony of that?" I ask with a laugh. "You have all the money in the world. You could decide to do or be anything you wanted and every door would just open right up to a guy like you. How is it possible you feel like a slave in that scenario?"

He shakes his head and looks over at me. "I never thought of it like that," he says. "I guess that's why I never talk about it to anyone. It's insane to be so privileged and feel so limited. I can't even say how I feel without knowing how awful and stupid it must sound to anyone listening. I sound like a spoiled brat."

"Yes, you do," I say.

His eyes widen and I shrug.

"The truth hurts," I say. "But you need to get your head out of your ass. You sound like you're thinking poor me, my parents care about my future so much they've built an empire around it, ready to hand it to me when I'm ready. Poor you? You have everything everyone in this world wants. You have the entire universe at your fingertips, and all you can think about is how tough it is to have all this pressure and all these expectations. Personally, I think it's bullshit."

I pull my legs back through the railing and sit criss-crossed, facing him. I want him to hear what I'm saying and understand that I am not trying to make him feel worse. I'm trying to make him see what he has.

"What's the worst thing that could happen if you didn't go to work for your dad?"

"He'd kill me," he says.

"You said that already, but think about it honestly. If he didn't kill Penny for running off and getting knocked up by the son of the guy who stole millions from his company, he's not going to actually kill you."

"Point taken," he says with a laugh. He turns his body toward me now, and we're sitting face-to-face on the platform.

"It goes without saying he'd be disappointed. It might take him years to forgive you, but that's his problem," I say. "Would he disown you? Throw you out on the streets with no money and no resources?"

Preston takes a deep breath. "No," he says. "He would probably threaten it, but I doubt he'd follow through with it. Not after he realized I was serious."

"Okay, so this hypothetical future Preston has money and resources galore," I say. "Disappointed parents, yes, but they'll get over it in time. After a few months of trouble and heartache, he has freedom. Just like that. What does he do with it?"

He rubs his hand across his cheek, his eyes bright. A smile teases the corners of his mouth. "I can't even imagine what I'd do," he says. "I've always wanted to travel. And I don't mean my parents' version of traveling where it's meeting after meeting and you only stay at five-star luxury resorts that you never even get to enjoy. I've always wanted to go to more exotic, spiritual places like Tibet or the

Amazon rain forests, with nothing but a backpack. No tour guides or concierge service. I would love to explore the kinds of things you don't see as a typical tourist."

My heart skips a beat. "That's one of my biggest dreams," I say, almost breathless. "I've never even been out of Georgia, if you can believe that?"

"Seriously?"

"Dead serious," I say. "Not even one foot out of this great state my entire life. But I have always dreamed of being able to travel, just like you're saying. Take a backpack and go exploring places off the beaten path. There are ancient Mayan ruins in Mexico deep in the jungle that I would kill to visit someday. It's never really seemed possible, though."

He reaches over and takes my hand in his. "Anything's possible right now," he says. "What about you? What's in store for future Jenna besides traveling the world?"

A flutter goes through my stomach as I look up at him. For the first time in as long as I can remember, I'm wondering if there really is something more out there for me. Something bigger than what I've ever dared to hope for.

"Graduation's coming up in May," I say. "After that, I don't know. I've put in some applications here and there, but I don't have my heart set on anything yet. That sounds incredibly dull, doesn't it? Graduate and get a job. Boring and not at all adventurous, but unlike you, I don't have a mountain of money sitting there to pay my bills when I get out of school."

"Okay, so let's pretend for a minute that money's no object," he says, turning my game around on me. "What would you do if you didn't have to be practical?"

I look away. "It's not as fun for me to pretend and

dream, because there's no safety net keeping me from hitting rock bottom," I say. "I have no choice but to be practical."

"That's not true," he says. "People take risks every day. They follow their hearts and take chances and don't let anything stand in their way. I had to say what I would do if I faced my fear of disappointing my parents. Now, you have to say what you would do if you faced your fear of taking a risk after graduation."

I take a deep breath. "There is one thing," I say. I pull my hand away from his and look back out over the ocean. "I've never told anyone this before, so you have to promise you won't laugh at me."

"I swear," he says.

"I would love to be an artist," I say.

He turns his head in surprise. "What kind of art? Like paintings and stuff?"

"No," I say, my cheeks flushing in embarrassment. "Nothing that normal."

"What?" he asks again. "I want to know."

"You know those little animals I'm always making with spare napkins and beer labels and stuff?"

He nods. "Origami?"

"Yes, but so much more than just that," I say. "I'm into all kinds of paper art. Quilling and paper sculptures. I even make my own paper."

He doesn't say anything at first, and when I glance over at him, his mouth is slightly open and he's staring at me.

"I know it's weird, but I got into it in high school when I was going through some rough times," I say. "It sets me at peace. Helps me find focus. If I could do anything I wanted and not have to worry about money, I would just create all day long. Is that crazy?"

"It's wonderfully surprising," he says. "I had no idea."

I shrug. "It's what I end up doing with most of my free time."

"Can I see some?" he asks.

My heart warms. I expected him to dismiss it as something ridiculous or silly, but the fact that he's interested enough to want to see some of my art touches me. "Maybe someday," I say. "It's just a silly dream, anyway."

"Our deepest hopes and dreams are never silly," he says, his voice low. "Want to know a secret?"

I give him a sideways look. "Okay."

"I have one of your little frogs," he says with a laugh. "I took it from the bar the other night."

My mouth opens and I turn to face him. "Are you serious?"

He's blushing like a kid caught with his hand in the cookie jar. "It's sitting on the side table in my apartment. I don't even know why I took it. You left and I was standing there, trying to decide whether to finish my drink or head home, and I picked it up. I couldn't figure out how in the world you made something so elaborate and perfect with the label off a beer bottle. I just couldn't stand the thought of someone throwing it away."

"Stalker," I tease, shoving him slightly.

He takes my wrist and pulls me toward him. Before I know it, his lips are on mine. Warm and soft and perfect.

Suddenly, we are alone in the universe, connected to each other heart and soul, our bodies drawn together like magnets. I don't think about consequences or fear. All I can think about is him. The weight of his hand on my wrist. The warmth of his tongue as he tastes me for the first time, coaxing my lips open.

His other hand slides around my waist and we move together, lifting to our knees on the platform, erasing the space between us.

I feel his kiss vibrate through my entire body, waking up some long-dormant desire to be closer, not just physically, but spiritually. To be seen for who I am, and loved anyway.

I lean into him, grip his muscled arms. Beg him to tighten his hold on me.

And he does.

Soft touches turn to hungry exploration, his hands sliding under my shirt and gripping my bare back, pulling me against the hard length of him.

I feel him smile against my lips, his nose nuzzling my cheek as I turn and bury my face against his shoulder. We hold each other tight as we catch our breath.

"I could stay up here with you forever," he whispers against my neck.

I smile and turn to look at him, seeing him in a new light. One that terrifies me so much my body trembles against him.

"You're only saying that because you're dreading having to climb back down," I say.

"I don't know. Maybe falling isn't such a scary thing, after all," he says, and kisses me again.

CHAPTER 12

JENNA

Storm clouds gather in the sky outside my apartment. They're the deep gray, ugly kind of clouds you know are getting ready to unleash hell any minute. I don't want to leave the comfort of my apartment, but I have less than an hour to get to downtown and pay my electric bill. It has to be done today or my power will be shut off for the third time this year.

Leave it to a small town like Fairhope to have an antiquated payment system that won't take credit cards over the phone. Most months, I'm barely scraping by, I usually end up taking extra shifts at Brantley's so I can pay bills that were due yesterday. If I want to keep my power, I'll have to drive over to the corporate offices downtown and pay in cash. I just barely made enough on the lunch shift to afford it, and after this, I'll have less than five bucks to my name until tomorrow night's shift.

It's not the most relaxing way to live, but I'm proud of

myself. I'm doing this alone, paying my way through school, keeping a roof over my head, and putting gas in my car. Most days.

I spend ten minutes looking for my umbrella before I finally give up and make a run for the car. Which is exactly when the rain begins to pour in earnest. Figures. The whole way there, I can barely see out the windshield even though I'm only going about ten miles per hour. It takes me twenty minutes to go seven miles, and I barely have time to park and run inside before the office closes.

As I'm dodging raindrops on my way in, I notice Preston's Escalade parked in one of the prestigious spots marked for the elite Wright family. His father owns this building, and most others along this strip, but their main offices are at the Wright Building across the street. I wonder for a moment what he's doing here on a Wednesday afternoon.

We haven't spoken since this weekend's kiss on top of the old water tower. After we both made it down safely, I drove him back to his apartment and we made out like teenagers for another thirty minutes, the windows fogged over, and our bodies sweaty. It was delicious.

By the time I made it home, though, the fear had already begun to take hold.

What was I thinking? I'd agreed to hang out with him for one night, thinking we'd both get so bored it would cure us both of this insane attraction. Instead, we'd connected on a level I never expected.

My stomach flip-flops now just thinking about it.

He's texted me a few times since then, but I've been

avoiding him like the plague. One more night like that and I'm going to be in serious trouble. Still, as I run past his car, I can't help but hope I run into him inside.

The security guard at the front desk frowns as I track water through the lobby, but it can't be helped. I'm a woman on a mission. Ten minutes remaining. I ride the elevator up to the sixth floor, tapping my toes the whole time, my eyes glued to the display of numbers as I make the short journey upward. I'm convinced this is the slowest elevator known to man when it finally dings and the doors open.

A woman with graying hair and a flowered blouse sits at the desk just beyond the glass double-doors of the electric company offices. She gives a tight-lipped smile as I walk off the elevator and pull the doors open.

This is not the first time she's seen me here, cash in hand, ten minutes before closing.

"Good afternoon, Miss Lewis," she says, glaring at the clock on the wall to her left. "You just made it."

"Thank goodness," I say. "It's pouring out there."

"So it appears."

I pull a stack of bills from my back pocket—mostly fives and ones—and lay it on the counter.

"Did you bring your bill with you?"

Crap. "No, I forgot it," I say. "Can you pull it up by my address?"

She sighs and nods, typing away at her computer for a moment as I recite my apartment's address. "Sixty-two dollars even," she says. "There's a five dollar late fee as well."

I count out sixty-seven dollars and tuck the remaining four back into my jeans. It will be ramen noodles again tonight, but at least I'll have electricity.

"Thank you, dear." She hands me a receipt. "Be safe out there. I hear there's a tornado watch until five-thirty."

"Thanks Mrs. Williams," I say. "Have a good weekend."

"You too," she says.

I head back out to the elevator and it opens right away. It's empty and I notice with frustration that there's a nagging disappointment in my heart. In and out with no sign of Preston.

But the elevator stops on five and guess who is standing there?

My heart does a double-pump, and I straighten. Preston's eyes widen and a sly smile spreads across his face.

"Hey, what are you doing here?" he asks as he steps inside.

I smile back. I can't help it. He has one of those smiles that is contagious. Besides, I can't stop staring at his lips and thinking of last night.

"Oh, you know me, I like to come downtown on the weekends and ride the elevators up and down for a cheap thrill," I say.

He laughs and steps beside me, his arm brushing against mine. "Well, in that case, maybe we should get crazy and head back up once we hit the ground floor."

I press my lips together and try not to act amused. "What are you doing here?" I ask. "I thought your dad's office was across the street."

"It is," he says. "He's got me running some meetings over here with the accounting firm a few days a week now."

"Sounds fun," I say.

"You can't imagine how much," he says, turning toward me. "My day is looking up, though."

The elevator makes it about half a floor down when the power goes out.

CHAPTER 13
PRESTON

The elevator comes to an abrupt halt and the lights go off for a second before the backup lighting kicks in and fills the small box with its dim glow.

I reach for Jenna, touching her arm. "Are you okay?"

Her eyes are wider than I've ever seen and her lips are parted. "I'm okay," she says. "Just surprised. Is this just a power outage?"

"I think so," I say. I open the small panel under the number pad and pull out a red phone. It begins dialing immediately and an elderly man picks up. "Hank? It's Preston."

"Mr. Wright? Are you stuck in that elevator?"

I smile. Hank has been working security here at the Fairhope Building for about forty years. "Yes, sir," I say. "Is the power out throughout the whole building?"

"The whole town, I imagine," he says. "The sky got dark and suddenly, everything just poof, went right off. Not sure when they'll be able to get things moving again. Let me make some calls."

"What about a backup generator?" I ask. "Isn't there some kind of auxiliary power in this building?"

Hank clears his throat. "Well, sir, now this building was never upgraded with a backup generator. That was something Mr. Trent was supposed to take care of, I believe."

I close my eyes and groan. Of course. Yet another mess Mason's father got us into when he embezzled millions of dollars from the Wright Corporation. I'd been cleaning up his messes for months.

"What can we do?" I ask.

When I glance over, Jenna is watching me with a look of panic in her eyes. I've never seen her scared of anything, so this is a surprise to me. I reach out for her hand and she bites her lower lip and shakes her head. Her arms are wrapped tightly around her body and she's got her back pressed up against the wall of the elevator so hard, I'm afraid it will leave a mark.

"You just sit tight," he says with a little laugh. As if we could go anywhere. "Everything will be alright. I'll be in touch as soon as I have a plan in place. We'll get you out of there."

"Hank, I'm not alone in here," I say, watching Jenna. Her body is literally shaking. "I have a young lady in here with me and she seems a little frightened. You guys do whatever you have to do to get us out of here as soon as you can, okay?"

"Yes, sir," Hank says and hangs up.

I set the red phone back on the receiver and step carefully toward Jenna. I put my hands on her shoulders.

"They're working on getting us out of here," I say. "It shouldn't take long. You doing okay?"

I realize she's soaked to the bone and shivering. I pull my sweater over my head and hand it to her. "Here, put this on," I say. "We need to warm you up."

She nods and slips the sweater over her head. It's too big for her, and damn, she looks good wearing my clothes. It's such a small thing, but after everything that's happened between us, it feels intimate.

I put my arms around her and her head rests against my chest.

"What did they say?" she asks. Her voice is trembling. "Is there a backup generator?"

"Not in this building," I say. I spare her the details about Mason's dad. "But everything will be just fine. The elevators are programmed to stop when the power fails and nothing is going to happen to us. As soon as they get the power going again, the elevator will be running normally."

"How long is that going to take?"

"I'm not sure," I say. "Hank, our security guard, said he'd call back when he knows something."

She laughs.

"What?" I ask.

"Just realized the irony of the fact that I came here to pay my electric bill so my power doesn't get cut off today and the second I pay it, the power in their own damn building goes out."

I smile. "Maybe they forgot to pay their bill, too."

She laughs and pulls away, her eyes shining with frightened tears. "Sorry. You must think I'm an idiot," she says. "I'm not normally claustrophobic or anything, but I do not like the idea of being stuck in an elevator five floors above the ground with a possible tornado outside."

"Tornado?" I ask. This is news to me. I had just gotten out of one of my long meetings trying to fix yet another mess Mr. Trent made a few months back, when I got on the elevator. I hadn't heard anyone say a word about a tornado warning or I would have taken the stairs.

As I hold Jenna in my arms, I am so grateful no one told me. I would hate it if she were stuck in here, alone and scared.

Plus, I am really starting to like the way she feels in my arms.

We stand in silence for a moment, but when I realize it could be a while before I hear back from Hank, I need to find a way to distract her.

"Sunday was—"

The phone rings and we both jump. Jenna steps back and grips the metal bar with both hands.

I answer the phone. "Hank?"

"Yes, sir, Mr. Wright."

"Please tell me you have some good news."

"I wish I did," he says. "Unfortunately, there's a pretty nasty storm out there. There's been reports of a tornado touching down out by the Wilkes' farm. From what I'm hearing, several houses just outside of town are completely gone."

I curse and run a hand through my hair. Jenna moves closer, but I hold my hand up for her to wait just a second.

"There are also a couple serious car accidents in town on account of the heavy rain. Emergency services have their hands full right now. I could call your dad and see if he can pull some strings to get someone from the fire department out here to see if they can get those doors open for you, but it's going to be a while before they get the power up and running."

"No, don't worry about that Hank," I say."We'll be fine in here. Let them do their job, but just make sure they know we're in here and not to forget about us, okay?"

Hank laughs into the phone. "Yes, sir. No way we're going to forget about you two in there, I promise. You want me to give Mr. Wright a call for you anyway? Let him know where you are and that you're safe?"

"That's not necessary, Hank," I say. "Keep us updated if you can."

"Will do," he says.

Jenna's eyes are full of questions as I hang up the phone. "What's going on?"

"It's not good news, I'm afraid," I say. "Tornado struck down just outside of town. Sounds like there's some serious damage to a couple of the farms and the power's out all over town. It could be a little while before they get to us."

"Shit," Jenna says. She leans against the wall of the elevator and slides all the way down to the floor, knees up. "Was anyone hurt?"

"I don't know," I say. "Hank didn't have much information yet. I guess everyone's heading out there to go help. There were a few car accidents in town, too."

"Oh man," she said. Her foot starts tapping and she chews on her fingernails. "Do you think the tornado is heading this way? What would happen if it hit downtown?"

Her eyebrows are scrunched up and she looks pale. I need to change the subject before she freaks out.

"I'm sure everything will be fine," I say. "If we were in any danger, Hank would be sure to get the fire department out here as soon as possible to get us out of here. I think they're mostly just cleaning things up and trying to get the power back on. The worst of the storm has probably already passed us by."

I clear my throat, hoping I'm telling the truth. I don't want to be stuck in an elevator five floors up during a tornado anymore than she does, but I can't imagine any better company in the world. Jenna all to myself? I like the sound of that, even if these aren't the best of circumstances.

"Penny looks good, doesn't she?" I ask, wanting to get both our minds off the situation.

"Yeah, she looks amazing," she says. Her teeth are chattering.

She wraps her arms around her middle again. She leans back against the wall of the elevator and then slides down to sit on the floor.

"Thanks for the sweater. I knew it was about to rain, but I couldn't find my umbrella, so of course I got soaked. The first thing I'm going to do when I get home is take a scorching hot shower."

I swallow hard at the thought of Jenna in the shower. I can practically see the water cascading down her naked body. Suddenly, it feels very hot in here.

"Turned out to be crappy weather for spring break," I say, trying to think of anything that will help take her mind off things.

"Makes Aruba sound a lot nicer, I imagine."

I smile. "Perhaps," I say. "One thing I learned growing up, though, is that the destination is never as important as the people you're traveling with."

She raises an eyebrow. "Did your family travel a lot growing up?"

I nod. "We took at least one big trip a year as a family. We never spent much time with our parents, though."

"Why not?"

I shrug. "They usually had meetings to go to or what I call business social events where it looks like a party, but is really just about networking and greasing the wheels. I didn't realize it until I got a little older, but my parents have always put business first. If the CEO of a company my dad was courting or working up some big deal with was going to Bora Bora on vacation in December with his family, suddenly my parents were, too, and what a coincidence," I say, a touch of bitterness in my voice. "They always booked two adjoining suites of rooms so they could have their own space separate from Penny and me. That way they could host social gatherings in their part of the hotel without keeping us awake or having to deal with us at all. The nanny, Miss Claire, always stayed with us and took us to the beach and stuff like that."

I look up and Jenna is staring at me with a strange expression.

"What?"

She shakes her head. "Hearing the sadness and regret in your voice when you're talking about suites of rooms in an exotic resort makes me feel so conflicted," she says with a laugh. "On one hand, I'm sure it's tough to grow up feeling like your parents never put you first. Constantly being passed off to a nanny couldn't have been easy when you just wanted to spend time with them. But on the other hand, it's hard for me to sympathize with you when you're talking about having free reign of a luxury resort that probably cost more a night than what my parents made in a month."

"I sound like a spoiled brat again."

She smiles. "A little bit," she says. "But at the same time, if all you wanted was some attention from your parents, I'm sure those vacations made you sad, too. It's just so foreign to me. My parents' idea of a vacation was to take us down to the local spring. There was this tiny little pond that sat right on top of a natural spring. The people who ran it set up a beach area and rented out intertubes and stuff. I think it cost about $1 to get in back then and that was a stretch for my family. A real treat was getting to go to the concession stand and buy a twenty-five cent candy bar and a soda," she says with a laugh. She's picking at the red nail polish on her fingernails. "The water was cold as hell, but so incredibly clear you could see straight down to the bottom."

"At least they spent time with you."

She snorts. "If you call that spending time," she says. "My daddy would always bring a cooler full of cheap beer and be passed out by noon and Momma, well, yeah, she spent time with us. She was too chicken to wear a swim suit in front of people so she always wore these ridiculously huge t-shirts that went down to her knees."

Jenna smiles like she's remembering some secret joy, and in that moment, she's the most beautiful person I have ever seen in my life.

"We should go there together sometime," I say. "Take a road trip. I'd love to meet your family."

She wraps her arms around her knees and lays her head against them. "No you wouldn't," she says. "Besides the spring is all dried up now from what I hear."

This is the most I've ever heard Jenna talk about her family or her hometown. There's a sadness in her voice that seems bone-deep and still raw. I want to ask her more, but I'm scared to push her.

"Well, the best part of going on vacation was getting to spend time with Penny," I say. "I wouldn't trade that for anything. By the time Penny and I were about nine or ten, our parents let us take some friends with us each time, which made things a lot more interesting. Especially as we got older and knew how to get into more trouble."

I laugh, remembering all the craziness we used to get into when we were teens.

Jenna smiles. "Like what?"

I search my memories for the worst of the stories. Or best, depending on how you look at it.

"Oh, okay, so there was this one time, we were spending two weeks in St. Lucia. My parents had strictly forbidden us from leaving the resort, but they were so busy with their meetings, they had no idea what we were up to. At this point, even though Miss Claire was technically still supposed to be looking after us, she was getting older and liked to take these really long afternoon naps."

"How old were you?"

I shut one eye and glance up at the ceiling, trying to remember. "Maybe about fifteen, I think. Could have been sixteen," I say. "Of course as soon as her head hit the pillow, we left the resort to go explore. It was me and Mason and Penny and her friend Summer. Have you met her yet?"

"Is she the one with the crazy colored hair?"

I smile and nod. "I think it was teal last time I saw her."

"Yeah, she's been in the restaurant a few times," she says.

"I haven't talked to her much but I know who she is. She seems cool."

"I think you guys would get along," I say. "She's a rebel like you."

Jenna gives me another look, but I ignore it for now.

"Anyway, so we head off-resort and end up at one of those scooter rental places, you know the type where you can rent a death-trap for about a hundred bucks an hour, no helmet?" She gives me a blank stare. "We rent four and head all around the local villages, shopping, getting ice cream, whatever. So then Mason has this crazy idea that we should ride up to check out the volcano."

Jenna's mouth drops open. "There was a volcano?"

I laugh. "Yes. It's on the far side of the island and took us about an hour on these scooters just to get there. We were definitely not supposed to be taking them out that far, but we were kids, we didn't care.

"We get to the tourist area of the volcano when Penny spots this side road that's marked 'Do not enter'."

"So of course you enter."

"Of course," I say. "And this narrow road takes us all the way up around to the opposite side of the volcano. The area where tourists are definitely not allowed to go. There were no paths or anything, but we got off the scooters and walked up as close as we could get to the edge. The bottom of our shoes were literally burning by the time we got up to the top. It was insane," I say. "But it was also one of the most intense and beautiful views I've ever seen. Mason pulled out a joint and we sat up there at the top of the giant active volcano and smoked a joint. We were almost finished with it when the police arrived."

Jenna's hand rises to her mouth and she gasps. "You're kidding me?"

"I wish," I say with a laugh. "Oh my God, we were so stoned. We could not stop laughing. They kept yelling at us in French, telling us we weren't allowed to be there. They actually put me and Mason in handcuffs," I say. "Penny fell on the way back down the mountain and burned her leg, though, and they ended up having to call in an air evac to get her off the mountain. She was in hospital for like three days. Still has the scars to prove it."

"Holy shit, I can't believe that," she says.

"Yeah, it was crazy," I say. "We totally lost those scooters, too. By the time we got back down to them, they were gone. Probably stolen. I thought my parents were going to kill us. I don't even want to know how much it cost them to get us out of that mess."

"So you weren't arrested?"

"Not officially. Once my parents intervened, everything was fine," I say. "After that, you would think they would have kept closer tabs on us during vacations, right?" I shake my head. "I did end up getting arrested in Paris that following Christmas for getting drunk and throwing an empty bottle of wine off the top of the Eiffel Tower. So stupid. I did a lot of dumb things back then."

"Did your parents get you off the hook that time, too?"

"Always," I say. "But it was less about what would happen to me and more about how an official arrest would reflect upon them and the family name."

"Must have been weird to grow up knowing you never really had to deal with any consequences," she says. "I can't imagine it. I probably would have been dead by now if I wasn't scared of getting thrown in jail."

I laugh. "Did you get into a bunch of trouble when you were younger? I have this very clear image of you as a young, rebellious teenager."

"I got into way too much trouble," she says. She avoids my eyes. "The kind that's much harder to get out of."

I study her. "What do you mean?"

She shrugs. "No one was ever there to bail me out when I fucked up," she says. "If I got arrested, there were real consequences, you know? Of course, that didn't stop me from making all the wrong choices."

"Like what?"

She takes a deep breath in through her nose and lays her head back on her knees. "Like skipping school and doing drugs with my boyfriend," she says. "I was fourteen the first time I got arrested for possession. My dad—"

She stops herself and the air shifts around us, as if some ghost of her past has returned to haunt her. The hairs on my arms stand up and my stomach twists.

"Your dad what?"

She leans her head back against the wall of the elevator and closes her eyes. "My dad was pissed," she says. "Let's just leave it at that."

"Did you go to jail or something?"

"Worse," she says. "Had to enter a rehab program for juveniles and go to school at the juvenile detention center for most of my sophomore year of high school. It was rough."

"I had no idea," I say. I try to imagine what my life would have been like if my parents hadn't been there to bail me out of every single bad decision I made.

"You would think I'd have learned my lesson the first time," she says with a laugh. "I got pretty messed up with drugs when I was younger. It got bad for a while, but I pulled myself out of it."

The conversation has very quickly gone from a carefree sharing of a silly story I thought would make her laugh to some real shit about her own life.

"How did you get out of it?" I ask quietly.

Her eyes meet mine and there are glassy tears in them. "My boyfriend, Aaron, overdosed on heroine," she says. "Christmas break our junior year. We were both out of our minds fucked up and he just went a little too far. I passed out at some point during the night and when I woke up the next morning, he was just laying there beside me, all the light gone from his eyes forever. That was a big wake up call for me. I've never touched drugs since that morning, and I never will again."

My heart pounds in my chest. I have never been in a situation like that, and I have no idea what to say to her to tell her how sorry I am that she went through that.

"That sounds terrifying," I say. "I'm sorry."

"We were stupid," she says. "We both knew we were walking the line, but we couldn't seem to stop ourselves. Every time we'd get high, we swore it was going to be the last time. We just needed one more hit and we were done," she says. "We'd clean up our act for about a week, maybe two, and then be right back at it."

"Addiction is tough."

"You have no idea," she says. "It's brutal. I would be doing okay, swearing I was done with that shit, but then something bad would happen and I felt like I needed it. I know you probably don't understand that at all, but it was so real to me. The smallest thing could send me back over the edge."

I don't know what to say. She's right. I don't understand that kind of addiction, and there's so much desperation in her voice, it scares me.

"It was a coping mechanism," she says. "A way to escape the shitty life I was living and get away for a while. I guess in some ways, getting high was my way of forgetting the consequences of my life for a while. Forgetting reality. You had money to bail you out. I had drugs."

She laughs, but it's a joyless sound.

I reach over and touch her hand. She looks up, surprised, but takes my hand and threads her fingers through mine.

"I have no idea why I'm telling you all this," she says, a tear escaping down her cheek. "I don't like to think about those days anymore. I don't very much like the person I used to be."

She sniffs and leans her head over to wipe her cheek against her shirt.

"You must think I'm a real piece of trash," she says, not looking me in the eyes.

Her words stab deep. "Not even one tiny bit," I say. "I was actually thinking how strong you are."

She looks up, her eyes now overflowing with tears. "Strong? No way."

"Yes," I say, gripping her hand tighter. "Do you know how many people can never get out from under something like that? How many people would still be getting high every weekend and falling deeper and deeper into that hole of depression? But not you. You made a very difficult change and finished school. You're in college, working practically full time to support yourself with no help from anyone else. I admire you, to be honest."

She rolls her eyes and sniffs. "How could a guy like you, with all that you have and all that you've accomplished, admire someone like me? I'm nothing," she says.

I move closer to her and put a hand on her cheek. She lifts her eyes to me, and I make sure I have her complete attention before I speak.

"Then you don't see yourself very clearly," I say. "You are one of the most beautiful, most amazing women I've ever known."

Her hand tightens around mine and for a moment, we're suspended a mere breath away from each other, the air between us shifting one last time as some of the walls she's built around herself fall away.

I run my thumb down her cheek, caressing her skin and wanting nothing more in this world than to pull her into my arms and kiss her.

As my lips touch hers, the power kicks back on and elevator begins to move.

CHAPTER 14
JENNA

The elevator comes back to life, and I nearly have a heart attack. I spring to my feet and clutch the handrail.

My heart is pounding, and it's not just because of the sudden movement. What the hell just happened here?

It's funny. I've heard people say before that there's just something that happens when you're stuck in an elevator. As if you have no idea if you're truly going to survive the night, you begin to spill your darkest secrets.

That has to be it. That's the only explanation I can come up with for why I just told Preston all that crap about my past. It was the one thing I didn't want anyone in my new life to know about me. Well, okay, one of the things. There are more.

But Aaron's overdose and my time in rehab is a biggie.

I'm ashamed of who I was back then. Ashamed of what I did and what I let him do. He died right there beside me while I was passed out. I did nothing to help him or save him.

It's one of those deep, dark secrets I keep hidden inside and never let out into the light. Why did I tell Preston?

I glance over at him and try to read his expression. Is he completely mortified? He's staring at the numbers going by on the overhead display, counting down to the first floor. Probably can't wait to be free of crazy Jenna and her sordid past.

I honestly can't blame him.

Most of the time, I feel exactly the same way.

The elevator dings with each floor. Five. Four. Three. Two. One. The doors open and Preston's mother rushes in and throws her arms around him. I scoot around them, anxious to get the hell out of this death trap.

I am normally not afraid of elevators, as long as they work. Broken elevators? Well, that just makes me think of plunging to my death in a fiery explosion.

Outside, the rain is still coming down hard and the sky is as dark as night even though it's only six-thirty. I wonder if the worst of the storms have passed or if there is more to come.

"I was so worried about you," Mrs. Wright says. She has both her hands on her son's cheeks and his face has gone beet red. "Why didn't you call us right away? I've been trying to get in touch with you for over an hour, wondering if you somehow got stuck in all this mess."

"I had my phone off for the meeting," Preston says. "I forgot to turn it back on."

"Stuck in an elevator for an hour and a half and you

forgot to turn it back on?" His mother clucks her tongue. "You should have called. I was worried to death."

"Hank here had it all under control. Didn't you, Hank?" Preston reaches his hand out to an elderly black man with graying hair and a nice smile. He's wearing a blue suit with a gold name-tag.

They shake hands and Hank beams at Preston.

"Thank you, Hank," Mrs. Wright says with a passing glance at the security guard. She turns back to Preston. "If we had known you were stuck in here, we would have rerouted everyone to get you out as fast as possible. Who knows what might have happened?"

His mother still had yet to even notice or acknowledge me, which was no surprise. Should I duck out and make a run for my truck? I feel stupid hovering here near the door, watching them.

"That's exactly why I told him not to call you," Preston says. "How are things going out there? Any news on the damage?"

"Oh, honey, it's just terrible," his mother says with a frown. "The Wilkes' farmhouse is completely destroyed. There's a lot of damage out that way."

"Was anyone hurt?" he asks.

"One of the Powell children is still missing," she says. "Their little girl, Anna."

"She's only four years old," Preston says.

I step closer at this news. A four year old little girl missing? I can only imagine what her family is going through right now.

"Where was she last seen?" I ask.

Preston's mom turns, noticing me for the first time.

"Oh, goodness, I didn't even see you there, sweetheart." Her eyes drop from my face to Preston's sweater, still draped on my body. She makes a slight face, but recovers quickly.

I take a deep breath. I'm used to that kind of look.

"Mom, you remember Jenna Lewis," Preston says. "She's a good friend of Leigh Anne's. We were stuck in the elevator together."

His mom's eyebrow twitches, and I'm sure she's wondering why in the world I was here with her son. Wisely, she doesn't ask.

"Of course I remember Jenna." She reaches her hand toward me. "You're the girl who took Penny to that awful pawn shop last year."

She says it as a matter of fact, and I cringe. We aren't exactly off to the best start. "Yes, ma'am," I say. I have no good excuse for what I did. Hopefully she understands I was only trying to help her daughter when she needed me.

"Well, that's all in the past," she says, a thin smile on her heavily made up face. "The little Powell girl was in her mother's arms when the tornado hit. They didn't have a storm shelter, so they were all huddled together in the hall closet when the roof was torn off the house. The force of the wind carried her little girl right out of her arms and they haven't been able to find her."

My hand flies to my mouth and my stomach feels sick. "Oh, God," I say.

"What can we do?" Preston says.

"Your father is meeting with some of the town council members. They're coming up with a plan to get folks back on their feet," she says. "A few people have already headed over to the Powell house to search for the little girl. I sure hope they find her soon. It looks like we might not be done with the storms for the night."

I pull my cell phone from my back pocket and dial Leigh Anne's number. She picks up right away. "Hey, are you okay?" I ask.

"Jenna, thank goodness, I tried to call you," she says. "Can you believe these storms?"

"It's awful," I say. Preston is still talking with his mother so I step toward the door. "Did you hear about the little Powell girl?"

"No, what's going on?"

"She's missing. She got carried away by the storm," I say. "Is Knox free? I was thinking maybe we could all head over there and help them search for her."

Preston puts a hand on my back and whispers in my ear. "Mason's already on his way in his truck," he says. "If they want to come with us, tell her and Knox to meet us here in a few minutes."

I turn to him, surprised he's coming to help.

"I don't think that's a good idea," his mother says. "The storms might start back up and I don't want you and Mason out there in all this."

"All the more reason we need to get out there looking for this girl," he says. "Go home, Mom. I'll call you when we have news."

She makes a deep sound in her throat and lifts her chin. "I don't know what has gotten into you and your sister both," she says. She doesn't explain herself further. She just kisses him on the cheek and nods to a man standing in the corner. He straightens and rushes to open the door for her.

The man grabs a large umbrella that's propped up against the side of the building and holds it over her head as she walks toward the car.

We watch as his mother gets into the back of a sleek black car with tinted windows. The tall man closes the door, rushes around to the driver's seat, and takes off just as the rain begins to pour harder.

"Jenna?" Leigh Anne says through the phone. "Was that Preston's mom? Where are you?"

"Yes, sorry," I say. "We're over here at the Fairhope Building downtown. Do you guys want to meet us over here and go looking for that little girl?"

"Of course," she says. "Let me throw on my boots and we'll head over. Do you need anything?"

"Bring some flashlights and umbrellas if you have them," I say. "And if you have a spare pair of boots, I'd appreciate it."

I look over at Preston in his nice black pants, loafers, and a shirt and tie.

"Maybe bring some old jeans and boots for Preston, too, if Knox has something he could spare."

"Sure thing," she says. "See you in a few."

We hang up and I stand at the doors with Preston, looking out at the heavy rain.

"I hope we find her," I say. "Can you imagine how terrified she must be right now out there all alone in this?"

"If she's even conscious," he says quietly.

At my side, I feel his hand slip into mine and squeeze. Warmth wells up within me. How could he have heard about my past and still even want to be around me? Have I completely misjudged him?

Or has the storm distracted him for now?

I stare out at the rain and wonder if my confession will mean the end of us before we even had a real beginning.

CHAPTER 15

JENNA

Mason and Knox pull up at almost the same time. Preston opens his umbrella and we run out to greet them together.

I climb into the truck with Leigh Anne. She hands Preston a plastic bag with some clothes and boost, and a look passes between us before he closes the door and runs up to get in the truck with Mason.

Something has changed between us, and I can't tell yet exactly how or what it means. All I know is that the more time we spend together, the more my walls start to come down. Walls I built for a reason. I watch him until he disappears into Mason's truck.

"Where are we headed?" Knox asks. "Out to the Powell place?"

"Yes," I say. "Preston's mom said there's already a group gathered there to start looking."

"What a nightmare," Leigh Anne says. "Can you imagine?"

"Is everything okay at your place, Knox? That's out toward that same side of town, isn't it?" He's put so much work into restoring his mother's old house, I would hate to hear that anything had happened to it.

"Yeah, but I'm trying not to think about it right now," he says as he pulls out of the parking lot, following Mason and Preston in the other truck. "I'll head over and check it out after we find the girl and things settle down a bit. Not much I could do about it anyway with it raining like it is."

"Where were you guys when it hit?"

"At my apartment," Leigh Anne says. "It didn't get too bad here in town. Just a lot of scary wind and rain. The power went out, but I think it's out all over town. What were you doing here?"

Like Mrs. Wright, Leigh Anne notices Preston's sweater right away and raises an eyebrow.

I roll my eyes. "Stop letting your imagination run away with you," I say. "I came here to pay my electric bill. I got on the elevator and Preston got on the floor below me. The power went out and we got stuck in there for a little over an hour."

"So much for your plan to stay far away from him," she says with a giggle.

"You're telling me," I grumble. "Of course someone leaked an invite to the party last night, after I told them I didn't want to see Preston for a while."

I glare at Leigh Anne and she looks up at the ceiling of the truck, biting back a smile.

"Maybe nature is trying to tell you something," Knox says with a laugh. If Leigh Anne wasn't sitting between us, I would punch him on the leg.

"It was a coincidence," I say. I don't mention the water tower last night, but yes, it does seem that there have been a lot of coincidences bringing Preston and I together lately. "Thanks for coming, by the way. It sounds like they can use as many eyes as possible out there right now."

"Don't try to change the subject," Leigh Anne says. "What happened in the elevator?"

"I'm just wearing his sweater because I was cold, okay? Don't make a big deal out of it."

She throws her hands up. "Who is making a big deal? I was simply asking how it went. Did you guys talk?"

"He didn't ask me out if that's what you're getting at," I say. I don't know why I'm so grumbly with her, except that maybe I'm a little embarrassed about what happened between us in that elevator. And last night on top of the water tower.

I never dreamed Preston would be so easy to talk to. So understanding. What does all of it mean? It's going to be hard to go back to being just friends after what we've been through.

I shake my head and stare out the side window. I can't think about that right now.

Still, the sound of his voice telling me I'm beautiful rings in my memory like a gift. I scrunch down in the seat and hide a smile at the thought, despite myself.

The Powell farm is only a few minutes outside the city limits, but it takes us nearly half an hour to get there in the pouring rain. Leigh Anne hands me an old pair of boots and I toss my sneakers onto the floorboard of Knox's truck and pull on the boots. They're a little big, but they'll do.

"Thanks," I say.

There are about six other cars in the driveway. A small crowd is gathered on what remains of the porch. Most of the roof on one side is gone. My heart is sick just looking at the scene.

A woman in a flowered house-dress stands on the porch, her face a splotchy mess of tears. A man in overalls and boots has his arm around her. They look up as the five of us approach.

"Oh my goodness, y'all are just such good people," the woman says. She starts crying all over again. "I can't thank you enough."

She buries her head in the man's overalls and he wraps his arms around her and rests his cheek against the top of her head.

They look familiar to me, and I'm pretty sure they've come into the restaurant before with their three kids. Their little girl's face flashes in my memory, and I feel tears creep into my throat. She's a pretty little thing with long, sandy blond hair and the brightest blue eyes. She always orders grilled cheese and asks for those little cherries from the bar.

I press my lips together tightly to keep control of my tears.

"What can we do to help?" Knox asks. "Do we have a plan?"

"I don't know how much we can do while it's still storming like this," a man says. I don't recognize him, but Preston seems to know him. They shake hands. "It's getting darker and the rain doesn't seem to be letting up any."

"We have to try," Preston says. He looks to the couple near the door. "Mr. And Mrs. Powell," he says, shaking the man's hands. "I'm so sorry about Anna. We're going to find her safe, okay?"

Mrs. Powell tries to smile, but sobs instead.

"How are the rest of your little ones?"

"They're doing okay. A little shaken up," Mr. Powell says. "They're over at my sister's for now."

"Good," he says. Everyone on the porch is now looking to Preston, as if he has suddenly outranked them and taken over as the natural leader of the situation. I'm impressed with how quickly he's taken charge. "Do you have any idea which direction the wind may have carried her? Where do you think we should start looking?"

"I don't know," Mrs. Powell says. "It all happened so fast."

"It's okay. Let's try to figure this out. Anyone know which way the storm was traveling?"

"It came from the northwest, I think," a redheaded man says. "And if you look out across the farm over that way, you can clearly see the path of the storm in the pattern of the debris."

"Good," Preston says. "Thank you, Dale. I think we should head that way, then. Southeast after the direction of the storm. Let's form a straight line starting here at the edge of the property and walk through slowly. Keep your eyes on the ground in front of you, pick up any easy-to-move debris to make sure she's not hiding underneath, trying to get out of the rain. Make sure nothing's got her caught or trapped. Let's get moving before it gets too dark out to see anything. Does everyone have a flashlight and an umbrella?"

"We have a few extra flashlights," Mr. Powell says. "I'll go fetch them."

Preston quickly divies the supplies among the group and gets us into a line on the southeast side of the property.

Within ten minutes of our arrival at the house, we are actively searching for the little girl. I keep my eyes glued to the ground, squinting through the rain, but my thoughts are locked on Preston.

I'm impressed and surprised by the way he took charge and moved these people to action so quickly. How long had those men been standing on that porch doing nothing but talking about how tough this was going to be?

He's a natural leader, a role I haven't seen him in before. It makes sense considering he's had his father to watch and take after all his life, but it still surprises me how easily he stepped into the role.

My feet sink into the ground with each step. Water falls so fast it's running like a river all through this stretch of farmland. There's debris everywhere. Pieces of the torn roof. A broken windmill. Branches from nearby trees. The field is a landmine of hiding places and dangers. She could be anywhere.

I lean down and lift up a big piece of wood that might be large enough to hide the body of a small child, but after almost an hour of walking in a straight line, I'm starting to panic. What if we don't find her?

What if she's hurt or bleeding? What if she hit her head and needs immediate medical attention?

We could be running out of time.

Preston walks beside me, and I take a moment to look over at him. He senses my eyes on him and meets my gaze. I see he's just as worried as I am.

"We've got to find her soon," I say, trying not to raise my

voice too much. The girl's father is at the end of the line. He looks terrified.

"I know," he says. "I'm really worried, and it's getting very dark out here. This rain just isn't letting up."

"Maybe we should spread out more?" I say. "Cover more area faster."

"That's not a bad idea."

He calls everyone in, and they stop and gather in a crowd around him.

"It's getting dark real fast, and I'm thinking maybe we'd do better covering more space," he says. "Mason, Leigh Anne and Knox, why don't you three keep on this path but spread out a little. Dale, Mr. Johnny and Felix, you three take Mr. Powell and head down to the south side of the field. There seems to be a lot of downed trees over that way. Jenna and I will take a look over in the wooded area on the other side of the field."

"Should we meet up at a certain time?" Dale asks.

Preston looks at his watch. "Let's give it another good hour and head back to the farm house and regroup around eight-thirty," he says. "If we still haven't found her by then, we'll make some calls and see if we can get some more help out here. Things should be a little more settled in town by then."

Everyone spreads out toward the assigned spots. Preston and I track our way through thick mud toward the tree line.

"What's going to happen if we don't find her in the next hour?" I ask.

"God help us," he says. "I don't know. I saw a few more cars pull up over at the house, so hopefully we can get more people looking and cover more ground. I've heard stories of people being carried half a mile by a storm like this. There's no telling where she is."

I have to double-skip to keep up with him. We're both completely soaked from head-to-toe. I've stopped used the umbrella. It wasn't helping anyway, and I wanted my hands free.

But as we reach the trees, the rain begins to let up. We both look toward the sky.

"Whew, that's our first break," he says. "Maybe we can look faster without the rain."

He props his umbrella against a tree and starts walking.

It's darker here in the woods and we swing our flashlights across the forest floor, looking for any sign of the little girl. I call her name several times, but hear no response.

Half an hour later, though, I see a tiny blue shoe stuck in the mud.

CHAPTER 16
PRESTON

Jenna calls my name, and I turn and run. We've been making our way through the woods for half an hour, spreading out just far enough that I can still see the light of her flashlight through the trees.

I run full force, my heart pounding, praying she's found the girl.

When I get to her, her eyes are full of fear and hope. She's pointing to the ground where a little blue shoe is peeking out from the sludge. I don't know whether to be scared or hopeful.

I reach down and grab the shoe from the mud. "This has to be hers," I say. "It's about the right size, don't you think? And what else would a shoe be doing out here in the woods?"

"Do you think she might be close?" she asks. She's out of breath and frantically shines her light all around us. Her hands are shaking.

"I hope so," I say. "Come on, let's look around this area."

We move faster, fueled by this new discovery. My eyes can't hold to one spot long enough. I feel jittery and anxious. I wonder if we should call out to the others, but if we're on the wrong track, I don't want to stop their search. A shoe could have been lifted from the house and slung over here by the storm.

Or she might have been wearing it.

Our lights scan the forest floor all around us. A few feet beside me, Jenna gasps and takes off at a full run.

The wind roars through the treetops overhead and pine needles fall all around us.

"Anna," Jenna cries out.

My eyes quickly follow her light to a large pine tree about twenty feet away that has fallen over, it's roots ripped from the ground in one large clump.

In the jumping light as she runs, I catch a glimpse of dark blue denim fabric covered with mud, a pale chubby leg sticking out, lifeless.

My heart tightens as we run toward the little girl. I cry out for the others as we run, but it's too dark to see anyone from here. We're too deep in the woods now and the wind is picking up again.

I get there first and fall to my knees, sliding through the mud and pinestraw that coats the ground.

The child is on her belly, her head tilted to the side. Her eyes are closed.

I put my hand on her back, sending up a prayer that she's still breathing. Hot tears spring to my eyes as cold rain stings my face.

"Anna?" I say softly, leaning down close to her. Her back

rises against my hand and I let out a sigh of relief. "She's alive," I say to Jenna.

She kneels next to me, her hand over her mouth. The little girl's arm is twisted at a terrible, unnatural angle and it's easy to see that it's broken. I'm scared to lift her in case there are other, unseen injuries, but I can't leave her here either. The storm is getting worse and we need to take cover.

In my pocket, my phone beeps a new alert. I take it out and curse.

"What?" Jenna asks.

"Another tornado warning," I say.

A warning means one has been spotted in the area. Not good. There's no way I can carry her in this storm all the way back to the farmhouse. By now, that has to be at least half a mile away, if not more. I don't want to risk being out in the middle of the flat field when it hits.

"What do we do?" Jenna asks. "Can we make it back to the house?"

"I don't know," I say. I look around, searching for any place we might take shelter.

"The tree," I say, nodding to the downed pine. "Pine trees have very shallow root systems and when they fall, the roots come up with them, usually leaving a hole in the ground. We can take shelter there until this passes. It's better than being out in the middle of the field, and if another tree falls, we'll be safe slightly below ground level."

Jenna nods. "Do you think it's okay to lift her up?" she asks.

"We don't have a choice," I say. In the distance, I hear a sound like a train whistle raging through the wind. "Hear that?" I shout. "We need to take cover. Now. Go over to the tree and make sure there's nothing in that hole," I say. "If there's debris, clear it out as best you can. I'll get the girl."

I slide both my arms under the child's body and lift her as gently as I can. She stirs slightly, moaning as I press her tiny body against my chest. I try to keep her arm as stable as I can against my chest and carry her toward the fallen tree.

Jenna climbs down and helps me lower the child into the hole. We settle ourselves on either side of her, creating a shield with our bodies, pressed close to the muddy wall of the hole. As the wind whips around us, Jenna holds on to me and we lower our heads over the girl.

The tornado passes dangerously close. Above our heads, tree branches fly through the air, cracking against the sides of other trees.

I don't dare look up to see what might be coming. I put my arm over Jenna's head, protecting her from anything flying around. We crouch low in the ground, our bodies soaked completely with red Georgia clay. The night is dark and unforgiving.

It lasts about five minutes. The five most terrifying minutes of my life.

Trees move and shake. A few nearby pines topple to the forest floor. The storm is loud and angry, dumping rain and leaves and pine needles all over us. A limb breaks off a nearby tree and lands on my back, scraping across my neck and arm. I can hardly breathe, clutching tightly to Jenna's hand.

When it's over, the area grows calm, the rain gone and the wind still.

Jenna lifts her head, her face streaked with tears and mud. "Is it over?"

"I think so," I say. I turn my flashlight back on and shine

it around. The forest is a mess of trees and branches, but getting into the hole was a good idea. Other than a few small limbs that landed on us, we are safe and alive.

"Are you hurt?" I ask Jenna. There is a deep scratch on her neck that is beaded with red blood.

"I'm fine. It's just a tiny scratch," she says. "Do you think it's safe to move her now?"

"Yeah, I think we need to try to get back as soon as possible. She needs medical attention."

I pull my phone back out and type out a quick text to Mason. I pray he and the others were able to find shelter. "We found the girl in the woods. She's alive but hurt. Meet at the house."

Together, we lift the girl from the muddy hole. I carry her in both arms, Jenna close by my side as we make our way back through the woods. My phone dings in my pocket and I ask Jenna to get it and check the message.

"It's Mason," she says. "He says they are back at the house. Everyone is safe. They're heading our way to help. He says there's doctor at the house."

"Thank God," I say.

We move as fast as we can without jostling the child too much. Mercifully, she's still unconscious and hopefully unaware of the pain she's in.

It takes us twenty minutes to find our way out of the woods and when we do, Mason and Knox are both there at the tree line with a four-wheeler.

They drive over to us and Knox carefully takes the child from my arms.

"I think her arm is broken," I say. I can't help the tears in my eyes as I watch them ride off with her.

I run a hand across my cheek and let out a deep sigh. I pull Jenna to me, her head resting against my chest as we both cry tears of relief. I kiss her forehead and she puts her hand in mine.

We walk in silence all the way back to the farmhouse.

CHAPTER 17
JENNA

Mason drives us back to the Fairhope Building, but we're all too exhausted to talk. We stayed at the Powell's house for a little while waiting on news of how Anna was doing. She was taken by ambulance to the hospital here in town, but the doctors say it's a miracle. Other than her broken arm and a few scrapes and bruises, she's going to be fine.

As exhausted as I am, I don't want to leave Preston after the night we've had. Something is growing between us, and even though it's unexpected, I don't want to say goodbye.

But at the same time, I'm terrified. I had decided to stay away from him at all costs, but somehow, fate keeps bringing us back together. It sounds stupid, but it's real. I feel it deep down in my bones.

We stand together beside my car, neither of us saying a word. The night air is strangely still and quiet after the storms. The power is still out through most of the town.

"I'm so glad—"

"You were really—"

We speak at the same time, stop, and then laugh. Conversation has been so easy between us the past few days, but now that we're alone again, there's a tension here that wasn't there before. A feeling of things unsaid, like we're standing at a line, trying to decide whether or not to cross it.

"What were you going to say?" he asks.

"That you were really great out there tonight," I say. I swallow, my throat thick with nerves. "You saved her life."

"You were the one who found her," he says.

"We make a good team, I think."

"Yeah, we really do," he says. His eyes are on my face, but I'm scared to meet his gaze. Afraid if I do, it will all come crashing down and I won't be able to resist these feelings growing inside.

"I'm just glad she's okay," he says. "I was so scared when I saw her lying there that she was..."

His voice trails off, but I know what he's feeling. I felt exactly the same way when I caught sight of her small body, lying there so still and lifeless.

"I can't even think what might have happened if we hadn't found her exactly when we did," I say.

"I know this is going to sound strange," he begins, his weight shifting from one foot to the other. "Maybe even crazy. But there's this feeling that we were meant to find her. That we were meant to be out there, together. Is that weird?"

I shake my head. "Not at all," I say. "If we hadn't been stuck together in that elevator or the power hadn't come back on exactly when it did. Or if your mother hadn't been there to tell us about the girl. If any one thing had gone differently, we might not have been there to find her before the second tornado hit," I say. "How can that be anything other than fate?"

With that one last word, I finally lift my eyes to his. The moment is electric. Something passes between us that shakes me so deeply, I feel as if I've been knocked off balance. I feel as if I'm falling, losing my grip on reality.

Can this be real?

I've never been one to believe in fate or wildly romantic notions of love or soul mates, but for a single moment, that's what this feels like. I'm standing here with the most unlikely man in the universe, feeling so drawn to him I can barely keep my feet on the ground.

Desire flashes in his eyes and he steps forward, lifting a hand to my neck and pressing his body against mine. We stare into each other's eyes, and I know this is the moment of decision. One crazy night on top of a water tower can be explained away as a moment of temporary insanity, but in less than twenty-four hours, our relationship has deepened beyond something casual. I know I should make some excuse, get in my car and drive away as fast as I can. But I have reached the end of my willpower. I can no longer resist whatever's happening between us.

My hands circle his waist pulling him closer. He lowers his lips to mine, tugging on the back of my neck.

Passion releases inside me, the floodgates of all the built-up emotion from this night opening with a vengeance.

His other arm circles around my back, his hand sliding under the sweater and finding my cold bare skin with his warmth.

My lips part and we kiss each other hungrily. I want so much more than just the taste of his tongue against mine and the feel of his hands on my skin. I want to explore every inch of his body. I want to feel him inside me.

But then I remember what I told him in the elevator, and fear brings hesitation. I pull away, turning my head to the side and leaning against the door of my truck.

"What's wrong?" he asks, breathless, his hands still reaching for me.

He moves close and leans his forehead against mine as our chests rise and fall together.

"What are we doing?" I ask. I feel dangerously close to tears.

"I believe it's called kissing," he says with a smile.

I shake my head. "That's not what I mean, and you know it."

"Are we back to the conversation about this being complicated?" he asks. "Already?"

I place my hands on his chest and push him back. I can't breathe with him so close. "Listen, I'm usually the last person in the world to start asking where things are going in a relationship, because I usually don't get this far," I say. "I like to keep things simple, but with us, it can never be simple. Can't you see that?"

"Jenna, I'm not some jerk looking to score with you," he says. "I think we could really have something here. I haven't wanted to be with someone this much in so long, I can't even remember the last time. What is it you're so afraid of?"

My heart skips a beat and panic rushes through me. "Everything," I say. "I've let you in on more secrets I never meant to share in the past week than anyone since I moved here. That scares the crap out of me. That stuff I told you in the elevator? That was just the beginning of it. There are so many things you don't want to know about me, Preston, and I'm scared that once you find out, you'll never look at me the same way again."

"So you think I'm just going to judge you on your past and walk away? You think what you told me back there scared me? Well, I'm still here, aren't I? Hearing about your past and everything you've survived just makes me want you more," he says. He runs a shaky hand through his thick dark hair. "Yes, starting something new is scary. Relationships are risky and messy sometimes, but when you find someone that makes you feel more alive than you ever have before, you don't just walk away."

"What kind of relationship could we possibly have?" I ask him. "Your mother already hates me. There's no way your father is going to approve of you dating a girl with a past like mine. I don't fit into your world, Preston. We have to at least think about that before we get to the point where someone is going to get hurt."

"I'm already there, Jenna," he says softly. The look in his eyes is pure torture, and I wonder how things got out of hand so quickly. He moves toward me and takes my hands in his. "I don't care what my parents think. And like it or not, you're already a part of my world. This doesn't have to be about the money or the things we've done in the past. I'm not asking you for any kind of commitment. Can't this just be about two people having fun?"

My eyes snap to his, my heart racing.

"I'm willing to slow things down if that's what you want. No pressure or expectations, but you need to know that I'm crazy about you," he says. "I have been for a long time now. And Sunday night? That was one of the best nights of my life. Every time I'm with you, I never want the night to end. And every time it does, I'm counting the hours until I see you again. If you don't feel the same way, tell me now and I'll walk away. But if you feel even half of what I'm feeling right now, I'm asking you to take a chance here."

The night grows still and I lose all sense of time and place. I'm terrified of what's happening between us, but I know that if I walk away from this moment, I will regret it for the rest of my life.

As I stare into his deep brown eyes, something inside me lets go. I allow myself to think of what it would be like to truly let someone into my life. To stop trying so hard to hide behind these walls, and just be myself with someone.

I reach up and wipe a streak of red mud from his cheek. "Okay," I say, a flood of excitement and fear washing over me. "But we keep it light. No expectations. No girlfriend and boyfriend. Just fun times until graduation."

"Deal." Preston smiles and gathers me into his arms. He swings me around and when he sets my feet back on the ground, we're both laughing.

"Now, come on," I say. "Let's go find some place to wash all this mud off."

"WHERE ARE WE HEADED?" PRESTON ASKS.

"That depends on whether you have any food at your place," I say. "I'm starving. We never got to eat dinner."

"There's nothing at my apartment," he says. "And with the power out, we're going to be taking cold showers. Unless..."

I raise an eyebrow. "Unless what?"

"Unless you want to go to my parents' house," he says, making a face.

I shake my head. "No way. I do not want to have to face your mother for the second time tonight."

"It's not as bad as it sounds," he says. "Plus, there's food and a generator powerful enough to keep the whole estate running for days. I swear, you'll never even see her. My parents are already fast asleep, trust me. We'll get you settled in the pool house, and I'll go forage for food in the main house."

I hesitate. A hot shower sounds much better than a cold one, but I don't want to risk running into his parents.

"There's a hot tub," he says.

I sigh. "Okay, I'm sold," I say. "But any sign of your parents, and I'm leaving."

"Fine, but there won't be." He motions to his Escalade. "Get in. We can just leave your truck here and come back and get it in the morning."

"Uh uh," I say, shaking my head. "I may be willing to take a chance on us, but that doesn't mean I'm ready for the whole town to be talking about us shacking up together after the big tornado. Why don't you follow me back to my apartment and we'll go from there?"

He laughs. "Fair enough."

He follows me a few miles back to my apartment and as I drive, I'm shocked at the damage throughout town. Trees around the courthouse are blown over and lying across the sidewalk. A child's tricycle is overturned, hanging out into the street. Garbage cans have toppled over, their contents scattered through people's yards. At least most of the mess is going to be easy to clean up, but my heart goes out to the families outside of town like the Powells and the Wilkes, whose homes have been destroyed.

I have to work tomorrow night, but maybe Preston and I can see if there's anything we can do to help during the day.

When we get to my apartment, I run up and stuff a change of clothes into my backpack before heading back down to his car. By the time we get to his parents' house, my imagination has kicked into overdrive. Hot showers. A hot tub. What exactly have I gotten myself into? And just how far are we planning to go?

I take a deep breath and let it out slowly. It's only a few months until graduation. Why not have a little fun before I leave? I'm tired of resisting him, and he's right, we do always seem to have a great time when we're together. No expectations, and no regrets.

All I have to do is make sure I don't fall in love with him. How hard can that really be?

CHAPTER 18
PRESTON

I wave to our security guard Jason and the iron gate leading to my parents' estate slowly retracts. I pull the Escalade into the driveway and park just outside the garage.

Jenna and I quietly make our way, hand-in-hand, around the side of the house and go through the back door of the poolhouse.

"Damn, I forgot my bathing suit," she says.

I consider suggesting she doesn't need one, but decide not to test my luck just yet.

"Don't worry. We have tons of extras," I say. I open the door to the guest suite and show her to the closet. There are dozens of swim suits hanging up, tags still attached.

She puts a hand on her hip. "You've got to be kidding me," she says. She flips the tag over on one of the suits and whistles. "You guys have four hundred dollar bathing suits in a variety of styles and sizes just on the off occasion someone stops by needing a suit?"

"It happens more than you think," I say.

"Shit, I'm sure," she says. "If I was a different kind of person, I'd be over here once a week accidentally forgetting my own suit so I could have a peek at this week's array of fine goods."

I laugh, but feel a little embarrassed. I'd never given those suits a second though until now, but to someone who doesn't have a lot of money, it must seem kind of ridiculous.

"I'm going to hop over to the other suite and take a quick shower to wash off this mud," I say. "There's a shower in here for you with shampoo and whatever you need. Unless you want to join me in the other room?"

One corner of her mouth curls into a sexy smile. "I'll meet you by the pool in ten minutes?"

Damn. Was worth a shot. "Sounds good," I say.

"And bring food," she calls after me.

I had almost forgotten about the food. It's like my brain doesn't totally work when I'm around her. I can't believe she's finally letting down her walls and spending time with me, but as I walk toward the main house, I realize what kind of corner I've just painted myself into with her.

We're dating, but I can't call her my girlfriend. We can't talk about any kind of future together. And once graduation comes in May, it's over between us.

Something heavy knots in my stomach. Isn't that what I wanted? Someone to just have fun with for a while? No talk of marriage or pressure to be anything but myself?

I grab a tray from the linen closet and pile it high with cheese, fruit, bread and sliced turkey. My stomach growls as I bring the food back out to the pool and set it on a table near the backside of the house. I rush inside to shower and change into my suit, but the whole time I'm in there, I can't help but shake the feeling of dread that graduation day is going to come much too soon.

CHAPTER 19

JENNA

Preston is already in the pool, and he turns as I walk out the door. His eyes travel from my head all the way down to my toes, and I squirm under his scrutiny. This isn't the first time I've worn a bikini around him, but this is the first time since our kiss that he's seen me so undressed. I feel incredibly naked and vulnerable for the first time in a long time.

"Damn. You look gorgeous," he says. He swims to the edge of the pool and pulls himself out of the water. His body radiates heat as he pulls me into his arms again.

"Is the pool heated, too?"

"Yes," he says. "I guess it seems pretty indulgent considering most of the town is without power right now."

"You think?" I say, teasing. Don't get me wrong, I have no problem with the idea of luxury. But it's so foreign to me the way his family spends money without a care in the world. What must it be like to live like that? Never worrying about your power getting turned off or your car breaking down.

Being able to spend thousands of dollars on bathing suits for guests who happen to stop by. I honestly can't even imagine it.

"Are you still hungry?" he asks.

"Hungry doesn't even begin to describe the way I feel right now," I say with a laugh. "Ravenous is more like it."

He motions toward the tray full of food.

"It's too cold out here, though," I say. "Mind if we take it back inside?"

"Not at all." Preston carries the tray back inside the pool house and sets it down on a coffee table in front of a large gas fireplace. He flips a switch on the wall and fire roars to life.

I laugh. "Now all we need is a bear-skinned rug and this would be truly decadent."

"I can have that arranged," he says with a wink.

I roll my eyes and make myself a sandwich, piled high with enough turkey to feed a small army.

"Want something to drink?" he asks.

I lift up a finger, asking him to wait while I chew the giant bite I just took of my sandwich. He smiles and taps his toes, pretending to check his watch.

"Sorry, I told you I was hungry," I say. "And yes, I'd love something to drink. What do you have?"

He steps over to a mirrored bar near the kitchen. "Pick your poison," he says. "Anything your heart desires."

I search my brain for the most obscure drink I can think of. "A manhattan," I say, not entirely sure what goes into that.

"Coming right up."

"Wait, seriously? Do you even know what's in that?"

"Whiskey, sweet vermouth, and bitters," he says.

"Okay, what about a gimlet?" I'm pulling out every old-school drink in the book.

"Gin and a splash of lime juice," he says.

"How about a mojito?"

"Rum, sugar, lime, sparkling water, and crushed mint," he says. "But I'd have to go back to the main house to get the mint."

I laugh and shake my head. "How do you know all that?"

He shrugs. "An added bonus of growing up with parents who like to drink and entertain," he says. "Plus, I like to play bartender on the yacht. Not that you'd know this."

He gives me a sideways smile, and I try to think up more obscure drinks.

"Can you make me a mint julep?" I ask. "I've always wanted to try one of those. It sounds so Southern."

"Bourbon, simple syrup, and mint."

I twist my mouth to the side. "Hmm. Yeah, I forgot about the mint part," I say. "What's your signature drink, then?"

"The Bone," he says, and I wonder how he keeps a straight face.

"You've got to be kidding me," I say. "Your signature drink is called The Bone?"

"Yes, and you're going to love it."

"What's in it?"

"Do you like Bloody Mary's?" he asks.

"Sure," I say.

"Then you'll probably like this," he says. "Give it a try. If you hate it, I'll drink it."

He takes the ingredients out one at a time. "Wild Turkey.

Lime juice. Simple syrup, which is really just sugar water. And the best part, Tabasco sauce."

My eyes widen as he pours it all into a cocktail shaker and shakes it up. He gets a heavy glass from the shelf above the bar and puts four cubes of ice inside before pouring The Bone over the top.

"Enjoy," he says, handing it to me.

I clear my throat and sniff the drink. I can definitely smell the Tabasco sauce. I bring the drink to my lips and take the smallest sip. To my surprised, it's actually pretty damn good.

"You like it?"

"I do," I say. "Did you make this up yourself?"

"Nah," he says. "Don't laugh, but I got it out of Esquire Magazine. Everyone loves it, so it kind of became my signature drink."

"You know, you should take that job over at Rob's that Jo was talking about. You'd make a good bartender. Plus, a good bit of eye candy like you would bring in all the ladies. It could be a very Tom Cruise moment for you."

He laughs. "That actually sounds like fun, but my parents would probably die."

"Probably, but who cares? You're the one who said you were looking to add a little adventure to your life, right?"

"I am," he says, putting one arm around me and pulling me closer.

The heat in the room kicks up a notch as our skin touches, the entire length of our bodies separated only by a tiny string bikini and a pair of swim trunks.

He leans down to kiss me, but I place my cold glass

against his back and he sucks in a quick breath and pulls away. "Holy shit, that's cold," he says.

"I'm still hungry," I say, wriggling out of his grasp and heading back to our little carpet picnic by the fire.

There's no doubt I want him, but I'm not sure I'm ready to cross that next physical barrier with him just yet. And tonight has all the ingredients of an impending sexual encounter. A romantic fireplace. A hot tub. A lot of alcohol.

I'm up for having a good time, but if I want to protect my heart, I need to take it slow.

"What are these for, anyway?" I ask, motioning to a pair of silver dogtags on a chain around his neck.

He lifts them up and shows me the name punched into the metal. "These were my grandfather's," he says. "He served in World War II and was a real hero. After that, he traveled the world, helping people recover from war. He was an amazing man."

"Sounds like it," I say. "When did he pass away?"

"Years ago," he says. "But I never take these off. I never want to forget what he meant to me."

I study him, realizing I have completely judged him wrong. There's so much more to Preston than I ever thought.

When we finish our meal, we head out to the pool. Steam rises off the top of the water. I slide in and all the aches and pains from our time trudging through the mud looking for that little girl disappear.

"This feels amazing," I say. "I've never been in a heated pool before."

"You've been missing out," he says.

We swim together, playing and laughing in the water for a

while, but the anticipation is growing. I think we both know where this is headed, but we take our time. After a while, though, he swims over to me, and pulls me into his arms. This time, I don't have a cold glass to distract him. We float near the edge of the pool, and I feel helpless to resist him. No matter how many times I've tried to deny what's happening between us, something always draws us back together, as if this is where we've been headed all along.

When he kisses me, heat spreads through my body like honey, thick and sweet. I circle my arms around his neck and run my fingers through his dark hair. Below the water, his hands explore my body, his fingertips sliding across my hips and up my back.

I can't reach the bottom of the pool from here, so I wrap my legs around him. As our kiss deepens, he grabs my hips and pulls me closer. The thick length of him hardens and presses against me. A moan escapes from my lips, and my resolve to take it slow disappears into the mist.

Slow is highly overrated, anyway.

"I want you," he whispers against my lips.

Desire blossoms through me, and I can't deny how much I want him, too. I answer him with a kiss. With a tightening of my legs around his hips.

"Not here," I say. "Let's go inside."

He nods and pulls himself out of the pool. I grab his hand and he lifts me from the water. Excitement and nervousness mingle inside me as we walk back to the warm fire in the poolhouse.

"See? A bear-skinned rug would be perfect," I say as he kisses me again.

His fingers find the strings of my top and untie them. He

tosses the wet piece of fabric to the side and his hands move up to cup my breasts. I close my eyes as his mouth descends on me, drawing my nipple into his mouth and teasing it with his tongue. One hand slides down my stomach and past the tiny elastic string of the bathing suit bottom. As his fingers find me, I'm stricken with both panic and pleasure.

Yes, I want him, but I'm not ready for this. Even with our agreement in place, I can already feel myself losing control. Losing my heart.

I can hardly force breath into my lungs.

"Wait," I say. I place my hands on his bare chest and push him back.

"What's wrong?"

I shake my head. "I'm sorry. I'm just not ready," I say. I cross my hands in front of my chest to cover myself. I take a step backward. "Can you take me home?"

His expression darkens. "Did I do something wrong?"

"No, it's me," I say. "I just need more time to wrap my head around this. I'll be fine. I just want to go home."

He nods and grabs a towel from a stack near the door.

"Thanks," I say, wrapping it around my bare body. I turn and rush back to the guest room, closing the door behind me. I lean my head against the wood and take several deep breaths. Shit. I'm not prepared for this. After the things I've shared with him already about my past and about my dreams of the future, moving forward sexually feels incredibly intimate. I don't know how to deal with this level of vulnerability. How can I keep my heart safe and my mind in the right place if he's already got me so off-balance?

I strip naked and toss the wet bikini into a hamper in the bathroom. I dress in my muddy clothes as quickly as I can and go back out to the main room to find Preston already dressed and ready to go. His face looks stricken, as if I've wounded him.

We don't say a word as we walk back to his car and he drives me home.

Outside my apartment, he places his hand on mine. "Are we okay?"

I nod and meet his eyes. "Yes. It's been an emotional day, and I think I'm just exhausted," I say. "I need a good night's sleep and everything will look better in the morning."

"I don't understand what I did wrong."

"You didn't do anything," I say. "I just need more time."

"I meant what I said earlier about slowing down if that's what you need," he says. "Just don't shut me out."

"I won't," I say. I lean over and kiss him softly on the cheek. "I'll talk to you tomorrow?"

He swallows and nods. I hate that I've upset him and probably confused the hell out of him, but I can't help it.

"Goodnight," I say, having no other words to offer him. I head up to my apartment and watch through the curtains as he pulls away.

CHAPTER 20

JENNA

In the morning, Preston knocks on my door with a peace offering. Two large coffees and a sack of bagels with cream cheese.

I invite him in, but he shakes his head.

"We have too much to do today," he says.

"We do?"

"Yes, it's still technically spring break, and I know you don't have to work today because Brantley's is closed due to the storm last night."

"Oh no, was the restaurant damaged?" I grab my cell phone and my keys and follow him out to his car. "I need to call Maria."

"I don't think it's anything serious," he says. "I heard my dad talking about the damage around town, and I think it's mostly just a small leak in the roof that caused a little water damage in the dining room. He thinks they'll reopen by the weekend."

I sigh with relief. After I dumped all my money into

buying my truck, I can't afford to be without a job for very long. I don't mention this to him, though.

"So what are we doing today?"

"If you're up for it, I thought we'd head over to campus and help clean up. There's already a group of students gathering in the quad to get rid of fallen tree limbs and trash that got knocked over in the storm."

"I actually slept like a log last night," I say. "I must have been exhausted."

I know this doesn't totally make up for me running out on him last night, but I'm glad he's not holding it against me.

We eat our bagels on the way to campus and spend the rest of the morning cleaning. The beautiful cherry trees I'd been admiring earlier in the week have been stripped of most of their blooms, but other than a few cosmetic things, most of the campus was saved from any significant damage.

"I feel sorry for the families that lost their homes, though," I say. "Can you imagine what they must be going through?"

"Penny's already all over it," Preston says. "She's been making calls all morning to get donations to help put the families up in a local hotel until their homes can be rebuilt. Insurance should take care of the rest."

"She's such a work-horse," I say. "Ever since she got back from her trip, she hasn't stopped working to help families here in town. I wish I could be more like her."

"You and me both," he says. He tosses a bag of trash into the dumpster and looks around. "I think we're about finished up here. Do you have any plans for the rest of the day?"

"Nothing specific now that work's off," I say. "I should

probably call Maria and make sure she doesn't need anything, but if she's good, I'm all yours."

Something flashes in his eyes, and my knees go weak.

"You know what I mean," I say.

"Make the call," he says. "If you have the afternoon free, I thought we could head over to one of our properties outside of town and ride the four-wheeler around for a while."

I raise an eyebrow. "One of your properties?"

"We have a few," he says with a laugh. "A few years back, Mason and I made a path through the woods so we could ride around out there. I keep a couple four-wheelers out there, and it's really fun in the mud."

I make that call to Maria and am relieved when she says she doesn't need me for a few days.

"Let's go," I say.

We pick up some lunch on the way, and then ride out to his family's cabin in the woods. Preston shows me how to drive the four-wheeler, and we spend the rest of the day sliding around in the mud together.

I'm surprised at how easy things are between us. How fun he can be. I realize I've been judging him the same way everyone else does, never realizing how much more there is to him than just his name or his wealth. He makes me laugh, and he's incredibly patient. It took me a few tries to figure out the controls on the four-wheeler, but he never once got frustrated with me.

I haven't met a lot of guys I could be myself around like this.

"This was really fun," I say when we pull up to the cabin. It's getting dark out, and I realize I don't want the day to end.

He wipes a chunk of mud off my cheek. "I've never brought a girl out here before," he says. "Most of the girls I've dated would die if I asked them to get dirty like this."

"I loved it," I say. "It must be so awesome to be able to do whatever you want and not have to worry about whether or not you can afford it. You're so lucky."

"It's no fun if you don't have someone to share it with," he says. He has that look in his eye again, and I know he wants to kiss me.

"Look, Preston, about last night—"

"Don't worry about it," he says. "I want to be with you on whatever terms you're comfortable with. I don't want you to feel rushed. I don't want you to have any regrets about us."

"You're almost too good to be true, you know that?" I say. Is there no end to his patience?

"I've never met anyone like you, Jenna." His hand caresses my cheek. "If we only have a few months together, I don't want to do anything to mess that up. If you don't want to have sex, I can live with that. I just want to be with you."

"You mean that?"

"Every word," he says. "Of course, if you change your mind, I'm open to the possibility."

I smile and wrap my arms around him. I lay my head against his chest, not caring that he's covered head-to-toe in mud. "I'll keep that in mind," I say. I look up at him and he kisses me softly.

Everything about him makes me want him more, but as we walk back to his car, I remind myself that when something seems too good to be true, it usually is.

CHAPTER 21
PRESTON

The next few weeks are some of the best of my entire life.

Dating Jenna is better than I ever imagined. When she's not working, we ride four-wheelers or play Frisbee on the beach. We play video games and watch movies at my apartment. I can't get enough of her.

But with every week that passes, I know we are that much closer to graduation. By mid-April, I can hardly imagine my life without her.

When we're not together, I'm counting the hours until I can see her again. She's started sleeping over at my place, and even though we have some hot make-out sessions, we never cross that line toward sex.

I'm trying to be patient, but as time passes, it's getting more difficult to hold back.

I'm afraid if I bring it up again, I'll push her away, so I pretend to be content with just kissing. But the truth is, I want so much more. And I'm not just talking about sex.

It's frustratingly unfair that every girl I dated before Jenna was ready to start shopping for engagement rings, but the one girl I want more than anyone before her won't even let me call her my girlfriend.

I wave to her across the quad and she smiles.

"How was class?" I ask.

"Fabulously boring," she says. "I'll be so glad when I'm done with school forever. Just a few more weeks."

Her words fall heavy on my heart. How can she be so excited when it will mean the end of us? It's impossible to tell if she's falling for me, or if this is all just a passing flirtation for her.

"What are you still doing on campus?" she asks. "I thought your last class on Thursdays ends at noon?"

"I was waiting for you," I say. "Do you have to work tonight?"

"Nope," she says, looping her arm in mine. "Did you want to do something?"

"Always," I say with a smile. "What do you say to an evening on the yacht? I know you said you've been avoiding it, but I promise there will be no frat boys this time. Just you and me. We can rent a movie, shoot some pool, whatever."

"Okay," she says. "I'm in."

"Really?"

"Yes." She steals my baseball cap and puts it on her head. "As long as I don't have to call you captain or anything while I'm on board."

"Aww, man, that's what I was looking forward to the most," I say.

She rolls her eyes and pushes my arm.

"I'm teasing," I say. "I promise. Nothing weird. I can have

the chef prepare something and have it ready for when we arrive."

"No chef," she says. "Let's order pizza. If I'm going to spend an evening on a fancy yacht, I need something to ground me in reality."

"Deal," I say.

IT IS THE PERFECT NIGHT TO BE OUT UNDER THE STARS. Jenna and I open a bottle of champagne and eat pizza on the main deck.

"I can't believe how huge this place is," she says. "It's like a floating mansion."

"I told you it was nice."

"Nice is an understatement," she says. "You have heated tile floors in the bathrooms."

She notices things I've never given a second thought to. It makes me wonder how much I've taken for granted in my life.

"Do you ever sail places? Or does it mainly stay docked here?" she asks.

"My dad sometimes uses it for business trips, wining and dining clients," I say. "When I was younger, we sailed down to the Florida Keys a lot. We went to the Virgin Islands a few times, but mostly Dad takes it out a few miles from shore to entertain."

"If we could just sail away and go anywhere in the world right now, where would you want to go?" she asks.

"Alaska," I say without hesitation. "It's one of the few

places in the world I've never been, but always wanted to see."

"Let's go," she says, a smile playing on her lips.

"Right now?"

"Sure, why not?"

I shrug. "I could probably make arrangements, but it would take until tomorrow."

She shakes her head. "You're serious, aren't you? Unbelievable."

"What?"

"Sometimes it just amazes me how the two of us can come from such different worlds, yet get along so well," she says. "I'm not even sure I would want a life like yours."

"Ouch."

"No, I don't mean to insult you, it's just, you have so many choices. If you can pick up and go anywhere at any time, how do you decide what to do next? It seems complicated."

"I guess I never thought of it that way," I say. "Maybe it will be different after I make it through school, but I never think of myself as having a lot of freedom. Mostly, I do what my parents expect of me. I don't know that I could ever just pack up and walk away from it like Penny did."

"Is there nothing you've ever wanted so badly you were willing to disappoint them?"

You. The word is on my lips, but I don't say it. My mother has made several casual references to my growing relationship with Jenna, but I always tell her it's not serious. But for her, I would do anything.

I don't answer her and instead of talking for a while, we lean back against our blanket and stare up at the stars.

I slowly reach out and take her hand in mine.

"There's something I've been meaning to ask you," I say. "Next weekend my parents are hosting a charity dinner at the country club. It's nothing big, just dinner and dancing. All the money raised goes to cancer research. I have to go, and it will be boring without you there."

"I don't think that's such a good idea," she says. "Charity dinners aren't really my thing."

"You said yachts weren't really your thing, either, and look how much you're enjoying it."

She laughs. "Yes, but it's just you and me here tonight. A charity dinner means a room full of rich people, including your parents who very much don't like me," she says. "That does not sound like my idea of a good time."

I roll onto my side, propping my head up on my hand. "I promise we'll make it a good time."

"So far, I think we've been doing a good job of keeping our time together separate from all that," she says. "No pressure, remember?"

"I know, but I don't think it would be such a bad thing to be seen in public together every once in a while," I say. "As a real couple."

My stomach knots with nerves as I say it. I know this isn't what we agreed upon, but with only a month left before graduation, I want to see if we're still going to hold ourselves to these limitations.

"We're not a couple, Preston," she says softly.

I run my hand along her cheek. "We spend all our time together. We kiss. We have fun. We do everything couples do," I say. Almost everything. "We don't have to define this if you don't want to, but I don't think going out to a dinner together is going to change anything in any significant way."

"Then why does it matter so much to you?"

I sigh and lean back against the blanket. "It doesn't," I lie. "It's not a big deal, really."

"Besides, I wouldn't have anything to wear to something like that," she says. "Something tells me jeans and tank tops aren't permitted."

I start to mention I would gladly buy her something to wear, but she distracts me by rolling onto her side and kissing my neck.

The conversation is lost to kisses after that, but like every night before this, the walls around her heart are still firmly in place.

CHAPTER 22
JENNA

A knock on the door pulls me from my sleep.

I must have fallen asleep in front of the TV the night before after work. A fast food bag with stale fries is still lying at my feet, a half-consumed coke beside it. The TV is blaring.

Damn, Jenna, get it together.

I swallow, my throat dry and aching, and walk over to the door. My entire body aches. Between working hard at the restaurant and playing hard with Preston, I'm sore in places I can't even name. Who the heck is here on a Saturday morning at ten? None of my friends would come around this early after they knew I was working late last night, and Preston and I hadn't made any plans to see each other again until tomorrow.

I peer out the tiny peephole and see a delivery guy dressed in a brown suit. UPS. I know I didn't order anything. I never have any money. So what is this?

I pull open the door and he smiles in a very chipper morning-person kind of way. "Good morning. Miss Lewis?"

"That's me," I say.

He shoves a large rectangular box at me and wishes me a good morning.

"You, too," I grumble, kicking the door closed.

I walk into my living room and set the box on top of the bar. I plant my butt down on my one barstool and look at the address label, trying to remember what in the world I must have ordered.

The return address is a place called Tootsies in Atlanta. I have never in my life heard of this place, so I double check to make sure UPS delivered to the right address and this wasn't meant for one of my neighbors. But no, it's addressed to Jenna Lewis with the correct address.

Something knots in my stomach.

I stand and go to the kitchen to make coffee. My eyes keep darting to the package, as if there might possibly be a bomb hiding inside. And maybe there is. I spend the entire morning avoiding the thing like the plague, terrified to open it. Terrified of what it might signify.

I take a shower, wrap one towel around my hair and another around my body. I lean against the edge of the door frame, staring coldly at the large box on my bar. Maybe it's just something I ordered and forgot. Something completely boring and of no significance, like air filters. But no matter how long I wrack my brain, I cannot remember a single thing I ordered, and definitely not from a place in Atlanta called Tootsies.

It has to be from Preston.

My brain registers this thought, dismisses it, and then, finally, accepts that there's no other explanation.

I scowl at the box and go back into the safety of my bedroom to dry my hair and get dressed for the day. I have to work in about an hour. I can simply leave the box unopened until tomorrow.

But as I go to leave, my stomach twists. I have to know what's in there.

I take my wine opener out of my work apron and run the small blade across the tape, slowly opening the big box. There is a black box inside with "Tootsies" written across the top in gold. I suck in a slow breath and pull the top off the second box. Black and white tissue paper conceals the present, but there is a note inside as well. With trembling hands, I open the note and read:

"I know you will be stunning in this dress. Please come with me. Yours - Preston."

I feel sick. I set the note aside and pull the tissue paper from the box. Nestled in the center of the paper is a silky black dress. I pull it out and it slithers from the box like a poisonous snake. It's gorgeous, of course. Expensive and exquisitely made. I glance at the tag. There's no price listed, but I don't need to see the price to know it's ridiculous.

Memories of my childhood come rushing back. I'll never forget the first time my mother came home wearing an expensive pair of red high heels. She claimed to have found them at a thrift store, but I knew better. Thrift store shoes have scuffs on the bottom, but hers were brand new.

Why would Preston buy this for me?

I stuff the dress back into the box and slam the top back

on it. Teeth clenched, I pull my cell phone from my back pocket and dial the restaurant.

"Maria, I'm sorry to do this to you, but I'm going to need a few minutes," I say. "I can come in now if you really need me there to set up, but if you can give me an extra half hour or so, I'd appreciate the time."

"Of course, what's up? Everything okay?" she asks.

"Yes," I say, my jaw tight. "I just have to take care of something."

CHAPTER 23
PRESTON

I am sitting on the couch playing the latest video game when someone knocks on the door. I pause the game and stand. It's been a boring Saturday morning, so I'm hoping it's one of my friends maybe coming to hang out, but when I open the door, I'm pleasantly surprised to see Jenna standing there. She's wearing her work uniform of plain black pants and a white button-down shirt, but even in these plain clothes, she takes my breath away.

"Couldn't wait until tomorrow?" I tease, leaning against the door.

She pushes past me, a black and gold box in her hands. "What the hell is this?" she asks, throwing the box on the table. She places her hands on her hips and turns to stare at me.

"Come on in," I say, trying to hide a smile. Damn, she's even hot when she's angry. I close the door and walk over to the table. The box is from the boutique in Atlanta where Penny loves to shop. I called her stylist yesterday morning and asked her to overnight something nice for Jenna. Had she sent something horrible?

"I mean it," Jenna says. "What were you thinking, sending me an expensive dress like this for an event I never even agreed to go to?"

I stare at the box, confused. "I was thinking you would wear it," I say. "Is there something wrong with it? I can send it back and let you pick something out yourself, if you'd rather do that."

"There's nothing wrong with the dress," she says. "It's beautiful. Exactly what a girl should wear when she goes out with a guy like you, I'm sure. But it's not the style of the dress that's the problem, it's the fact that you felt the need to buy it for me. Do you have any idea how insulting this is?"

My stomach turns. Wow, she's really angry with me. "Insulting? For me to buy you a nice dress?" I shake my head. "How is that insulting?"

She lets out a huge sigh and places a hand on the box. "Where do I even begin? There's the implication that you felt the need to dress me," she says. "Like I won't fit in unless I wear exactly the right thing. Like nothing I own is good enough for a guy like you. And second, when a guy like you gives a girl like me something expensive I could never be able afford on my own, it feels like payment for services rendered, if you know what I mean. Or a bribe to get into my pants."

I put my hands up. "Whoa, hold on a second. You got all that just from a gift?" I ask. "That's not at all what I meant when I sent this to you. Do you really think that's the kind of guy I am?"

Her shoulders fall slightly and she turns her eyes from me. "I don't know," she says. "Maybe. That's the way it makes me feel, Preston. I already told you I wasn't sure I would feel comfortable at an event like that. Sending me a dress I could never afford in a million years just makes me feel cheap."

"You said you didn't have anything to wear. I thought this would help make you feel more comfortable," I say. "If I thought, even for a second, that this would upset you, I never would have sent it. It's really not a big deal. If you don't like it, we'll just send it back."

"It's not about whether I like the dress, Preston. It's about you thinking I needed your help in the first place. I don't like the implications."

"You are blowing this way out of proportion," I say. I'm trying my best to wrap my brain around the real problem, but I honestly can't understand what has her so upset. "I was trying to do something nice for a girl I care about."

"You were trying to make sure I look like everyone else there," she says.

"No, I swear to you that was never even in my thoughts," I say. I've never had a girl complain about me spending money on her before. In fact, they usually complained I didn't spend enough. What in the world did I do wrong? I can't shrug the feeling there's a lot more to this than she's letting on. But how do I get the truth out of her when she's so closed off? "If you don't want the dress, it's fine. I'm sorry. I was trying to be thoughtful."

"What I don't want is for you to think you can buy my affections with fancy gifts," she says. "Or dress me up like some little couture robot doll so that I fit in with your crowd when it's clear that I don't belong there."

I scratch my forehead and swallow. "Is that what this is about? You think I'm trying to control you? Damn," I say.

"That's complete bullshit, and I think you know it. If all I cared about was having a girlfriend who looks like she belongs, I would have just asked one of the dozen boring girls I've been out with since Christmas."

"You do that, then," she says, pushing past me again. She puts her hand on the doorknob, but I reach over and touch her shoulder.

"Jenna, what I'm trying to say is that I don't want any of those other girls. All they care about is how much money I have and how we look together," I say. "It's always the same with them. Every single date I went on before you, I felt like it was only a matter of time before they mentioned something they were hoping to get from me. A ride on the private jet. A free trip to the Bahamas. Jewelry. One of them even started talking about us getting married and building a house together right on the beach. On our first date. That's all they seemed to care about, like I wasn't even a real person to them. Just a bank account. You're not like that."

"So why in the world would you think sending me an expensive gift would make me happy?"

The meaning of her words finally sinks in, and I feel like a complete idiot. I've treated her exactly like I always treat my dates, showering them with gifts to make them happy and to make them want to stay with me.

"I don't know," I say. "Shit, I wasn't thinking. It's just that when you said you didn't think you'd feel comfortable at the event, I wanted to help. I don't ever want you to be anyone but you. I swear."

She draws her lower lip into her mouth and her hand drops down to her side. "You really mean that?"

"One hundred percent," I say. "I don't ever want money

to come between us, but it's tricky. I can't suddenly not have it, but at the same time, I don't ever want you to feel like I'm trying to buy you. We've been dancing around this issue since we first kissed, and honestly, I think there's more to this than you're telling me. Maybe we need to sit down and really talk about it. I'm not trying to be a jerk, but I'm not used to people being mad at me for spending money on them. I need to know why you're really upset. You don't get mad when I take you out to a nice dinner."

"A nice dinner is one thing. Spending more than two months of rent money on a dress I'm going to wear once is something completely different."

"Maybe we need to set some ground rules, then. But let's talk through it next time before you just assume I'm trying to turn you into some brainless, what did you call it? Couture robot?"

She looks up and I see the anger she was feeling is gone from her eyes. She shakes her head and gives me a half-smile. "Okay," she says. "Maybe we should talk about it. I have to get to work, though. Another joy of not having a bank full of money."

"Hey, I work, too," I say with a smile.

She rolls her eyes. "Yeah, it's exactly the same," she says. Her eyes dance in the light, and I know she's forgiven me.

I pull her into my arms and kiss her forehead. "What time do you get off work?"

She wraps her arms around my waist. "Probably close to midnight," she says. "What are you doing tonight?"

"Counting the minutes until midnight, apparently," I say, and pull her into a kiss.

CHAPTER 24
JENNA

I am counting the hours until I can clock out and head back to Preston's. I owe him a serious apology. I feel ridiculous for storming over there like a child, complaining about a gift, but I feel so much better after he told me his reasons for sending it.

I completely overreacted, but seeing that dress made me feel like I'm living my mother's life all over again. That's not his fault, though, so why did I lash out at him? What is wrong with me?

I guess in the end, I've been really proud of myself for making it work on my own here in Fairhope. I don't want him to swoop in like some fairy god-boyfriend and suddenly start taking care of me. I saw how that worked out for my mom when she started her affair with the rich guy she used to work for. It was nothing but trouble for all of us involved.

Part of me wants to believe the differences in our finances aren't important, but at the same time, it's a real issue for me. We come from completely different worlds.

How can I possibly expect him to understand what it's like to be worried about where your next meal will come from? That's not even something that's registered on his things-to-consider in his entire life, while for me, it was an every-day concern growing up. Hell, who am I kidding? Sometimes it still is.

So tonight we're going to talk about it.

Something I've been dreading since the moment his lips first touched mine. I don't want him to know how difficult things are for me sometimes, or where I came from. I'm scared he'll either feel sorry for me or try to fix me. Both would be horrible and embarrassing beyond belief. I don't want him to take care of me or buy me things, and I'm afraid once he really knows what kind of family I come from, he'll go running for the hills.

Of course, if he does, then at least I'll know what kind of guy he really is and what he finds important.

He says he's looking for someone different, but what if it's only temporary? What if he's just going through some rebellious phase, trying it out for a change to get away from the types of women he's been dating? If that's the way it is, I know it will only be a matter of time before dating the girl from the wrong side of the tracks loses its novelty and he's falling right back into the arms of someone more his type.

Then where will I be?

I finish filling the sweet teas for Table 6 and load them up on my tray. I need to get him out of my head for the next few hours so I don't end up dumping an entire tray full of drinks on someone's head. Maria is a forgiving boss, but she's already been looking at me funny all evening. I know I'm not on my usual A-game, so I make an extra effort to keep my head on straight and forget about Preston for the rest of my shift.

It's a slow night for a Saturday, at least, which is bad for money, but good for my current state-of-mind. I wish Leigh Anne was working tonight, too, but she's already flown to Boston to spend the weekend preparing for the trial. Knox went with her this time, which makes me happy. She could use all the support she can get. It's only a month and a half until the scheduled court date, and even though she's putting on a brave face for all of us, I know she's nervous as hell.

The hostess, a sweet high school girl named Phoebe, ushers a group of couples about my age to one of my empty tables. I sigh. I recognize a few of them from school and from the looks of it, they have already been out celebrating the last weekend of spring break. One of the girls can barely walk in her mile-high heels. Her arm is slung around her boyfriend's shoulder and he's practically carrying her to her seat.

I toss a glance at Maria, who already has her eye on them. I can't tell if the rest of them are too far gone to be ordering more drinks, but I always hate making judgment calls about this sort of thing. It's always the waitress who takes the blame if she has to tell them no. I wish they had just gone straight up to the bar so Colton could deal with them. He's much better at handling their verbal abuse if that's what it comes down to. Me, I'm not in the mood.

I take a basket of bread to the table next to them, plaster a smile on my face, and walk over. "Hi, I'm Jenna. I'll be taking care of you this evening," I say. "Can I get you started with an appetizer or some of our famous sweet tea?"

"Jenna, you beautiful thing, bring us a round of Long

Island Ice Teas," the guy on the end with the drunk girlfriend says.

I try to catch Maria's eye over the top of the booth, but she's gone back into the kitchen. "Sure," I say. One drink. "Can I see your ID's, please?"

"Oh come on, you're not going to be like that, are you?" he says. "We're good."

Crap. I really don't need this tonight. "I'm sorry," I say with a smile that probably looks as fake as it feels. "Manager's orders. If it were up to me, I'd let you slide, but she'd kill me if I didn't check."

"Okay, but it's coming out of your tip," he says with a wink. Like it's such a cute thing to say.

He lifts his butt from the seat and pulls out his wallet. None of the other three at the table make a move. I take his ID and check the date. He's only legal by two months, and I get the sneaking suspicion his friends are underage.

"Thank you," I say, and look to the other guy, hoping he'll get the hint and everyone else will follow suit.

No such luck. The other guy sets his hands on the table and looks up at me like he has no clue what I could possibly be waiting for.

"What can I get for you?" I say as sweetly as I can.

"I asked for a round," the first guy says. "That means one for each of us. And we'll take one of those big combo appetizers."

I feel tired. I hate that they're actually going to make me ask them for ID a second time. What is with these people?

"I'll be happy to put those orders right in for you," I say. "As soon as I see everyone's ID."

The guy slaps a hand down on the table, and I jump.

"What the heck is your problem?" he asks, loud enough that several of the other guests around us turn to look. He motions toward his date. "Don't you know who this is?"

I take a deep breath and count to three before I speak. "No, but if she would show me her ID, I'm sure I'd figure it out."

"This is Sheriff Hathaway's daughter," he says. "She doesn't need to show you her ID. We came in here to have a good time, but if you can't help us out, maybe we should get your manager involved, after all."

I press my lips together and hold my tongue. This is the worst part about being a waitress. Not being able to speak my mind when someone is being a dick.

I don't answer the guy or even respond to his threat. I simply walk away.

Maria is in her office typing away at her calculator. She doesn't even look up when I knock. "Table 7 giving you shit?"

"Of course. They refuse to show ID, but want to be served," I say. "I think they've all already been drinking. The guy says his date is the Sheriff's daughter?"

Maria laughs, not missing a beat with her calculations. "I swear, they get dumber every year. He really thinks that's more likely to get them served when they're underage?"

"Are they?"

"Refusing to show ID should have been a dead giveaway. You're slipping, hon," she says. She finally looks away from her receipts and pushes her rolling chair out from the desk. "What's eating at you tonight? You've barely been here all evening."

I sigh and lean against the door frame. "Boy trouble," I say. "What do you want me to do?"

"I'll deal with it," she says. "You just take care of your other tables and close out when they leave. I'll let Phoebe know I'm cutting you early. Everything okay?"

"It will be," I say. "Thanks, Maria."

"You're welcome," she says. "You deal with whatever you need to deal with, because I need my best girl around here."

She smacks me on the ass as she heads out to the dining room.

&s.

THE ORDER IS UP FOR ONE OF MY OTHER TABLES, SO I GET everything set up on the tray and head back into the dining room. As I drop their food off, I listen in on Maria's conversation with the group at Table 7. They are much nicer to her, but of course, she's the kind of person you don't want to cross.

The much nicer couple at Table 4 orders a bottle of red wine, and I make my way to the bar to ring it up.

"Fun evening?" Colton asks. He's cleaning glasses and walks to my end of the bar.

"So much I can hardly stand it," I say with a smile. "Can I get a bottle of Sterling Cab?"

"Maybe," he says, one eyebrow raised. "If you come out with me after our shift tonight."

I laugh and lean over the counter. "In your dreams," I say.

Colton and I have been carrying on a mild flirtation for the past year. Okay, maybe more than mild. We slept together a few times last summer, but it was more of a friends-with-benefits type of situation. I know from experience that can only last so long before real feelings get involved and someone gets hurt, so we put some space between us for a while. Lately, though, he's been flirting a lot more. Must be spring fever.

It's not that I don't like Colton. I think he's a fun guy with a good heart, but he doesn't make my arms break out in goosebumps the way Preston does. No guy's been able to make me feel that way in a very long time. The fact that I have no interest in taking Colton up on his offer for a good time makes me realize how much I want to see things through with Preston.

Which scares the ever-living crap out of me.

"Why not?" Colton asks. He sets two wine glasses and the bottle of Cabernet down in front of me and leans in closer. "I know we agreed to cool things off and just be friends, but I was hoping since we're both still single, maybe we could hang out some. Rekindle some of what we had last summer."

"As enticing as that sounds, I'm actually kind of seeing someone," I say. It's the first time I've actually said it out loud to anyone, and butterflies start fluttering around in my stomach, causing all kinds of trouble.

Colton's mouth drops open and he steps back. "I had no idea," he says. "Don't tell him I propositioned you. I don't want some thug coming in trying to beat me senseless."

He says this with a wink and I narrow my eyes at him.

"What makes you think it's some thug?" I ask.

He laughs. "You know I'm just teasing you, Jenna," he says. "I'm sure he's a real nice guy. He's certainly a lucky one, whoever he is."

"Thanks," I say. I take the bottle and glasses off the bar. He really is a sweet guy. Life would be so much simpler if I was into someone like him instead of Preston Wright. No one in this town is going to believe it. In fact, I don't even want to think about what the people in this town will say. "I'd better get this out."

"See ya later," he says. "And if things don't work out with this mystery guy, give me a call."

I laugh and head back to my table to serve the wine.

The table where the two couples were earlier is empty now, and I wonder if Maria kicked them out, or if they left of their own free will. Either way, I'm glad they aren't my problem anymore.

I finish up with my last three tables and get my work done in the kitchen by eleven, so I decide to text Preston and let him know I'm finished early. He texts back immediately and says he's going to swing by and pick me up, which gets the butterflies going again.

He's waiting for me when I step outside. The evening air is chilly and I shiver from both nerves and cold. Preston is leaning against the side of his expensive black sports car. I might be annoyed at that if he didn't look so amazing standing next to it in his dark denim jeans, a plain white v-neck tee, and a navy blue blazer. He smiles as I walk out the door.

"A full hour early. Couldn't wait to see me, huh?" he says. "I have that effect on women."

I try to hide my smile. "Maybe I just wanted to get this over with so I could go out and have some real fun."

He places a hand on his chest. "That hurts, Jenna," he says, eyebrows furrowed. "That hurts deep."

I playfully punch him on the shoulder. "Maria let me off a little early," I say. "Where do you want to go?"

To my left, a bottle breaks against the pavement. I turn and peer into a dimly lit area of the parking lot. Someone laughs and footsteps scatter against the asphalt.

"Wherever you want," he says. "Ladies choice. You're always welcome back at my place."

I try to shrug off a strange feeling in the pit of my stomach, but it won't go away. A car starts up and lights come on, shining straight at us. The engine revs and the car pulls out, barely missing a van parked beside it. I move closer to Preston and he puts his arm around me, his face turned toward the lights of the approaching car.

They swerve toward us, again barely missing the back-end of Preston's car as they come along beside us. The windows are rolled down and the guy from my trouble table earlier leans his head out, one arm resting on the door.

"Let's get out of here," I say to Preston.

"What's going on?" he asks.

But it's already too late to make a quick escape. "Well, if it isn't the whore who ruined our night," the dick says. He throws the car into park and steps out. "Wasn't expecting to see her with you, Preston. I knew you were dating again, but have you really reached the bottom of the barrel so quickly?"

"Jason, sounds like maybe you've had a little too much to drink," Preston says. He carefully steps in front of me and protectively puts an arm out. "Can I get you guys a cab or something?"

"Nah, man, I'm fine," the guy says. Apparently he and Preston know each other. "We were hoping to get some food and have a good time inside, but your little friend here had to go tell her boss on us."

Someone inside the car mutters the word bitch just loud

enough for us to hear.

"Can we just get out of here, please?" I whisper to Preston, but he's already taken a step toward the guy.

"I don't think you're in any condition to drive," he says. "You're definitely not in your right mind if you think you can call my girlfriend a whore and get away with it."

Did he just call me his girlfriend? My eyes snap to his face, but he's staring straight at the Jason guy, his shoulders tense.

Jason laughs. "Man, I knew your family was going through some hard times what with Penny's little escapade, but I didn't realize you'd gone off the deep end, too," he says. He looks back at the other guy in his car and runs his thumb across his nose. "What? Did the two of you make some kind of pact to start dating the worst losers you could find?"

"You really should learn to shut your mouth," Preston says. "Don't think for a second I won't kick the shit out of you if you make another crack at Jenna or my sister."

"You? Kick the shit out of me? You're joking right?" Jason laughs again and takes another step toward Preston.

I don't like the way the tension out here keeps building, and I definitely don't want to see a fight break out between these two. I've been called a lot worse than a whore and a loser in my life, and I know myself well enough to know I'm neither of those things. It isn't worth fighting over.

I tug on Preston's arm, but he shrugs me off.

"Don't test me, Jason," he says. "Let me call you a cab so y'all can get home safely."

He pulls his cell phone from his pocket, but Jason smacks his hand and the phone goes flying to the pavement, the screen cracking as it hits.

Preston's jaw tenses and his hand closes into a fist, but he doesn't throw a punch. "I'm going to let that slide, because you're obviously a stupid drunk, but you need to get your act together before you really piss me off."

"Oh yeah?" Jason says. He looks back at his friends as if to say watch this. "You want to know what I think of your girlfriend, here? I think she must be one amazing fuck if you're willing to stand up for a piece of trash like her."

Preston rears his fist back and sends it flying through the air at Jason's face. It lands with a loud thud and Jason falls back three steps until his butt hits the door of his car. Preston opens his fist and shakes it out.

"I warned you, man," he says.

Jason shakes his head and takes a moment to recover before taking his revenge. He's shorter than Preston by a couple inches, but he's bigger in every other way. His meaty fist flies toward Preston, but he's too slow and Preston easily side-steps him and grabs his wrist, pulling it behind Jason's back. He puts his other hand on the back of Jason's neck and forces him to bend forward.

Jason curses and tries to pull away, but Preston has a good hold on him now. The two girls and the other guy get out of the car, but thankfully don't join the fight.

I stand there watching them, my mouth open in disbelief. I have never had a guy stand up for me like this, and even though I'm normally the kind of girl who likes to fight her own battles, I'm glad Preston was here when I walked out into this parking lot tonight. Had these guys been out here waiting for me to get off work?

"Don't you ever talk about Jenna like that again, you understand me?" he says.

"Shit, man, I'm sorry," Jason says. "I was just joking around."

"Here's what's going to happen," Preston says calmly. "First, you're going to hand over your car keys. Second, you're going to let me call you a cab so you can go home and sober up. Third, you're going to never speak to me or my friends again until you get yourself some manners. Do I make myself perfectly clear?"

"Fine, whatever, just let me go. You're hurting me."

Preston lets go and pushes Jason toward his car. He holds his hand out flat. "Keys."

Jason rubs his face where Preston hit him and reaches into the car to grab his keys. He dumps them in Preston's palm.

I bend down and retrieve Preston's cell from the asphalt, but there's a huge maze of cracks all along the screen. It won't turn on, so I take mine out of my apron and hand it to him instead.

He makes a quick call to the local cab company and throws a twenty on the ground at Jason's feet. For the second time this week, I'm impressed at how well Preston handles even the toughest situations.

"Don't call my dad, okay?" the Sheriff's daughter pleads with Preston. "He'll kill me if he finds out I've been drinking tonight."

Preston doesn't answer the girl. He turns and tosses me the keys to Jason's car. "Do you mind parking that real quick?"

I catch the keys and nod. "Sure," I say.

I pull the car into a parking spot near the front entrance and lock it up. With the keys still inside.

CHAPTER 25

JENNA

Preston and I climb into his car and leave the restaurant—and the four jerks still waiting outside—in the dust.

"Does that kind of stuff happen to you a lot?" he asks.

I shake my head. My heart's still pounding from the confrontation. "First time," I say. "Thank God you were out there. I don't know what I would have done if I was out there alone. I park out back where it's much darker. Do you think they were out there waiting for me to get off my shift?"

"I don't know," he says. "It sounded like they were drinking out in the parking lot, though. Who knows."

"So you're friends with that Jason guy?" I really hope the answer is no.

Preston makes a face. "Friend is too strong a word. We went to high school together, and we've been at a lot of the same parties over the years, but I wouldn't really say we were friends. And definitely not after tonight. What a douche."

I laugh. "You handled it well," I say. "Where did you learn

to fight like that?"

"One perk of having money. You get to send your kids to classes like karate and kickboxing instead of actually spending time with them," he says. His jaw tenses, and after our conversation about how his parents ignored him even on vacations, I take it this is a really sore spot for him.

"Well, my parents were poor and they still didn't spend any time with me," I say, leaning back against the seat. "I did fun things like stealing my dad's lighter and burning grass and leaves in the backyard. Totally not as cool as karate lessons."

Preston laughs and looks over, a flash of something in his eyes that makes my stomach flip. He takes my hand and squeezes it before having to take it back to shift gears.

"Where do you want to go for this big talk we're going to have, anyway?" he asks. "Want to just go back to my place?"

"Let's go somewhere neutral," I say. "Like the beach. But first I need to go home and change clothes."

He turns on Main Street and navigates to the side of town where my apartment is. I don't say much the rest of the ride, wondering just how big of a talk this is going to turn into. Things were so much easier when I had my walls up and thought there was no chance of a relationship between us. Talking about my past and why his gifts bother me so much makes me a lot more nervous. Those are the types of conversations that either lead to pity or dumping, or at the very least some kind of discussion about where this is all heading between us. I'm not sure I'm ready to go there.

He parks in front of my apartment building and I jump out. "I'll be right back."

"Wait," he says. He opens his door and gets out. "I'm coming with you. I've never seen your apartment before."

I stand there, open-mouthed for a second. "Um, it's not exactly the Taj Mahal or anything," I say. "You're not missing anything, I promise."

"I want to see your paper art," he says.

I take a deep breath. He really was paying attention the other night. "Okay, but you stay in the living room. No peeking."

He laughs and follows me up the stairs to my door. I live on the second floor, just a few doors down from my best friend, Leigh Anne. The apartments are small and nowhere near as fancy as where Preston lives, but I'm proud of my place simply because it's mine. I know someone like Preston could never understand that, and I hate that there's this awkward feeling of shame as I open the door.

No, not exactly shame. Maybe embarrassment is a better word. I'm embarrassed over things that normally wouldn't matter to me, like the fact that I got every single piece of furniture at Goodwill or yard sales on the cheap. There's a large scar across the entire top of my small kitchen table, which is the only reason I got the set for less than fifty dollars. The couch pulls out, which is a nice bonus if someone needs to come stay with me, but the upholstery is stained with wine or juice on one side and the cushions are well-used. I flip the lights on and can't help but glance at him to see his expression as he takes it all in.

Everything is neat and tidy, but I don't think there's one thing here that isn't used.

I stifle the desire to make apologies, almost angry I feel the need to make excuses about the quality of my things. Why the heck am I bringing someone into my home if they are going to make me feel bad about what I have?

But Preston doesn't seem to mind the furniture. Instead, he walks over to a picture sitting on the bar, a smile growing on his face. "Is this you?"

I make a face. "Yes."

"How old were you?"

"Six or seven, I think." It's a picture of me in my parents' backyard. They had gotten one of those little plastic baby pools at Walmart for me that summer and I think I spent every single day sitting in it, pretending I was some glamorous starlet sitting by her pool in L.A. In the picture, I have on a bathing suit that's already way too small—probably another hand-me-down I'd already been wearing for two summers—and a pair of cheap sunglasses. A pair of long clip-on earrings dangle from my ears and my arm is full of bangle bracelets. My legs are crossed and I'm holding a cup of juice up like it's a martini, a toothless smile plastered on my face.

"I love it," he says. "You have such a great smile. You look really happy."

I bite the inside of my lip. I do look happy. That's one of the reasons I love that picture and keep it with me, to remind myself that it's not healthy to only remember the bad things. Sometimes as a child, I was happy.

"Have a seat if you want," I say. "There's beer in the fridge if you want one. I'm gonna go change."

"You sure you don't want some help?" He smiles and wiggles his eyebrows.

I laugh and shake my head. "I'm sure."

I head toward the one bedroom in the apartment, glancing back at him before I disappear inside. He's still staring at the picture of me, a smile on his lips.

CHAPTER 26
PRESTON

Jenna's smile gets me every time. Even as a child, she had something special. A charisma that reaches down inside you and pulls the joy from your heart. I set the picture down on the bar and look around to see if there are more pictures, but this is the only one from her childhood. There's a picture of her and Leigh Anne out at Knox's from last summer on the side table by the couch and a framed picture someone took of all of us around Christmas last year at a party at Knox's bar.

There are no other pictures of her family or childhood.

I don't see any of her paper art out here in the main room, and I wonder if she keeps it hidden in her bedroom. The thought of her naked in there is incredibly distracting, but I hope after she gets dressed, she'll let me in to take a look at some of her work.

Her phone rings and I turn, looking for it. It's sitting on the table with her apron, and I call out to her. "Jenna, it's your phone. Want me to get it?"

"What?" she calls back, her voice muffled through the door.

I cross over to the table and pick the phone up just as it stops ringing. The caller ID says Dylan, and underneath, it says there are eighteen missed calls from him. I stare at the name. Who the heck is Dylan, and why is he calling her so much?

Jenna pokes her head around the corner, a smile on her face. "What did you say?"

She sees the phone in my hand and frowns.

"I'm sorry," I say, setting it back down on the table. I wish I hadn't seen this or picked it up. "I said your phone was ringing. Who's Dylan?"

Her eyes darken and she takes a deep breath. "Hang on, I'll be out in a second."

I step away from the table and wait for her, worry growing in my stomach. From the darkness of her expression, there's something going on with this Dylan guy, whoever he is. An old boyfriend? Jenna and I have never had the "ex" talk before, mostly because she already knows about my two exes. Other than Leigh Anne and Bailey, I have only ever dated a handful of girls and never went beyond a first or second date with any of them.

I don't know the first thing about Jenna's past, but I can't shake the feeling that her past just called.

When she comes out of her room, she's wearing a pair of faded jeans, torn at the knee, and a baggy off-white sweater that hangs down off one shoulder in the sexiest way. A large black tattoo of roses and other flowers covers her shoulder. The sleeves of the sweater hide her hands and she brings them up over her middle.

"Dylan is part of what I wanted us to talk about tonight," she says. "But not here. Let's go to the beach. It's nice out tonight."

I nod and let her gather her things. I don't want to push her about the artwork now. I just hope after tonight, I'm invited over to her apartment a lot more often.

We drive in silence to the beach and start walking. I have brought her out to a section of my family's private beaches so we won't be bothered by anyone. The wind is strong, but it's not too cold out. The sky is completely clear, a million stars overhead as we walk a good hundred yards without talking. I am carrying a blanket I pulled from the trunk of my car, and I nod to a spot just out of reach of the waves.

"Want to sit for a while?" I ask.

Other than the night of the tornado, things between Jenna and I have been carefree and fun. Weightless. But there's a heaviness tonight, as if the words yet to be spoken between us carry the ghosts of our past. As if what we say tonight determines the rest of us, and what we might become.

"Sure," she says. She still has her arms wrapped around her body like a shield, or a barrier. As if to say keep your distance.

I lay the blanket out on the sand and sit, giving her plenty of space.

Jenna sits across from me, her knees up and her body bent over them, all closed up. She's staring out at the water instead of me, and I hold my fists tight, wondering what could possibly be so bad or so serious that she's shutting down like this. How can I make her feel more comfortable?

How can I let her know I'm ready to hear what she has to say, without making her feel rushed?

I turn my body toward the ocean, my legs straight out with my hands behind me, propping me up.

"I love the beach in the spring," I say. "The water's too cold to bring the tourists, yet, but the air is getting warmer. It's peaceful."

"I used to come to the beach a lot when I first moved here," she says. She rests her chin on her crossed arms and stares out at the waves. "I love it out here at night when no one's around. I love that feeling of just being invisible, like no one in the world knows where you are or what you're doing at that moment. It's like a secret between me and the universe."

I don't miss her reference to being invisible. Didn't she say something similar at the water tower? She chooses such lonely places sometimes, which is the opposite of what I would have guessed about her a few weeks ago. She's always so full of life. Why would she want to feel invisible?

"Do you still come out here?" I ask.

She shrugs. "Not as much," she says. "Too much work and not enough time. But it's nice."

I want so badly to touch her, but I know now is not the time. I have so many questions, but I have no idea how to get her to talk about the things that matter. So I give her time, letting her stare and think and be. After a long stretch of silence, I notice there are tears on her cheeks.

"Jenna, you can talk to me," I say. "I know you think I'm just some rich kid who has no idea what you've been through, and you're probably right, but that doesn't mean I don't care. I want to understand what I did wrong so I don't do it again."

She turns her head to the side and wipes her eyes with the sleeve of her sweater, still wrapped around her hands. "I try to avoid these kinds of conversations at all costs," she says. "But I can't keep denying there's something going on between us."

When she looks back toward me, our eyes lock and my mouth goes dry.

"I want there to be more," I say.

"Me too, but I'm scared," she says. "Preston, you and I come from worlds that are so unbelievably opposite from each other, I don't even know where to begin. This is all happening so fast."

I don't know what to say. I'm scared, too, but my fear comes from a different place. I'm not afraid to be with her. I'm afraid to lose her.

"Dylan is my brother," she says.

I sit up and turn my body toward her, one arm slung over my knee. "I thought maybe he was an ex-boyfriend or something," I say. "I wasn't trying to be nosy, but I asked if you wanted me to answer it and when I picked it up, it stopped ringing. It said there were almost twenty missed calls from him. Is something going on between you two?"

"He's been calling me a lot lately, but I can't bring myself to pick up the phone," she says. "Sometimes he leaves messages saying I need to call him back, but I never do."

"Why not?" I try to think of any reason I would ever avoid Penny's calls. We've had our arguments and our differences, but they never last long between us.

"Things with my family are very complicated," she says. She doesn't offer more, and I can sense her fear and hesitation. I wish I knew how to comfort her.

"Jenna, I know this can't be easy to talk about, but I want to know where you're coming from. I want to understand what you're so afraid of," I say. "I want to take this to the next level, but that means you need to tell me what's going on in your head. There's no question we have a lot of fun together and there's this connection between us that can't be denied, but that's all surface stuff. You have to let me in. What are you so afraid of?"

She closes her eyes and her jaw tightens. "Preston, I know this is not something you can relate to, but I have worked so hard to build a life for myself. I had to fight and work for every single thing I have right now. My scholarship. My apartment. My independence. As long as I can focus on those things, I know I'm going to be okay," she says. "But I wasn't counting on this. Whatever it is we have, it's so completely unexpected. I didn't plan to meet someone like you and have actual feelings that went beyond a good time. I don't know how to deal with this."

"So you're scared if you let me in, I'll somehow ruin what you've got going? That doesn't even make any sense."

"I'm scared you'll swoop in and mess with my head," she says. "Knock me off balance. If I start to factor you into my life in any real way, how will I recover if you're suddenly gone? What happens if we break up and I can't get back on my feet? It's so much easier when I only have myself to rely on."

"We haven't even been together for a month, and you're already planning for us to break up?"

"How else can this end?" she asks. There's anger in her voice and her body is rigid. "The richest guy in town does not start dating a poor girl like me and plan to stick around. That's some kind of fairy tale, and I don't believe in that shit."

"Jenna, you have got to stop looking at me like I'm some guy up on a pedestal. I'm not just some rich guy who takes everything for granted," I say. "Why can't you see past the fact that my family has money? Why does this matter so much to you?"

"Because I grew up with nothing, okay? I'm the girl who was always on free lunch at school and wore hand-me-downs or shopped in thrift stores. My dad is a piece of shit who could never hold down a job for longer than a couple months at a time and pawned or sold every single semi-nice thing we ever had so he could buy beer," she says. She's yelling at me. "My brother and I, we never knew for sure if we were going to come home to find our dad drunk and passed out on the couch or an eviction notice on the door of whatever apartment or trailer my mom was renting to get away from him. I've never known the kind of stability you have. Not even close. I never had anything I could really call my own until now. What I've built for myself here in Fairhope, this is the first time I've felt like a real person who could be proud of herself. I don't want to lose that. Can't you see that you put all that at risk?"

I stare at her, my heart aching for the fact that she has no idea how strong or how amazing she really is. And the fact that she thinks I would come in and ruin that for her hurts so badly, I can hardly breathe.

"This is why opening some box from a boutique in

Atlanta with a thousand dollar dress is offensive and hurtful," she says. Her voice is calmer, but her hands are shaking. She presses them against her legs. "It felt like you were saying I'm just like all those other girls, when I'm not. Not even close."

"I didn't mean for it to be like that," I say. "I know you aren't like those other girls, Jenna. That's why I want to be with you. Not because of money or how you grew up, but because of who you are."

"When I saw that dress, it made me feel like I wasn't good enough as I am," she says. "Like in order to fit into your world, I have to learn to dress a certain way or act appropriately."

"I swear I didn't mean that at all," I say. "It's just a stupid dress."

"The money you spent on that dress could pay my rent for a month or more," she says. "And I struggle every single month to make those payments. Don't you see how that creates a major imbalance between us? If we started really dating, how long before you decide to start helping me with rent? Or buy me a new computer? Or hell, someone said you bought Bailey a freaking car for Christmas one year."

"I'm sorry, I don't understand why that would be such a bad thing," I say, frustrated that I don't even know how to defend myself against these arguments. "If you're struggling, why would it be so horrible if I helped you out?"

She stares at me, her eyes are gleaming with tears. "Because I don't want to take your money," she says.

"Jenna." I touch her arm. "What's really going on here? I know there's something you aren't telling me."

She shakes her head and looks away. Finally, she turns back and takes in a deep breath. "I don't want to accept any gifts from you, because that's what my mother used to do when she was sleeping with some rich guy."

I inhale. This is what I've been waiting for. Some kind of truth about why this is so important to her and why she's so messed up about it. "I'm listening, Jenna," I say softly. "You can tell me."

She closes her eyes and a tear rolls down her cheek.

"I can't even believe I'm going to tell you this," she says. She hesitates for a long moment, and finally her shoulders relax. "When I was little, we had nothing. My mom cleaned houses and my dad couldn't hold on to a job for long. When dad had a job, things were okay for the most part. We'd have food on the table, and things would feel normal for a little while. But we always knew it was just a matter of time before things fell apart again. He'd get fired for coming in late or for mouthing off to his boss, but with him, it was never his fault. He'd come home, yelling about how stupid his boss was or how unfair it was they'd let him go or how they'd had it in for him from day one. It was always something.

"That's when he would start drinking again and the real problems would start. The longer he went without work, the angrier he got. When I was really young, it was mostly a lot of shouting between my parents. But as I got older, it turned more physical."

"He hit you?" I feel sick to my stomach. I had no idea she'd gone through all this.

"Not at first," she says. "At first, it was just my mom. He'd beat the crap out of her and she'd give it right back, punching and throwing and scratching. When it got really bad, she'd pack our things and we'd move out. We never knew if it would be for a few days or a few months, but she always went crawling back to him, promising that this time, everything would be different."

"But it wasn't."

She shakes her head. "Oh, it would get better for a while. He'd find a job and the cycle would start back up again," she says. "When I was in junior high, though, my mom started working for this agency that would send her to clean for all the richer families in town. The money was more stable, so we all thought things were looking up. That's when she started coming home wearing things I knew she couldn't possibly afford.

"A pair of new sapphire earrings. A Coach bag. Red high heels. She always said she it was luck that she'd found them at the thrift store in such new condition. I believed her for a while. She was my mom, right? I wanted to think the best of her. But I knew better. As time went on, the gifts got more extravagant. Diamonds. Designer dresses. Her lies got more extravagant, too. The woman I'm cleaning for was just going to throw these out, she'd say. As if rich people just toss their diamonds into the trash."

She laughs, but it comes out as more of a choked sob. I reach out to her, putting my hand on her leg.

"It took my dad longer to figure it out, I think. He was so wrapped up in his own world, he didn't care enough about her to notice. But eventually he did. He confronted her about the gifts, calling her a whore. She denied it, of course, but one day he followed her to work. Walked right in on her having sex with a married man who owned a huge mansion on the side of town. Turns out the agency my mother was working for had nothing to do with cleaning houses."

She buries her face in her hands and begins to sob.

"Jesus, Jenna, I had no idea," I say, the truth of why my gift hurt her so badly finally dawning on me.

"Later that night, they had this complete knock-down, drag-out fight that left my mom in the hospital for nearly a week. My father took a knife to her face, saying that no one would hire an ugly whore and that it served her right for doing what she did. My brother tried to break it up and my dad punched him so hard, he broke Dylan's nose. When he started after me, Mom picked the knife up off the floor and told him to get out and never come back."

"Oh my God," I whisper. "Was your mom okay?"

"Eventually, but her face is scarred for life," she says. "I had just gotten out of rehab and had been going through some of my own dark times when everything went down between my parents, but once Mom got out of the hospital, she swore everything was going to be different for us. She picked up some extra jobs, got us into a really nice rental house in a good neighborhood. I was working by then and saving up every dime I could. My brother graduated and got a job working construction around town, so he was able to help out with the rent. But the truth is, she never recovered from what my dad did to her. It broke her spirit, I think.

"She started drinking and popping painkillers all the time," she says. "I tried to talk to her about going into rehab and getting help, but she wouldn't listen."

"How old were you then?"

"The fight happened when I was a junior in high school," she says. "We spent most of my senior year in that rental house, but one day, about a month before graduation, I come home from school to find my dad sitting there on the couch, his arm around her like nothing ever happened."

My hand goes to my mouth. "How could she take him back after all that?"

She shrugs. "I have no idea," she says. "She told me she was tired of trying to build a better life without him, and that sometimes, you just have to understand your place. That night, she packed up the rental and moved back into my father's trailer. I couldn't stand to go back there, so I went to stay with a friend for a while. I worked extra shifts and saved every penny I could. I got the Hope scholarship and enrolled here at Fairhope Coastal. As soon as I had enough for a small apartment, I moved here, got my job at Brantley's and never looked back. That was almost four years ago."

"You haven't been back to see your parents?"

"I haven't spoken to them since the night I graduated high school," she says. "They didn't even come to my graduation, so I went over there afterward to tell them I was leaving town, but they didn't even care. My dad was so mad at me for walking out, acting like I had no right to be angry with him for what he'd done. And my mom, I think she was upset I was leaving, but she couldn't stand up for herself against him anymore. I left that night and promised myself I would never be like them."

"Jenna, I'm so sorry," I say. "I can't even imagine how hard that must have been."

"Leaving was the easy part," she says. "It was figuring out how to survive until I could be out on my own that was hard. I've lived in my apartment here in Fairhope longer than any other place in my life. I've paid for it with money I earned from a job I've kept since the day I moved here. I know it sounds like some small thing, but I'm proud of that. I don't want anything to mess me up or take that away now."

"I would never do that to you," I say.

"I know that, but I need you to understand that it's taken everything I have to create some stability in my life. I had to completely walk away from everything I'd ever known and learn how to start over. I don't want to fall into the kind of life my mother had, Preston, taking gifts from rich men she was screwing. I can't be any part of that."

"I don't want this to come between us," I say. "I swear, I'll never pay for anything if you don't want me to. I won't ever treat you like that again."

"I'm not sure that's enough," she says. "Because it's always going to be there between us. Do you really think I'll be able to casually complain to you about having to eat ramen noodles for the fifth night in a row without you feeling the urge to fill my fridge with groceries?"

I look away. I hate to admit she has a point. I've never dated someone who struggled with money, but yes, if I heard her complaining about not having food, it would only be natural for me to want to help.

"That's what I thought," she says before I even get the chance to speak for myself. "You're so used to showing affection through gifts and taking care of things. It might start with dinner or groceries, but it would escalate. My truck would break down and you'd want to buy me a new car. I'd be late on rent and you'd want to cover it or have me move in with you. I can't live like that, because it would feel like I was becoming her."

I sit quietly for a moment, thinking about what she's saying. I've gotten so used to paying for things for my girl-friends and even my friends that it's become a part of my nature. I have extra, so why not? It never occurred to me that someone could be offended by that.

"I want you to know I'm listening to everything you're saying, and I think I understand how you feel, but I hope you can see that what we have is nothing like what your mother got involved with. I'm not buying you things so you'll sleep with me. The things I do for you aren't payments, they're expressions of affection. It's completely different."

"I know that," she says. "I know it's not fair for me to blame what I'm feeling on you, but you have to at least try to understand where I'm coming from. My mother liked to pretend she belonged in those diamonds, but it was all a lie. If I put on that expensive dress, I'd feel the same way."

"What if we came up with some ground rules? I never offer to pay any of your bills or buy you expensive gifts, and you promise to invite me over for ramen noodles."

She smiles and wipes a stray tear from her cheek. "You really don't want to have to eat ramen," she says. "Trust me."

"If it means I get to hang out with you, I'll eat ramen noodles every day for the rest of my life," I say. I reach over and take her hand in mine. She's trembling and cold so I wrap both hands around hers and pull her closer. "You are nothing like your mother, Jenna. She was with all those men because they had money. That's not why you're sitting here with me right now. I know that and you know that. You're here because what's happening between us is real."

I run a finger along her cheek and she looks up at me, our hearts racing.

"Even after you know all this about my family and my past, you still want to be with me?" she asks softly.

"More than ever," I say.

I pull her to me, and her kiss says everything.

CHAPTER 27

JENNA

I shiver even though the wind coming off the waves is warm for spring. My hair is blowing all around my face and Preston gently runs his finger across my cheek, pushing a strand of hair behind my ear. He cups my cheek in his hand and leans forward.

My eyes close as our lips meet. I have never felt so open and vulnerable. I can't tell if the buzzing across my skin is from fear or excitement. All I know in this moment is that I want him. Despite everything I once believed about him—and about myself—I trust him. If he could listen to that story and still want to be with me, knowing that my mother was a prostitute and my father an abusive nightmare, he must really care about me.

It could be the biggest mistake of my life, but I know I couldn't walk away from him if I tried.

His tongue slides across mine, and his fingers tug on my hair, pulling me closer. Heat flares through me, lighting me up like a bonfire. Our kiss deepens. My hands find the waist of his jeans and slowly pull his shirt out. I want to feel his skin against mine. I lay my palm flat against his stomach and his warmth feels like heaven.

I push him back against the blanket, my legs sliding over the top of his until I'm above him, straddling him with both hands firmly against his chest. His breath comes hard and fast, and the look in his eyes is pure hunger.

The wind whips my hair back and forth, wild in the shadow of the sea behind us. I hesitate, my breaths matching his. My desire matching his. I know if we go any further, we will go all the way. And unlike the other men I've been with in my life, I know this time it will be different. There will be no turning back from this one. No pretending it meant nothing come morning. If we do this, it will leave a mark on me forever.

"Jenna, I want you," he says, his voice low against the sound of the wind in my ears.

I have never connected with someone on this level. Never told anyone how much my past has wounded me. In some ways, that connection makes this more terrifying than ever. If I give myself to him now and he breaks my heart, I don't know how I'll ever manage to put it back together.

But isn't that what love is all about? Taking risks, even when you know it's dangerous?

I take a deep breath and stare into his deep brown eyes. It's time I stopped denying the truth. I want him so badly, not even a hurricane could move me from this spot.

My heart is beating so fast against my chest, I'm high on the adrenaline. Who knew anticipation could be the strongest drug out there?

Slowly, I reach for the edge of my sweater. With a single,

fluid motion, I lift it up and over my head, tossing it into the sand beside us. I'm not wearing a bra and the moment the air hits my nipples, they tighten.

Preston's eyes flash with desire and his hands move to my waist, his fingers digging into the skin just above the edge of my jeans. His lips part and his eyes roam over my body. Beneath me, I feel him growing harder.

I tug at his navy coat, sliding it from his arms. When my hands roam over his chest, I can feel his pulse drumming against my fingertips. He's wearing a white t-shirt and he sits up slightly to pull it over his head. He flings it to the side and lifts his hands along the skin of my back., exploring greedily. His mouth finds mine again and on instinct, my hands go around his neck. I wrap my legs around him tightly, grinding my body against his as our mouths do all the talking.

His bare chest against mine is on fire except for the cold metal of his grandfather's dog tags that press against my stomach. I run my hands through his hair, down his back, across his shoulders, wanting to memorize each muscle. One hand moves between us and he cups my breast. He tilts me backward and lowers his mouth to me, his tongue drawing circles of fire across my taut nipple.

I lean my head back, my eyes closed, letting my desire for him pulse through me. The waves crash on the shore a few feet away and I find myself rocking against him to the rhythm of the sea, our bodies reduced to nature.

His mouth moves to my other breast, leaving one nipple cold and exposed in the spring breeze. The contrast between warm and cold rips a moan from my throat. I'm not sure how much more of his teasing I can take.

I push his shoulders back and take his mouth again. My

fingers dig into the flesh of his back as my hips rock against him. Preston lifts me up and lays me back against the blanket. He runs his hands up and down my stomach, and my skin jerks in anticipation as his fingers find the button on my jeans. He slides them down over my hips and legs, tossing them aside to join our pile of discarded clothes. He lowers himself beside me, propping his head on one hand as he lazily runs his fingers across my skin. He traces the outline of my tattoos, his eyes following his fingertips. I feel completely exposed, heart and soul.

When he reaches the lace rim of my underwear, he traces along it from side to side, and the space between my legs tightens, growing wet.

"You like to tease, huh?" I say, breathless.

His eyes shoot back to mine, a smile teasing his lips. "I have wanted this so badly for so long, I don't want to take a single moment for granted," he says.

His choice of words brings unexpected tears to my eyes. My heart swells with emotion, and it suddenly hits me how far gone I already am. How much I am already falling in love with the most unlikely guy in the world.

CHAPTER 28
PRESTON

My fingers slide along Jenna's body, exploring every inch of her velvety skin. I almost can't believe we're here, and that she's finally opening up to me.

When she pushed through my apartment door earlier this afternoon, her face red with anger, I thought I'd screwed up beyond repair. I thought she was bringing me here to tell me it was over between us, closing herself off to me like she has done so many times before.

I never expected her to tell me the truth about her past. I had no idea she'd suffered so much as a child, or how hard she's worked to get where she is now. If I lost everything today, would I be so strong?

My body hungers for hers, but I don't want to rush through this. I don't want to give her any chance for regret. I want to make it last, and prove to her that I'm not just looking for a one-night stand or a good time.

I want to remember every touch, every kiss of this first time with her.

My fingers keep dipping to the top of her underwear. I want so badly to push them down and find the wet center of her desire. I want to watch her face when I touch her.

But I'm so hard, I'm not sure how much longer I can hold out. I want her with a hunger I've never known before.

When she reaches for the belt on my jeans, I rise to my knees and let her unbuckle it. The leather makes a zipping sound as she pulls it from my pants. The area around our blanket is a mess of discarded clothes, but there are a few key pieces still to go.

Her fingers are cold against my flushed skin as she slides them under the waistband of my jeans and unbuttons the top. I stand and pull my jeans off. My erection tents my boxer-briefs and I kneel beside her, knowing we are dangerously close to the moment I've been dreaming of for months.

I couldn't still the beating of my heart if I tried.

She comes up to meet me, our bodies pressed together in the wind. We touch and explore, our tongues teasing and tasting as our hands roam.

And then one hand slowly dips to my waist. Her eyes meet mine in one breathless moment as she slips her hand under the elastic waist and takes me into her hand. I inhale at the soft touch as she moves up and down, caressing me slowly.

"Now who's teasing?" I ask, barely recognizing my own voice.

"I'm just getting started," she says.

The thought of what else we could do to each other throws me over the edge. I loop my fingers in the top of her underwear and pull them down. She wiggles her body until they are resting on her foot. She gives them a little kick and they sail into the sand.

I take a deep breath and pull my boxers down, and just like that, we're naked together for the first time, me hardening to the point of pain against her stomach as I kiss her.

She pulls away and bends over, searching for her shorts. I bite my bottom lip, my eyes devouring her perfect form as she crawls across the sand in the moonlight.

Jenna pulls a condom from her back pocket and tosses it to me. I smile and open the condom. My family definitely doesn't need another surprise pregnancy, but I'm surprised Jenna brought a condom with her tonight. Had she known where this was heading all along?

"I brought it just in case," she says, as if reading my mind.

"Good thinking," I say, even though I have two in my wallet. Just in case.

She lays back against the blanket and watches as I slide the condom on.

I position myself above her, still on my knees. With one hand, I grip her thigh and pull her legs open slightly. She writhes, but opens to me as I slide my hands up her leg until I touch the patch of soft blond hair. She breathes in and her eyes widen as I slip one finger inside her. God, she's so wet. I can hardly catch my breath as I touch her, exploring her until she moans and her body tenses, lifting up against my palm.

She reaches for me, pulling me down on top of her.

"No more teasing," she says. "I want you."

I am helpless to do anything but obey. I position myself at the tip of her opening and with eyes locked, I slowly push into her.

Her body grips me, warm and wet and tight. I begin to move and she opens even more, wrapping her legs around me, lifting her body to meet mine with each thrust.

I start out slow, wanting to make sure she's comfortable, but I'm so close to the edge already, I'm having a hard time controlling myself.

"More," she says, her voice husky with desire. "Harder."

I groan and push into her. Her nails dig into my back and she pulls my lips to hers. We move together, sweat making us sticky and wet even in the cool spring air. Our bodies press tightly, hard and fast as the tension inside me fills to a breaking point.

I pull my mouth away from hers and bury my face in her neck, breathing hard as I come in one last, fevered thrust.

Jenna runs her fingers through my hair and kisses my neck as my body shudders, and then stills.

I move beside her, one leg laying over hers, covering her body from the wind.

When my breath settles, I softly kiss her neck and cheek. She smiles and runs lazy circles across my arm.

"Did you come?" I ask.

She shakes her head. "No, but don't take it personally," she says. "I don't usually from just intercourse."

"Really?"

"Women are slightly more complicated than men, in case you haven't noticed."

I smile and nod. "Oh, I've noticed," I say."But I'm not letting you leave this beach without feeling the way I feel right now."

She giggles, but then moans as my fingers find their way back to her.

Her legs spread open as I touch her, but I never take my eyes off her face. Her eyes close, and I watch for every sign of pleasure. Tense eyebrows, moans, a sharp intake of breath. I let her sounds and movements guide me until her body begins to writhe with each touch. My breath speeds up again as her back lifts from the sand, arching upward as her hips grind against my hand.

Her hand tightens around my arm and her nails dig in as her mouth opens and a pleasured moan sounds deep in her throat. Her body bucks against me and a rush of wetness floods over my fingertips. I continue to caress her until her body settles back against the blanket and her legs hang limply against me.

When her eyes open, she smiles and laughs. She buries her head against my arm, so I pull her closer, our legs tangling together. I reach over and wrap the edges of the blanket around us like a little cocoon.

We stare into each other's eyes for a long time, smiling and kissing, and I think this must be as close to heaven as you can get on this earth.

"That was amazing," she says. "I've never had anyone do that before."

I study her. "What? Give you an orgasm?"

She shakes her head. "No, I mean, I've never had a guy make sure I was taken care of after they already got off."

I laugh. "I hate that term, got off. It sounds so cheap for what just happened."

She lifts a hand to my cheek and runs her fingers across my skin. "Thank you for listening to me tonight," she says. "I try to avoid talking about my past and my family, because I don't want people to define me by where I came from."

"I understand that more than you know," I say. "I know we come from completely different worlds, but I struggle with that, too."

"I think I'm seeing that more and more," she says. She turns slightly so she's laying flat on her back, looking up at the stars.

I join her, slipping my arm under her head as we lay in our cocoon, watching the stars and listening to the lull of the ocean.

"I just hope you can understand that where I come from doesn't define me any more than it does you," I say. "I'm more than just my parents' money or my name."

She snuggles in close, one hand on my chest right above my heart.

"If I thought that was all you are, I never would have come here tonight," she says.

I hold her in my arms for what seems like hours, wishing our whole lives could be as simple as this. Praying we can remember the way we feel right now when the storms come again.

CHAPTER 29
JENNA

I roll over in my bed, expecting to find a warm body, but the space is empty.

I open my eyes and sit up, sick at the thought of Preston leaving without even saying goodbye. I am not used to having a guy sleep over, but after our time on the beach, it seemed natural to invite him back to my place for the night. I thought things would be different with him.

His clothes are gone from the floor, and I collapse back onto the bed. Dammit. Have I made a huge mistake?

I sigh and pull the covers off my naked body. As I begin to stand, the door to my bedroom flies open. I scream and grab the first thing I can think to use as a weapon from the bedside table—a paper mache sculpture of the white rabbit from Alice in Wonderland. I lift it over my head, ready to strike.

Preston nearly drops the tray he's carrying. He's laughing so hard, the glass on the tray is rattling.

"Preston, good Lord, you scared me to death," I say. I fall

back against the bed and wrap the discarded sheet around my body. "I thought you left."

"I did," he says. His eyes are dancing. He comes around and sets the tray of food and flowers on the bed. "I had to go out and get breakfast. Your fridge is totally empty, by the way. I wanted to surprise you."

"Surprise me? You nearly gave me a heart attack," I say, laughing. "I thought someone had broken in."

"And what? You were going to beat them with a paper rabbit?" His face is all smiles.

I realize I'm still holding the rabbit in a death grip. I set the little guy back on the table and straighten his pocket watch, which is now crumpled and distorted. I bring a hand to my mouth, unable to stop laughing. "Poor little guy," I say. "He was only trying to protect me."

"And now you've maimed him," Preston says. He sits close to me on the bed.

I turn and smack his arm. "You should have at least told me you were up and getting breakfast," I say. "I thought you'd gotten spooked and abandoned ship."

"Not a chance," he says. He thread his arms around my waist and pulls me closer. His lips descend on mine and warmth rushes through me.

I let go of the sheet and come around to straddle him, pressing my body against his. Our kiss deepens. I run my hands through his hair and wish like hell he hadn't gotten dressed.

He groans and pulls away. "I made breakfast," he says.

"Made? Or bought?" I say, eying the tray. There are two perfectly made egg and cheese biscuits sitting on a plate with hash browns. "You're either capable of performing miracles in my kitchen or you bought that and put it on a plate."

He laughs. "Do you have to call me out on every single thing?"

"Always," I say.

"I can't even tell you how much I adore that about you." He kisses me again, his hands roaming over my bare skin, growing needier.

It's my turn to pull away. "After breakfast," I say. "I'm hungry."

"I have plans for us after breakfast," he says.

I slide off his lap and sit back against the pillows, pulling the sheets back up to cover my chest. I motion toward the tray and Preston moves it between us. "What plans?"

"You'll see," he says, mischief gleaming in his eyes. "Now eat, you're going to need your stamina."

I raise an eyebrow and take a bite of my biscuit, happiness filling me like a warm light.

DESPITE MY BEST EFFORTS TO CONVINCE PRESTON TO spend the whole day in bed with me, I'm dressed and sitting in the passenger seat of his car by eleven.

"Where are we going?"

"I'm taking you to get a dress," he says. There's laughter in his tone.

"We talked about this," I say. "I don't want to go to some boutique, and I don't want you to buy me anything."

"I promise I'll let you pay for it yourself," he says. "Trust me on this."

I sit quietly as he drives us through town. It's quiet because nearly everyone in this town goes to church on Sundays. I know from working a thousand Sunday shifts that in an hour, most of the church-goers will end up at Brantley's for the Sunday buffet. I'm so happy to not be at work today that I'm willing to let him take me to whatever shop he wants.

My mouth drops open when he pulls into the parking lot of Jolene's Thrift Shop. I smile and shake my head. "You sly little devil," I say. "How did you know this is my favorite shop in town?"

He shrugs and hides a smile. "I pay attention."

"Not enough," I say. "Jolene isn't open on Sundays."

"She is today," he says. He gets out of the car and closes the door before I can question him.

To my surprise, Jolene is waiting for us. She opens the door as soon as she sees us. "Well, come on in, I ain't got all day," she says. She winks at me as I pass by her into the store.

"What is going on here?" I ask.

Jolene motions to Preston and shrugs. "If you need me, I'll be in the back watching TV," she says. "And I was just kidding. Take all the time you want. I have nothing else to do all day but relax. When you're ready for me to ring you up, just holler."

She shuffles back to the plain wooden door that leads to her apartment.

"What did you do?" I put my hands on my hips and stare at Preston.

"You don't want a fancy boutique? Fine by me," he says. "But if we're going to be seeing each other, you have to let me do nice things for you every once in a while. And believe it or not, I can be creative beyond spending money."

I bite down on my lower lip, trying not to smile like a silly girl. I thought sex would complicate things, and it probably has in ways I just don't understand quite yet, but I love that he took the time to arrange this for me. It proves he really was listening last night.

"You have the whole place to yourself for as long as you want," he says. "And we don't even have to worry about people coming in and putting in their two cents or asking us what the big occasion is. Just you and me. If you agree to be my date at this dinner, you can wear anything you want. All I care about is you being there and being comfortable."

I tilt my head and study him. "You may change your tune once you see the look on your mother's face," I say.

"If you could steer clear of tube tops and overalls, it would be in our best interest," he says. "But other than that, go wild."

I laugh and give him a big hug. "Thank you," I say.

"Is that a yes?"

"Yes," I say, wondering if this is the dumbest thing I've ever done in my life. "It could be fun."

"As long as we're together, I know it will be," he says. "Now go forth and shop."

"What are you going to do?"

He points to the well-worn leather recliner near the dressing rooms. "I'm going to park myself on this recliner and watch," he says. "I would not be opposed to seeing you model some dresses. The tighter and shorter, the better."

I roll my eyes and make my way to the dress section. Since I moved to Fairhope several years ago, I've been in this store nearly once a week. I adore thrift shops, which I guess is odd considering my past experience with hand-me-downs. But searching for treasure in a place like this is different from someone giving you a bag full of clothes that barely fit because they know you can't afford your own.

I like the anonymity of thrift shops. I don't know who these clothes used to belong to, and I don't care. I can find things on the cheap and alter them to fit my own style. I've been known to rip sleeves off jackets and holes in jeans, or shorten the skirt of a dress. When you grow up never having anything new, you find ways to make it seem new and different. I'm handy with a sewing machine and bought a used one when I was fifteen that I still have in my apartment.

I flip through the dresses on the rack and an orange taffeta bridesmaid nightmare of a dress catches my eye. I glance over a Preston, who is reclined on the leather chair and reading something on his phone. If he's really not bothered about the time, we might as well have a little fun. I take the orange dress off the rack and go through the rest quickly, choosing every hideous dress I can find.

"I'm heading back to the dressing room," I call out, both hands full of hangers.

Preston barely looks up from his phone, and I smile. I pile into the dressing room with all my treasures and undress quickly down to just my underwear. I pull on that first taffeta dress and stand back, admiring the worst of it in the mirror. The dress has huge puffy sleeves, is about two sizes too big, and there's a dark chocolate stain near the bottom. Or at least I hope that's chocolate.

I wonder how far I can take this before he goes running for the hills. There is no way he would let me walk into a fancy dinner wearing this dress. His mother would probably strangle him.

The thought makes me laugh out loud.

I open the door and lift the long ruffled skirt as I walk toward where he's sitting.

"What about this one?" I ask. I smile widely. "Isn't this adorable? It would be perfect, don't you think?"

Preston glances up from his phone and his eyes widen. The sheer terror on his face is priceless. He clears his throat and takes a deep breath. I can literally see the debate going on inside his head. "It's cute," he says, his voice a couple tones higher than normal. "If that's the one you love, let's get it."

I hold back my laughter. "Do you think?" I twirl around and fluff the ruffles. "You don't think it's too orange?"

He scratches his cheek. "It's a little more colorful than what I was expecting," he says. "But you'll look beautiful no matter what you wear."

I can't hold it back any longer. He actually thinks I'm serious, and I can tell it's killing him. I laugh and hold the skirt out from my body. "I'm kidding, Preston. Would you honestly let me buy this and wear it to the party?"

He lets out a long breath and laughs. "Thank God," he says. "That dress is hideous."

"Isn't it?" I say turning again. "It's probably been in someone's closet since the eighties and they finally brought it up here to try and sell. I look like a pumpkin."

"The sexiest pumpkin I ever saw," he says, his eyes dancing with laughter.

"Okay, if you think I look sexy in this dress, you've got it worse than I thought," I say.

"Oh, I've got it bad," he says, raising an eyebrow.

My stomach flutters and I inhale. The tension between us is delicious and warm, and all I can think about is the way the muscles in his back rippled against my hands as he hovered over me last night.

"There's more," I say, breathless.

"I can't wait," he says. "Please tell me they aren't all as bad as this one."

"Worse," I say as I lift the skirt and run back to the dressing room.

CHAPTER 30
PRESTON

Each time Jenna comes out of the dressing room, she reaches a new level of hideous.

By the fifth dress—a terrible shiny gold skirt with a black sequined shirt—we are laughing so hard my stomach hurts. "That's the one," I say, doubled over in the recliner. "All you need is a tiara and some bright pink lipstick and you will be perfect."

"I was thinking more like a top-hat and some really long gold earrings," she says. She holds her hand over her mouth and nearly collapses from laughter.

"Wait, I think I saw a black top-hat." I stand and walk over to the men's section. There's a dusty black top-hat sitting on the head of a mannequin wearing a powder blue tuxedo. I take it from the unfortunate guy's head and walk back to Jenna.

Her cheeks are flushed and her blue eyes are lit up. I move close and place the hat on her head. She tilts her chin up, and I'm struck by her beauty. By her ability to be so free and joyful. I know there are demons in her past, but that's part of what makes her so beautiful to me. She hasn't let her past rob her of joy, and the more I get to know her, the more I realize just how strong she truly is.

"I need a picture," I say.

She poses for me and I snap a few shots on my cell phone.

She wraps her arms around my waist and pulls me close. "Thank you for bringing me here," she says. "It means a lot to me."

"I just want to be with you. Nothing else matters."

I claim her lips and her arms tighten around me. The hat falls to the floor behind her, but we don't stop to pick it up. Her gold skirt makes whispered swishing sounds as she presses against me, and I would love nothing more than to rip this ugly dress from her body and take her again right here. If it wasn't for Miss Jolene in the next room, I probably would.

"I still need to find a dress," she says, her voice low and sexy and breathless.

I press my forehead to hers. "What? Something better than this?" I say. "Not possible."

She smiles and makes the sweetest little moan of a sound in her throat. "It is the best one so far," she says. "But I don't want to make the other women at the dinner too jealous. I'll already be on the arm of the hottest guy there."

Jenna pulls away and nods back toward the blue tuxedo.

"You should try that on," she says. "It looks just about your size."

She smiles and disappears into the racks of ladies dresses. I turn and study the powder blue tux. I laugh and shake my head. My mother would have a heart-attack. But then again, why should Jenna have all the fun?

As she searches through the rest of the dresses, I take stroll through the aisles of men's clothing. I expect everything to be equally as terrible as most of what Jenna has just spent the last hour parading in front of me, but I'm surprised to see some nice clothes in here. A pair of Guess jeans drapes over a cheap metal hanger and I reach for the price tag, turning it over between my fingers. Fifteen bucks? Damn. They hardly look worn.

Guilt nags at me. How many pairs of hundred-dollar jeans have I just tossed in the trash after only wearing them a few times? A couple times a year, my mom used to make me go through my closet and throw some old clothes in a bag to donate to charity, but I never really considered that people would pay for used clothes. I honestly have never given two thoughts to the prices on the clothes I buy, but watching Jenna now seriously looking through the racks for something nice enough to wear to this dinner, I realize how stupid I was to buy her that expensive dress.

I've been so caught up in my own world, complaining about dating women who only want me for my money, but never realizing how much I've let my money define me. How much I've taken it for granted. It makes me wonder how many people I've offended by offering to pay for things in the past. I usually think nothing of it to pick up the tab at bars with my friends or out at dinner. I always figured it was expected of me, but now, after hearing Jenna out, I'm wondering if it makes me seem like a jerk who's always throwing his wealth in people's faces. I never considered it would make people feel like I was saying I'm somehow better than them.

I think back on all the parties I've thrown in the past couple years. All the reckless spending when there are so many out there who are less fortunate. No wonder my sister Penny is always on our mother to spend more of her charity dollars here in Fairhope instead of sending the money overseas.

And no wonder every girl I've gone out with only cares about money. I have flaunted it so much in the past three years of college, I've let it become the single most important aspect of my character.

But how can I change? The thought of giving most of my money to charity like Penny makes me feel sick to my stomach. I like being able to buy whatever I want, whenever I want. I like having nice cars and cutting edge technology. Does that make me a bad person? At this point, I honestly don't even know.

Once you start to realize how much less everyone around you has, it makes everything about loving money feel wrong and greedy. But at the same time, I can't imagine giving it up.

Maybe I should take a small page out of Penny's book and spend some time living a more simple life. How hard could that really be? If it makes me appreciate the money instead of taking it for granted, wouldn't that be a step in the right direction, at least?

I browse the small section of men's suits. There has to be something here that will fit. I had planned to wear my tailored black Versace suit to the dinner, but there's no rule saying I can't wear something new. Or new-to-me. I take a few things off the rack and head back to the one small men's dressing room in the back of the store.

The first few suits are awful. The pants are too long or the material is way too scratchy. But the third option isn't half bad. It's dark grey and a quick check of the label shows a designer I don't recognize. The price tag reads fifty dollars. I adjust the collar of a plain white dress shirt and stand back from the mirror. It's not too bad, really.

When I come out of the dressing room, Jenna is standing in front of the three-way mirror in a knee-length black dress that takes my breath away. It's simple and unadorned, but fits her like it was made for her body.

"What do you think of this one?" she asks. She is staring at herself, turning at various angles to get a better look at the dress. She hasn't noticed what I'm wearing yet.

"It's perfect," I say, breathless. The back dips low enough that her tattoos become a show-piece, better than any jewelry she could have found to go with it. I want to run my fingertips across the roses the way I did last night.

She finally glances over, then does a double-take. Her lips part and then slowly curl into a smile. "Did you find that here?" she asks.

"Yeah. What do you think?" I join her at the mirror and in my eyes, we look like the perfect couple.

"It's fantastic," she says. "We look good together."

I slip my hands around her waist, running them over her hips and pressing my body against her back. I rest my chin on her head and smile at our reflection in the mirror. I have wanted her for months, and it's hard to believe I finally managed to break through her resolve. I'm falling for her faster than I ever could have expected, and in this moment, I want to tell her how much she means to me. But the relationship is still so fragile, I'm afraid to push her.

"Are you going to buy the suit?" she asks.

"I think I am," I say. "It will be my first thrift-store purchase. I'm kind of proud of that."

"You should be," she says with a smile. "You can finally get a taste for how the other half lives."

She spins around and puts her arms through mine. I kiss her again, our bodies rocking slowly, as if music is playing. I want this moment to last forever. As long as it's just the two of us, alone in our cocoon, nothing can keep us apart. But I can't shake the nagging suspicion that the demons of her past are never too far behind.

CHAPTER 31
JENNA

Outside, I hear Preston's car drive away, his headlights shining briefly through the gauzy curtains of my front window. He skipped his family's weekly brunch to spend the day with me, but agreed to meet back at their house for dinner. I don't envy the conversation he's bound to have with them about me. If he even decides to tell them about our relationship yet. Either way, they're going to find out next weekend at the dinner.

I grab a beer from the fridge and walk out to the small balcony just off the living room of my one bedroom apartment.

I light a cigarette and watch as the smoke is lifted away by the wind. It's eerily peaceful, considering the furious storms that passed through here earlier this week. Inside, there's a different kind of storm brewing in my heart.

We had agreed to keep things light, but here I am now, falling in love with him. Fate brought us together, and even though I never used to believe in that sort of thing, this feels right.

But as much as I want to be with him, I worry how much longer we can keep this up without our differences pulling us apart. I'm terrified I'll go to this charity dinner with him and he'll see me standing there beside the girls who really belong there, and realize how much I don't.

Everything has come so easy for him, is he really going to be willing to work on us when things get hard? When the storms of my past roll over me like they did when that gift arrived?

Nothing has come easy for me. I had to fight my way through life from that first newborn squeeze through the birth canal. How could a guy like Preston ever understand me?

And yet, I've seen a side of him that's so beautiful and unexpected. He's a natural leader, but it's more than that. The night of the tornado, he could have easily gone back home with his mother to the safety of their giant mansion with its decked out storm shelter—probably equipped with a generator that could power half the town and a full suite of games, dvds, and more food than his family could eat in a year—and left the search to us normal folks.

But he didn't. Preston hadn't even hesitated to help. He didn't worry for two seconds about his own safety. He trudged right along side me in the mud, his mind focused on finding that little girl. And if it wasn't for him, we might not have found her at all.

He was a hero.

And last night at the restaurant, he stood up for me. He listened to every word I said on the beach without running for the hills when I told him how messed up my family is. And, oh God, the way he made love to me still makes me shiver.

So far, he's made all the right moves. It feels too good to be true.

The deeper we go, the more I start looking over my shoulder for lightning to strike.

I smash my cigarette into the ashtray and go back inside. I wash my hands and get a stack of delicate papers from the hall closet. I set my workstation up on my kitchen table and turn the radio on. I need to think. I need to get my hands dirty and focus on the details of the folding and cutting. I need to get my mind off the worries and just meditate. Try to find a way to believe in the good things that are happening between us.

I open a plastic bag full of brightly colored strips of paper, and begin folding them in half, dabbing a tiny dot of glue on one end to hold them in place. The work is repetitious, but I fall into a peaceful trance as I go through the motions. Fold. Glue. Fold. Glue. When I have a collection of petals, I arranged them on a square piece of cardboard I've painted a dark gray.

I create delicate flowers in a variety of colors, folding and arranging the paper until a scene begins to form on the page. I let my mind go blank and fill my lungs with deep, deliberate breaths. After an hour, the beating of my heart has stilled and the demons have slipped away into the shadows.

But thoughts of Preston are still there. How easy it has been to open up to him. How much more we have in common than I ever thought possible.

A tear forms on my eyelash and I blink, letting it run

down my cheek as I stare at the scene I've created. A farmhouse made entirely of blue paper takes up a large portion of the left side of the page. A field of bright paper flowers adorns the stretch of farmland to the right. In the center of the field, stands a little girl, her hair in messy blond pigtails. She's wearing a red dress that's slightly too big for her scrawny frame. Her small face is lifted toward a stormy sky, but she has one hand delicately placed on top of a flower petal. It has taken me four hours to create this piece, and it was only after I'd finished that I realized I hadn't created a scene with the little Powell girl at all.

The girl in the field is me.

The scene is a perfect reflection of how I feel. A child standing her ground amidst the storm, trying to see the beautiful things in life. Trying to find the joyful things that hold her feet to this earth.

With a black marker, I sign the lower right corner with my initials—JAL—and on the back, I give the piece a title.

Storm Coming.

I tack this latest creation on the shelf in my bedroom and crawl into bed, thinking it's funny how fate does what it wants sometimes, despite our best efforts to deny it. Like the petals of the flower in my picture, the wind carries us where we are meant to be.

I just hope the storm waits just a little longer before it descends on us. I'm not ready to let him go just yet.

CHAPTER 32
JENNA

"Help me with the zipper?" I ask.

"I would help, but it will take me ten minutes to get out of this chair," Penny says with a laugh. She rubs her hand across her pregnant belly and smiles.

Leigh Anne stands and comes over to zip the back of my black dress. "I love this dress, is it new?"

I smile, thinking about our romantic trip to Jolene's. I never would have imagined there could be such a thing as romantic thrift-store shopping, but I had the best time.

"I found it at Jolene's," I say. I bite my lower lip and turn to her. It feels awkward to talk about Preston with her since she dated him for so long in high school, but it feels wrong not to confide in my best friend. Plus, Penny is his twin sister. She probably doesn't want to hear me get all gushy about her brother. "Is it weird if I talk about Preston? Because it feels weird."

"Don't look at me," Penny says. "I haven't seen Preston this happy in so long, I can't even remember. You can talk about him all you want to, as long as you don't go into detail about your sex life."

Leigh Anne laughs and shakes her head. "Seriously, Jenna. I have no problem with it at all," she says. "I'm happy you're giving him a chance. You are both my friends, and I want you to be happy."

She sits back down on my bed and picks up a piece of one of the butterfly projects I've been working on lately. She turns it over in her hands, studying it. "This is really beautiful, by the way," she says. "You made this completely from scratch?"

I slip on a dangly black earring and nod, watching her in the mirror. "Yeah. I made the paper myself, which took days since I needed so many different colors and weights," I says. "But I think it's turning out really pretty so far."

"It's unbelievable," Penna says. "Hand me one of those. They are so delicate and beautiful. You should sell these."

I shake my head and wrinkle my nose. "I can't imagine anyone would pay for those little things."

"I think you'd be surprised," she says. Leigh Anne takes one of the fifty or so I've made so far out of the box and hands one to her. "I bet you could find hundreds of parents who would love something like this for their little girl's rooms. I know I would."

"Seriously?" I ask. "I'll make some for the baby's room if you want. What color?"

"I'll pay you for them," she says. "We've decorated the room in lavender and white and gray, but have kept it very simple. A cluster of butterflies on the wall above the crib would be gorgeous, don't you think?"

"I think it would be perfect," I say. "Maybe I'll stop by

your place this week and take a look at the colors so I can match them."

"Anyway, you were saying something about Preston?" Penny asks.

My cheeks warm at the thought. "He did the sweetest thing for me," I say. "I told him I was uncomfortable with him buying me an expensive dress for this dinner, so he had Jolene open her store for us last weekend so we could have the place all to ourselves. We had such an amazing time. I never knew how much fun he could be."

"I can't believe you found such a perfect dress at Jolene's. It looks tailored to your body," Leigh Anne says. "I love it."

"So you don't think I'm going to look completely out of place at this thing?" As much as I didn't want to walk in there with a thousand dollar dress paid for by someone else, I also don't want everyone at the dinner to look down on me because of what I'm wearing. It's a very confusing set of emotions. "I've never been to something like this before."

"I think you look lovely," Penny says. "That's all anyone will notice."

"Thanks," I say, still not completely convinced. "You know the best part? Preston is wearing a suit he bought at Jolene's, too. Isn't that cute?"

Penny raises an eyebrow. "He is?"

I nod and dab some sheer gloss on my lips.

"I have never known Preston to show up at an event without a designer suit," she says. "You must really be getting to him."

"I think he just wanted to make me feel more comfortable."

"The fact that he's thinking of how you feel over himself or anyone else is a huge step for him," she says.

My stomach flutters. I hadn't thought of it like that, but it makes me both nervous and excited.

"I just hope I don't make a fool of myself in front of your parents and their friends," I say. "I wish you were coming, too, Leigh Anne."

"No way," Leigh Anne says. "I've been to enough of those things to last me a lifetime. If it was a dinner for Penny's charity, I'd be there in a heartbeat, but I'm glad to be sitting this one out."

Nerves zing through me. "Why? Are they usually that bad?"

She wrinkles her nose. "I'm sorry. I didn't mean to make you even more nervous," she says. "It's not that they're horrible, I just find those kinds of events boring. Plus, I always wondered why charity dinners like this are so popular. Wouldn't it just be better to give the full amount to charity instead of spending a fortune on a dress and dinner just to attend? Half the money goes to putting the event together in the first place."

"Don't even get me started," Penny says. "The events really do raise a lot of money in the end, but that's because the tickets are nearly five thousand dollars a person."

"What?" I spin around, feeling like I'm going to be sick.

"Don't worry, our parents already covered the tickets for all six of us," Penny says, waving it off like it's no big deal. "I just wish the full amount was going straight to cancer research instead of lobster and champagne."

I sit down on the edge of the bed, deflated. Five thousand dollars a ticket? I had no idea it was so expensive just for me to attend. And the fact that Preston's parents paid it is making me feel light-headed. I take several deep breaths. It's not like they spent the money on me, exactly. It's for a good cause, most of the money going to breast cancer research. But the realization that I'm going to be in a room full of people who don't hesitate to hand over thirty grand at the blink of an eye makes me feel completely out of my league.

Is this what our relationship is going to be like? This past week has been all about the two of us, mostly hanging out at the beach or at my apartments, but tonight is the first time I've really ventured into his world. I can't ask him to stop donating money to charity or giving parties on his father's yacht. I can't expect him to stop driving nice cars or wearing designer clothes. If I'm truly going to give this a shot, I'm going to have to learn to deal with his level of wealth in a way that doesn't have me running to the bathroom every five minutes to throw up.

"Are you okay?" Leigh Anne asks. She puts a cool hand on my forehead. "You look like you're going to pass out or something."

I shake my head and take another deep breath. "I'm going to be," I say. "I feel so stupid for letting this get to me. I'm just not used to being around people who have that kind of money."

"You're going to be fine," Penny says. "Honestly, you'll be sitting at a table with Preston, Mason and me. We'll eat, dance and have some fun, and then maybe we'll head back to the house to go swimming or something fun. I don't want to stay out too late. I've been feeling off all day."

We both turn to look at her, our eyes wide with worry.

"I'm fine," she says. "I'm just nine months pregnant is all."

"Just a few more weeks," Leigh Anne says, smiling at Penny. "Hard to believe there will be a tiny baby in our lives so soon."

"I know," Penny says. "I can't wait to see what she looks like and hold her in my arms."

I smile over at Penny, trying to remember that this is the most important thing. Time spent with friends who love you no matter what you have in your bank account or who you were before you came into their lives. I never really had a family I could love and trust growing up, but somehow, here in Fairhope, I've created my own little family.

I try to concentrate on that thought as the limousine pulls up outside.

"That's our ride," Penny says. She stretches out her hand and Leigh Anne and I both rush to her side, helping her up from the chair in the corner. "Thanks," she says with a laugh. "Come on, Jenna, let's go have some fun."

Leigh Anne kisses my cheek and follows us outside. "Have a good time tonight," she whispers in my ear as she pulls me in for a hug. "You really do look beautiful."

I hug her back and go to help Penny down the stairs.

CHAPTER 33
PRESTON

"What are you wearing?" my mother asks when I climb into the limousine.

"It's a designer I've never worn before," I say with a secret smile playing on my lips.

"I thought you were going to wear your Versace," she says. "The material on that suit doesn't look nearly as nice. Where on earth did you find it."

I consider for a moment whether it's worth the argument if I tell her the truth. I decide to take a page out of Penny's book and stop worrying so much about what my mother thinks.

"Jolene's," I say.

She thinks on it a moment, and then her eyes grow wide. "Here in town?" she asks. "Are you talking about that awful thrift store on the corner of Main and Hunter?"

"Yes, that's exactly what I'm talking about," I say. "But it's not awful. She has a lot of really nice things in there."

"Used clothing, Preston," she says. "Lord knows who

wore that suit before you did. Please tell me you had it cleaned."

"Jolene has everything cleaned before she puts it out on the floor, Mom," I say. "And while it's just the two of us, I'm going to ask you to be nice to Jenna this evening. It would mean a lot to me."

She gives a dramatic sigh and pours herself a gin and tonic. "I am trying to be supportive of both you and your sister," she says. "Even if I don't completely agree with your choices when it comes to romance."

"Thank you," I say.

"I do hope you'll reconsider giving Piper Hendricks a call, though," she says. "She's a much better match for you."

"Mother, don't you think I'm a better judge of that than you are?"

"I'm not so sure about that. I loved Leigh Anne for you, of course, and Bailey was precious, but Jenna Lewis? Do you even know the first thing about her family? She has nothing, Preston. Girls like that are only after guys like you for one thing."

I grit my teeth and count to three before I speak. "I know you believe what you're saying, but you have to trust me on this," I say. "For the past several months, I've been going out with the type of girls you want me to be with— pretty, polite, good family upbringing—and I've never been so bored in my entire life. Did you know that the last girl spent exactly thirty minutes with me before she started suggesting places she wanted me to fly her to in our private jet?"

Mom lifts her chin and takes a careful sip of her drink.

"All of these so-called perfect girls care more about our

money than getting to know me," I say. "Jenna's not like that. She couldn't be farther from that. We have fun together, and she never asks me to spend money on her. It's nice to be with someone who likes me for me."

"Well, I'm glad you're happy," she says, patting me on the leg. I'm not sure she's really heard a word I've said.

When the limousine arrives at Jenna's apartment, I get out to help Penny and Jenna down the stairs and into the car. I've never seen Jenna so dressed up before, and even though she can take my breath away wearing a tank top and jeans, she's stunning tonight in her black dress.

Her blond hair is sleek and perfect, pulled back a little on top with the rest of it falling across her shoulders. She smiles nervously as I take her hand and bring it to my lips.

"You look perfect," I say.

"How much shit did your mom give you about the suit?" she asks, which makes me laugh.

"A little," I say. "But it was fun to watch her squirm."

We ride to the country club, my mother on her best behavior. She even compliments Jenna on her earrings, which it turns out, she's borrowed from Penny.

I can tell Jenna is nervous, but she has no reason to be. Throughout the entire evening, I can barely keep my eyes off her. We dance and sip champagne before we join Penny and Mason at our designated table. We have been seated with a few other couples, including my ex-girlfriend Bailey and her new boyfriend, Judd.

Judd is one of my parents' scholarship recipients in medical research at Fairhope Coastal, working on a cure for leukemia. The more time I spend with them, the more I realize I couldn't have picked a better partner for Bailey. She lights up around him in a way she never did with me. I'm happy for her.

After the main course is served, I excuse myself to go to the restroom, but before I turn the corner into the hallway, I hear my name. I freeze, listening to the two women talking.

"Did you see the girl he brought with him tonight? I just know I've seen her somewhere before," one woman says.

"She's a waitress over at Brantley's," the second woman says. "Hasn't got a penny to her name, if you know what I mean. I heard she's slept with half the senior class at FCU."

"What in the world is he doing with a girl like that?" The woman makes a tisking sound with her tongue.

"Well, I think we both know what he's doing with her," the other woman says. "The question is why he thought it necessary to bring her to an event like this. His parents must be mortified."

Anger rages through me. Everyone thinks they have our relationship all figured out, but they don't know anything. I straighten my jacket and walk around the corner.

The two women stand up straighter, their faces flushed at the sight of me.

"Preston Wright, don't you look handsome this evening."

"We were just talking about you."

"I heard," I say. Their faces go slack. In the South, it's not considered polite to call people out when you happen to hear them spreading gossip about you, but I can't help myself. "It's none of your business what's going on with Jenna and me, and I don't appreciate you spreading lies about her."

The woman on the right sucks in a jagged breath, preparing to apologize, when her eyes shift to a spot behind me. She purses her lips and turns away.

I turn around to find Jenna standing behind me.

"Can I talk to you for a moment in private?" she asks through clenched teeth.

I nod and walk with her to the back patio. A few smokers stand in a cluster on the other side, but we are able to find a quiet spot near a bench.

"This is exactly why I didn't want to come here tonight," she says. "Whether it's true or not, everyone in that room looks at me and sees a woman like my mother. Someone who will sleep with anyone for money."

I take her hands in mine. "That isn't true. Those two women are assholes who like to gossip," I say. "Who cares what they think?"

"Usually, I wouldn't give a damn about those women and their ideas of who I am or what I do with my private time," she says. "But coming in here, dressed up like I want to be one of them? It makes me feel like a cheap knock-off. It makes it look like everyone's right about us and that all I care about is your money."

"Don't let this ruin our night."

"You can't go around defending me for the rest of our lives," she says. "You can't go around to everyone in town and tell them that hey, Jenna's not after my money and I'm not using her for sex. It only makes it worse when you try to explain it. And besides, I'm used to people saying bad things about me. It's you I'm worried about."

"Me?"

"Yes. You have a reputation to uphold in this town," she says.

"I don't give a shit about my reputation."

"Yes, you do," she says. "After what happened with Penny,

you've got the whole world looking over your shoulder, waiting to see if you're going to be a leader or a loser. I don't want them to judge you because of me."

"If someone is going to judge me because I am with the hottest girl in the whole room, let them judge," I say. I lean down until she looks up and meets my eyes. "I honestly don't care about any of that. If someone is too shallow to realize I'm the lucky one in this relationship, then that's someone I don't care to know."

She studies me, finally letting the hint of a smile cross her face.

"Let's get out of here," I say.

"You'd really leave for me?" she asks.

"Of course," I say. "All I want is you by my side."

"Good," she says. "Because one more stare or hushed whisper as I walk by and I'm going to end up punching someone in the face. Then you'd really be screwed."

I laugh and put my arm around her neck, pulling her close to me.

We take off our shoes and sneak away to the beach, a bottle of wine and two plastic cups between us. For the rest of the evening, it's just us, alone in the moonlight.

But I know we won't be able to shut the world out forever, and I can't help but feel our time is slipping away.

CHAPTER 34
JENNA

We are lying in bed naked, our bodies pressed close together, talking about the virtues of kung-fu movies when Preston's phone rings.

"Don't answer that," I say. "I want you all to myself until morning."

He leans over me and grabs his cell from the nightstand. "I have to," he says. "I'm an impending uncle."

I smile and run my hand along his torso as he answers.

"Hello?"

I glance at the clock. It's after two in the morning, and I realize it's a very real possibility this will be the call he's been waiting for.

When his eyes practically bulge out of his head and he stumbles out of bed, knocking over a small table with a display of paper kittens, I know the time has finally come.

I laugh and watch as he tries to juggle the phone while getting dressed. He nearly trips and falls three times before he hangs up.

"Penny's in labor?" I ask.

"Yes, what are you doing? Get dressed," he says. He collects a wad of clothing from the floor and throws it at me.

I shake my head from under a pair of yoga pants. "No, I wouldn't feel right," I say. "I don't want to intrude on private family time."

I toss the clothes back toward the end of the bed as he's pulling on his shoes.

His shirt is buttoned wrong and his fly is open.

"Come here," I say, crawling to the end of the bed on my knees. I fix the buttons on his shirt and brush my hands through his tousled hair.

"Thanks," he says, kissing me on the forehead. "You wouldn't be intruding. I want you there. Besides, you have to come."

"Why?"

"Do you really think I can drive in my current state?" he asks. "I'm so excited, I can hardly dress myself."

I roll my eyes, but grab my clothes and run into the bathroom to get ready.

Ten minutes later, we pull up at the Wright Women's Hospital—yes, named for Preston's family who donated the money to build a dedicated maternity wing. An actual valet comes out to park the car for us, which feels kind of ridiculous since the parking lot is literally fifty feet away.

"Your family is already upstairs," the tall man says as he holds his hands out for the keys to my truck. "They said to tell you she's in room 313."

Before I can argue or offer to park my own truck, Preston is in the lobby searching for the elevators. I shrug and hand the keys to the man.

"Thanks," I say.

"Yes, ma'am," he says.

I join Preston at the bank of elevators. He's staring at the descending numbers on the display as if it will help the elevator get here faster.

I slide my hand into his and squeeze. He takes a deep breath and squeezes back.

We make it to the third floor within a few minutes, and Preston knocks on the closed door of room 313.

His mother opens the door and pulls him into a huge hug. "So happy you're here," she says. "I can't believe this day is really here. Who would ever have imagined I'd become a grandmother so young?"

Preston smiles and kisses his mother on the cheek. "How is she doing?"

"As well as can be expected," she says. "She's refusing any pain medication, which I think is just preposterous."

She steps away to let Preston in and notices me for the first time. Her eyes dip to our clasped hands and for a brief moment, I watch as she composes herself.

"Jenna, dear, I wasn't expecting to see you here so late," she says, her voice tense.

Preston pulls me into the room and rushes to Penny's side. She's sitting on a giant exercise ball, leaning over onto the bed while Mason rubs her lower back.

Mason holds a finger to his lips and points to a machine on the other side of the room. A green line is spiking toward the top of a meter. After about thirty seconds, it falls back down to the bottom of the meter and Penny looks up.

"They're getting a lot more intense," she says.

Preston releases my hand and sits down on the bed across

from her. "I got here as fast as I could," he says. "How's it going?"

"I'm in labor, what do you think?" she says.

"How far apart are the contractions?"

"About a minute apart, so you've got approximately forty seconds to talk to me before I turn into a raging bitch," she says.

Preston laughs. "And how is that different from any other day?"

Penny laughs and playfully hits him on the shoulder. She squeezes his arm. "I'm so glad you're here," she says. She glances at me over her shoulder. "Hi, Jenna. I thought I heard mom giving you crap when you walked in."

"Penny, don't talk like that," her mother says, crossing her arms in front of her.

"I don't think the baby can hear me, Mom. And even if she can, she's going to have to get used to the word crap. It's a staple of my vocabulary."

Her mother sighs and turns around. She starts fussing with Penny's overnight bag, folding and refolding the same nightgowns.

"Jenna, come over here," Penny says. "Tell me a story to take my mind off this pain."

I step over and hover near the bed. I don't feel like I belong here in this intimate family moment, but no one else —besides their mother—seems to think I'm out of place.

I try to think of something that will keep her mind occupied when the next contraction hits.

She moans and leans over again, pressing her head to a wet towel clasped in her hands.

"Okay, so here's a story," I say, edging closer to the bed

and sitting next to Preston. "This one time when I was younger, probably about thirteen, I heard about a party a few high school girls were throwing. I wasn't invited, of course, young pipsqueak that I was, but I was also a rebel and didn't like to be told no. So I waited until my parents were asleep and crawled out the window of my bedroom, which let me tell you, was quite the task since it wasn't much bigger than I was at the time.

"I walked about three miles down this dirt and gravel road wearing nothing but a pair of worn flip-flops and my best sundress. I had managed to snag a tube of my mother's red lipstick, and I remember slathering it all over my lips like I was Marilyn Monroe or something. The whole way there, I thought about how I was going to walk up to that party and own the place. Like those seventeen year old girls were going to realize I was cool all of a sudden and invite me in to drink a beer."

Mrs. Wright clears her throat loudly, but I don't even look at her. I guess beer is another word she doesn't want her precious grandchild to learn on her first day in the world. But Mason motions for me to keep talking.

I glance at the monitor and see the contraction reaching its peak.

"So I walk all this way and by the time I get there, my legs are covered in dust. One of my flip-flops is completely broken, so I'm walking barefoot in the gravel, working on some blisters that are going to hurt like hell come morning.

"I stroll up to this big house with cars parked all down the street," I say. "There's music blasting from the open windows and inside, I can see all the cool older kids dancing and drinking, having a good time. But then I catch my reflection in the window of an old truck parked beside me. The lipstick is smeared around my lips and my hair is slicked back way too tight. Compared to the other girls, I realize my pretty red sundress with the daisies on it looks like a child's dress. At that point, I had no boobs to hold it up, so it hung down in front because it was probably a good full size too big on me. My legs were dirty and there were scratches down one leg where I'd had to climb through a stretch of blackberry bushes to get to the main highway. I looked completely ridiculous, and let me tell you, there were plenty of times since I wish I had a picture of how I looked that night to remind me just how silly we can be when we're trying to please other people instead of just being ourselves."

Penny lifts her head. There's moisture beaded on her cheeks and she's flushed pink, but she smiles at me.

"What happened?" she asks. "Did you go to the party and show them all how cool you were?"

I shake my head and lean across the bed to take her hand. "Nah. They would have just laughed at me. I ended up hiding behind that truck for another few hours, just watching them," I say. "Wishing I could figure out a way to be popular."

I take the wet cloth from her hands and dip it in the cool basin of water on the tray behind me. I wring it out and lean back on the bed, dabbing the coolness across her cheeks and forehead.

"Did you ever figure it out?" she asks, resting her cheek against the bed.

I look around the room, thinking how I'm one of the few private citizens lucky enough to be at the bedside of the richest twenty-something in Georgia. "Yeah," I say. "Turns out all along, I just needed to learn to be myself."

Penny smiles and grips my hand as her eyelids flutter closed.

I stay by her side for the next six hours as her contractions become more intense. Mason and Preston take turns getting her ice chips and rubbing her back. She changes positions, sometimes walking around until a contraction hits, and sometimes back on the ball.

"Penny, this is enough of this nonsense," her mother says around eight in the morning. "There's no reason for you to be in so much pain. I could have the anesthesiologist in here in fifteen minutes and you wouldn't feel a thing."

Penny lifts her head and she and Preston share a meaningful look.

"Mom," Preston says, putting his arm around his mother's shoulder. "Why don't we take a break? Let me take you down to the cafeteria for some breakfast and a cup of coffee?"

"I don't need a break," she says, lifting her chin.

"Yes, you do," he says. He glances at me and I nod. "I'll be back in half an hour or so."

Mason is in the waiting room talking to his mother, which leaves Penny and me alone in the room.

"I'm so glad you're here, Jenna," she says. "I was about to go insane with the two of them fussing over me like I was some invalid. You've made the hours go by with your stories."

"Glad my most embarrassing moments can help you laugh through the pain," I say, smiling. "I almost didn't come. I didn't want to intrude on your privacy."

Penny holds her hand out to me, and I help her to stand. Her huge belly leads the way as she stands, her entire body off balance. She wraps her hands protectively around her stomach and smiles.

"You're not intruding," she says. "Besides, from the way Preston talks about you, I wouldn't be surprised if you became a part of this family some day."

I nearly choke on my own surprise. My body goes cold and rigid, and I suddenly feel like I can't catch my breath. Has it been this hot in here all morning?

Penny laughs as she walks around the room, leaning on me for balance. "You look like I just punched you in the gut," she says. "Is that really such a horrifying idea?"

I don't even know what to say. "I guess I just haven't gotten that far," I say. What exactly has Preston told her? We've only been together a month.

"I didn't mean to scare you," she says. "Later you can just chalk it up to the ramblings of a woman in distress, but I've never seen him so happy or so in love."

I suck in a breath. "In love?"

"Don't tell me he hasn't said those three little words, yet?" she asks. She winces and grips my hand tighter.

I wrap my arms around her and let her lean her weight against me as the contraction ramps up. She's squeezing my hand so hard my knuckles turn white, and I start to lose feeling in my fingers.

"Keep breathing," I remind her. "Open your mouth and take deep breaths, in and out."

I feel her release the tension in her jaw and take a breath into her lungs. Her body relaxes slightly and the contraction passes. She begins to walk again.

"No," I say. "We haven't crossed that milestone yet. We're

not even really a couple." But even as I say the words, I know it's ridiculous.

"Do you love him?" she asks.

The question catches me so off-guard, I have to remind myself to keep putting one foot in front of the other as we pace around the room.

"Never mind," she says. "You don't have to answer that. I already know you do."

Another contraction seizes her and I am glad her eyes are closed so she can't see the tear that rolls down my cheek.

CHAPTER 35
PRESTON

Rachel Marie Trent arrives at noon, a healthy eight pound baby girl with a mop of dark brown hair and her mother's nose. I am the proudest uncle alive.

We give the small family of three some quiet time alone before we sneak back into Penny's hospital room. The baby is so tiny and pink, and when Penny hands her to me, I can't even describe the joy that flows through me. And the terror that I'll drop her or break her somehow.

She's so delicate and small. When I touch my index finger to her hand, she reaches up and wraps her tiny hand around it. I rock her back and forth in my arms.

I have never held a baby before in my life, but I love her instantly.

"Hello, little one," I whisper. I look up at Penny and there are tears in her eyes. "You did good," I say with a smile.

"I'm just so happy she's healthy," she says. A sob escapes from her throat, and she lifts her hand to her mouth. Mason puts his arm around her and sits close to her on the bed where she's propped up with half a dozen pillows behind her back.

"She's our little warrior," I say. I think back to the night Penny found out she was pregnant. She'd been so worried she had done something to hurt the baby in that accident, but like a miracle, she couldn't be more perfect.

I look around for Jenna to see if she wants to hold the baby, but she's not here.

"She left," my mom says, watching me closely.

"Left?" I ask. "When?"

"A few minutes ago when you took the baby," she says.

"Is she coming back?"

"I don't know," Mom says. "Why you brought her here in the first place is beyond me. I realize you're going through a phase right now, but this should have been our time together."

Penny and I exchange looks.

"I was so glad to have her here," Penny says. "I don't know if I could have made it through this without her."

"Well, that's just rich," Mom says. "What were the rest of us doing here, then? Twiddling our thumbs?"

"Mother, if you think I'm going to let you steal one ounce of happiness from this day, you are delusional," Penny says. "Get it together, or get out."

Mom sucks in a breath and lifts her chin, but before she can say another word, Dad appears at her side, his hand on her shoulder

"Let's not bicker," he says. "If Preston and Penny want their friend here, I'm glad she was able to come."

"I just don't understand why she was even with you at two in the morning," Mom begins.

Dad's hand on her shoulder tightens and she takes in a long breath.

"No matter," she says, waving a hand in the air as if brushing away the thoughts in her head. "Now let me hold that precious grandbaby."

She gently scoops the newborn into her arms and bounces her up and down.

Penny looks at me and shrugs. Our family has been through a lot of transition in the past seven months or so since Penny first found out she was pregnant. She would never have been able to stand up to our mother like this before she left Fairhope with Mason and found her independence. I'm proud of her, but also a little disappointed in myself for not being able to shrug off my mother's negative words.

It's no secret she doesn't like Jenna. Her first strike was helping Penny pawn a diamond tennis bracelet Dad gave Mom for their ten-year wedding anniversary in order to pay for a sick child's surgery. Her second strike was agreeing to go out with me.

Of course, Mom thinks Jenna surely cast some kind of voodoo magic spell on me to get me to go out with her, but she has no idea of the truth. She's going to completely lose her shit when she finds out how hard I'm falling for Jenna.

And worse, Dad probably will too.

They are careful around the subject, because they are terrified I'll make a repeat of Penny's disappearing act. But I know the moment they begin to sense how serious things really are between us, they'll start pushing me to break things off.

I excuse myself and go to look for Jenna. Why would she have left without telling me where she was going?

I check the cafeteria on the first floor to make sure she didn't go down to grab some lunch. She'd been at Penny's side through most of her labor and had barely eaten anything since we got here.

But she's not in the dining hall.

I step outside and ask the valet if he's seen her. He nods and points to an out-of-the-way spot between two columns at the end of the driveway.

"Thanks," I say, relieved she's only stepped outside for a few minutes.

But all my relief vanishes when I step closer and see her tear-streaked face.

I sit down beside her and wrap my arms around her shaking shoulders. She's holding her cell phone in one trembling hand, and I look over to see her brother's name on the display.

"Jenna, what's wrong?" I ask, fear heavy like a stone in my stomach.

She looks up, her blue eyes bloodshot and red from crying. She can barely catch her breath, so I wait patiently, rubbing her back until she calms.

"What happened?" I ask again.

She takes a breath and releases it in jagged bursts. "I came out here to give you guys some family time alone," she says. "I turned my phone on to check my email and there were sixteen missed calls from my brother back home. I've been avoiding him for so long, I figured I better call him to tell him to stop calling because I don't want to talk to him, but—"

She begins to cry again, and I hold her close. Something is terribly wrong, and my heart is aching for her.

"Did something happen back home?" I ask softly, not wanting to push her.

She nods and pulls away, wipes her face on her sleeve. She shakes her head and closes her eyes. More tears roll down her cheeks.

"He said it was my fault for running away. For not staying and making sure she was taken care of. He said he's been trying to get in touch with me for months so I could come home and try to talk some sense into her," she says. She's talking so fast, and I still don't understand what's happened that's so bad.

"What did he say was your fault, Jenna? Tell me what's going on."

She sniffs and looks up at me, her blue eyes full of thick, heavy tears.

"Preston, my mom died last night."

CHAPTER 36
JENNA

I'm numb as Preston drives me back to my apartment. I focus on the rumble of my truck's engine, the laughter of a child blowing bubbles in her front yard, a flock of black birds flying overhead. Anything but the words my brother shouted at me through the phone as he blamed me for our mother's death.

But they creep in anyway. I hear them over and over, drinking his words down into my stomach like poison.

The sun is shining and the heat in the truck is suffocating. I roll the window down as we ride, but find I still can't breathe.

Preston holds my hand, talks to me in low, soothing tones, but I can't hear what he's saying. I have descended into a void of loneliness and sorrow so deep, it feels like I'm no longer part of this bright world around me.

He parks and opens the door for me, takes my hand, and leads me slowly up the stairs. My thoughts have focused down to a single phrase chanting in my brain.

My mother is dead.

My mother is dead.

My mother is dead.

Every footfall brings it around again, and I'm surprised when I look up to see I'm standing in the bedroom of my apartment, my bag already open and half-packed. I don't even know what I've put in it.

Preston is in the living room, and I can hear the soft tones of his voice as he talks to someone on the phone. I step around the corner and listen to him telling someone he'll be gone for a few days for the funeral.

My stomach knots, and I think I'm going to be violently ill.

When he sees me, he ends his conversation and walks toward me. "I can drive you," he says. "I've already made arrangements at a hotel where we can stay, unless you want to stay with your family."

I shake my head, my jaw tensing.

"You can't come with me," I say. "I don't want you there."

He places his hands on my shoulders. "I want to be there for you," he says. "You're in no shape to drive all that way alone."

"Don't push me on this." There's more anger in my voice than he deserves, but the thought of Preston meeting my father and seeing the life I lived with his own eyes makes me insane with anger.

"Jenna, you don't have to go through this by yourself."

I push his arms away and walk back to the bedroom. I pull a random handful of clothes from my closet and stuff them into my duffel bag. "You can't fix everything, Preston,"

I say. "I know you think going will help, but I don't want you there, okay?"

"No, it's not okay," he says. "You're in shock, and I don't want you driving when you can barely pack a bag."

I stare down at the heaping mess overflowing from my bag, and the tears threaten to spill again.

He's right. I'm in no shape to drive. No shape to bury my mother. No shape to face my father and brother, who have decided to put this all on me.

But I cannot let him come with me. It's one thing to hear stories of my childhood, but it's something else entirely to actually witness the horror with your own eyes.

I cannot handle my father's drunken form of abuse with Preston watching it all go down.

I can't bear to let him watch me fall apart.

I dump the contents of my bag on the bed and start over.

"When is the funeral?" he asks.

"I don't know yet," I say, almost mumbling. I don't want to talk about it. I just want to pack my things and get on the road. I don't want to be still. Movement keeps the truth from sinking in, and I don't want to believe it. Not yet.

"Slow down," he says, taking my hand and pulling me back toward the bed. "Do you want to talk about what happened? How did she die?"

I close my eyes, picturing my mother with her nightly bottle of bourbon and her cabinet full of sleeping pills. She called them her happiness cocktail, and she liked to mix them. No amount of warning on my part could ever get her to stop.

"I'll be fine," she'd say, her speech already slurring after the first pill. Usually a Xanax. "I need this, baby girl. It's been a long day."

With my mother, every day was a long day.

When I was still at home, I'd sometimes water down the bourbon or sneak Tylenol into the pill bottle. Sometimes she didn't even notice, but when she did, she yelled like I'd murdered someone.

"I don't want to talk about it," I say. I twist my wrist from his grasp and go into the bathroom. I start throwing my makeup into a plastic bag.

"Please don't shut me out right now," Preston says. "I'll do whatever you need me to do. Do you want me to call anyone? Leigh Anne?"

"I want you to leave," I say, channeling my despair into fury. I know I'll regret it later, but right now, I just need to be alone. I don't want anyone around when the meltdown comes, and I feel it nipping at my heels like a shadow.

"Jenna—"

"You said you'd do whatever I want," I say, finally looking him in the eye. "I want you to go. I don't want to sit here and have some kumbayah moment while we discuss the details of my mother's overdose. I don't want you to book some fancy hotel in my hometown for me. I don't want you to take care of me at all. I just want you to go."

He leans his head against the door frame. I know I'm being childish and lashing out at him when he is only trying to help, but all I can think about is that perfect little scene of him holding his twin sister's newborn baby in his arms, smiling and cooing at her while the whole happy family looks on, smiling and full of joy.

I have never had that, and I never will. I almost resent

him for that happiness. That sheltered life with his complaints about how much his parents' hopes and dreams cut into his own ideas about the future. When I told my father I was leaving to go to college, he laughed at me. He said I wouldn't survive a semester on my own.

My mother had cried, saying I was a selfish little brat who only ever thinks of herself. She said I was abandoning her, leaving her there without another female voice of reason in the house.

And I had left. I'd gotten out of there so fast, I probably left a trail of smoking tire marks in the driveway.

I abandoned her and she drank herself to death. Dylan was right. It is all my fault she's gone, and there'll be hell to pay for it.

I push past Preston, who is still standing in the doorway of the bathroom, watching me.

I toss my makeup and toiletries into the duffel bag and go through my clothes again. I'll need something black for the funeral. Something I can burn afterward.

I take a plain black dress from a hanger and toss it into the bag.

"Are you seriously just going to stand there, breathing down my neck?"

"I don't know what else to do," he says. "I know you're hurting and confused. I know you said you don't want to talk about it, but maybe it would help if you did."

"What do you want me to say?" I shout. I'm so angry, I need to break something. I want to destroy everything, and just tear through this room like a tornado. My hand circles around the base of a lamp on my bedside table, and I hurl it across the room. The cord rips out of the socket and the lamp crashes against the wall, breaking into tiny pieces that scatter across the carpet. "That I knew my mother had a drug problem, and I left her there anyway? That I refused to take her calls for the first full year I lived here? That I'm a horrible person who wouldn't even drive three hours to see her when she went into the hospital six months ago the first time she overdosed?"

I take my newly packed bag and hurl it toward the closet. I grip the sheets on my unmade bed and rip them off.

Preston grabs my wrist as I reach for the paper mache white rabbit.

I look up at him and see tears forming in his eyes. All the anger and energy that pushed me forward dissipates into sorrow, and I collapse to my knees.

Preston follows, wraps his arms tightly around me.

"I'm so sorry, Jenna," he whispers over and over as I cry. He rocks me back and forth, stroking my hair as the tears pour down my cheeks.

I cling to him, unable to make sense of the emotions at war within me.

I sink lower, unable to hold myself up, feeling drained of life. Preston sits and leans against the edge of the closet, cradling me in his arms until the tears have run their course, and I drift off to sleep.

CHAPTER 37
JENNA

I arrive at my father's house by ten. I turn the lights off before I pull into the driveway. I need a few extra minutes before he realizes I'm home, if he's even sober enough to be coherent.

Twenty-four hours ago I was making love to Preston with the future spread out before us like an undiscovered treasure map. Twelve hours ago, I was holding Penny's hand through each contraction, ushering a new life into the world.

Now, my heart is stripped bare of those hopeful moments, and all I can see or feel is the heavy sorrow of my past.

I don't want to be here, but I owe my mother that much at least.

I let my head fall back against the worn headrest and force air into my lungs, gathering up the strength to go inside and face the nightmare that awaits.

Preston wanted to come with me and the thought of escaping my parents house and shacking up in some swanky suite downtown was more tempting than I cared to admit to him. But the horror of having him see this part of me won out, and I convinced him to stay in Fairhope.

I think of Penny's words at the hospital this morning when she said I might someday become a part of their family. Now, with the evidence of my humble beginnings staring me straight in the face, I almost laugh at the thought. Jenna Lewis, a true rags to riches Cinderella story.

I shake my head and sigh. That will never be me. No matter how hard I try, I will never shake the stink of this place off me.

I linger in the truck for a few minutes with the windows down, the smell of my mother's favorite wisteria blossoming around me. My father liked to remind her it was only a weed, but she didn't care. Even weeds can be beautiful, she'd say.

The scent brings a memory of one of the good days rushing back. It hits me like a anvil to the chest.

I was maybe seven or eight at the time and my parents were on one of their many breaks. We'd moved to a tiny apartment on the edge of town. It was a terrible, dirty place with one bedroom and a kitchen so small there wasn't room for two people at once. Mom had picked it solely because of the wisteria. She took one look at the stretch of woods behind the apartment building with its trees covered in purple flowering vines and knew it was the place for us.

I always suspected it had a lot more to do with the three hundred a month price tag than the flowers, but who was I to argue with my mother at that age? Besides, we were away from my father, and that made it better.

When they were apart, my mother was a different woman. She rarely drank and did things for us like cook eggs in the morning before school or walk us to the bus. On Saturdays, we would go to the park and she'd read romance novels while my brother and I played until we could hardly stand on our worn-out little legs.

One Sunday, I remember waking up to the sound of my mother's singing. It was early and the sun had only started to raise its head and paint the sky. I yawned and padded out to the living room, drawn by the siren song of her papery voice, so ethereal and thin, she sounded like an angel.

She'd looked up from the table and smiled. "Come sit with me, baby girl," she'd said.

A heaping pile of wisteria littered the kitchen table.

"What's all this?" I'd asked.

"I woke up this morning and decided we needed a little something to brighten up the house," she'd said. My mother, always with a cigarette in hand, had sat at the table the rest of the morning clipping and cutting those blooms and forming them into pretty purple bouquets. She'd spread them around the apartment, setting the biggest one beside my sleeping bag on the floor of the one bedroom my brother and I shared.

I remember staring at that bouquet for hours every night when I lay down, wondering if it was some kind of sign that happier times were here to stay.

A few days later, though, my father had barged in and stomped every purple blossom into the carpet with his boots. He said he'd had enough of my mother's nonsense, and that if she didn't come home, he'd burn the apartment down around us.

We left our little apartment a few days later and moved back here to my father's trailer.

Every time I smelled wisteria, I thought of those days with my mother, and how rarely I'd ever heard her happy enough to sing.

Being back her now only makes it more clear to me that Preston and I could never really be happy together. It's been wonderful for a while, just like that apartment, but this is really who I am. I will never be able to shake the demons of my past, and it isn't fair to drag him into that hell. He deserves more.

"Jenna?"

My brother's voice startles me from my memories, and I clap my hand to my chest. "Dylan, you scared me to death."

"What are you doing out here in the dark?" he asks, the smell of beer on his breath.

"Just thinking," I say.

"Well, grab your stuff and come on in," he says. "Wasn't sure you'd show your face around here. Too little, too late, don't ya think?"

He doesn't wait for me. Instead, he walks toward the house, stumbles up the stairs, and disappears inside.

Weary, I climb down from the sanctuary of my truck and follow him into the house.

The sweet smell of flowers is replaced by the overwhelming smell of sweat and smoke. My father is sitting in his favorite recliner, his big belly sticking out beneath a dingy white tank top. He's gained a good fifty pounds since I last saw him, and his hair is balding on top.

"Well, if it isn't the prodgical daughter," he says, not even bothering to get up and welcome me home.

I know better than to correct him. No matter how wrong

he is, my father is always right. I learned that the hard way a very long time ago.

"Hi, Daddy," I say.

There's a cigarette clutched between his fingers. Next to him, an ashtray overflows with discarded butts. Three empty packs are stacked up neatly beside it, and I wonder how long he's been sitting in that same spot, chain smoking and watching fishing on TV.

"So glad you decided to grace us with your presence, your highness," he says. He scratches a spot under his armpit and wipes his fingers across his shirt.

The man repulses me, and it takes every ounce of willpower I have not to turn around and drive straight back to Fairhope without so much as a glance behind me.

"Well, don't just stand there." He waves his hand back and forth. "You're blocking the TV."

Some greeting after being gone nearly four years. I step deeper inside the house and look around at the terrible mess that's accumulated. The sink is full of dirty dishes that look like the food is cemented on. The floor is grimy and covered in dust and mud. There's a basket of clothes next to the couch with four or five balled up sacks of fast food trash lying on top.

How long had they been living like this? If mom just passed away last night, she must have been living in this filth for a while. It wasn't like her. She'd always kept the house tidy and neat. She had to in order to avoid my father's abuse. Cleaning was woman's work, he'd always said, never bothering to lift a finger to help.

I start to say something about the state of the place, but

think better of it. Instead, I set my bag on the floor and go into the kitchen to start on the dirty dishes.

I turn the water scalding hot and scrub as hard as I can, washing away the dried-on ketchup and bits of ash from discarded cigarettes. I unleash my anger on these poor dishes, thinking it's no wonder my mother drank so much. In her eyes, she had no escape. This life was what she deserved, so she gave herself a life sentence and served until it drained every ounce of hope from her body.

When I'm done with dishes, I start on the floors. I mop the kitchen, scrub the bathrooms, wipe down the windows. It takes hours and despite barely having slept in the past two days, I'm wide awake.

It's nearly two when I force myself to go back in the living room. The TV is still on, but Dylan is passed out on the couch and my father is snoring in his recliner. A cigarette smolders in his hand. I carefully take it from him and smash it into the overflowing ashtray. I grab a garbage bag from the kitchen and throw away the butts and empty packs. It's so disgusting, I vow never to smoke another cigarette again in my life.

I clean up the discarded fast food wrappers and toss the clothes back into the washing machine.

It's close to four in the morning before I finally run out of things to clean and drag my weary body to the bed in the back room. I lay, fully clothed, on top of the flowered bedspread and wonder how my mother survived as long as she did.

MORNING COMES TOO FAST. MY MUSCLES ACHE AND AT first, I can't remember where I am. Those few moments are the best part of my day before the realization that I've come home rushes back.

I shower and dress, search the fridge for something to eat, but find it bare of everything except beer and a half-eaten bologna sandwich.

"Don't bother," Dylan says, coming up behind me. "I don't even know why you bothered cleaning up the place. It'll just look like crap again in a week."

"Heaven forbid you actually picked up after yourself."

"I never said I minded it the way it was."

I roll my eyes and shut the refrigerator door. "How long has it been like this?" I ask. "Mom never used to let the house get this bad."

He shrugs and lights a cigarette. He takes a swig from his beer, not seeming to care that it's only nine in the morning. "After you left, things started going downhill, I guess. She'd been working two jobs since Dad got laid off at the factory and said she didn't have the energy to come home from cleaning all those houses and clean up our mess, too. After a while, Dad got tired of arguing with her about it."

"You should have..." I don't finish what I was about to say, but Dylan finishes for me.

"What? Called you to tell you how bad things had gotten?" He laughs and tips his beer up until it's drained. "What did you think I was calling you for every day for the past six months? Just to say hi?"

I run a shaky hand through my tangled hair. I don't want to feel responsible for this, but the guilt is eating at me. If I would have come home to visit, even once, I would have seen for myself how bad things had gotten.

"She didn't want you to know, anyway," he says. "She was real proud of you for going to college, even if she wouldn't say it in so many words."

I am silent. I lean back against the kitchen counter and hold my arms tight against my body.

"What about rehab?" I ask. "I thought she got cleaned up."

"She was sober about three months," he says. "Came home from rehab and dumped nearly fifty dollars worth of bourbon right down the drain. I thought Dad was going to lose his mind when she did that. She had me sell all her left-over pills. Even let me keep half the money."

I close my eyes and try to still my tongue from lashing out at him. He almost sounds proud of earning that extra cash for himself.

"It didn't stick, though," he says. "I figured it wouldn't. She took her part of the money and bought this little laptop. Started searching the Internet for better jobs and going out on interviews. You should have seen her. She even went over to the Walmart in Perry and bought a new set of clothes for the interviews. They looked real nice on her."

"What happened?"

"She couldn't get a job," he says. "Nothing better than cleaning houses or waiting tables. She was looking for a desk job, but that was ridiculous since she can hardly type and barely knows her away around a computer. Besides, with her face all scarred up, no one wanted her sitting at the front desk, greeting customers. But she tried real hard. She'd sit here at the table all evening after she got off work, pecking away on the keyboard, looking for something better to come along. I guess after a while, she just got tired of waiting."

"Where did she get the pills?"

"Pawned the laptop," he says. "Bought some stuff off a guy down the street who got hurt at work and is out on disability."

"You knew this and didn't do anything about it?"

"Well, damn, Jenny." I cringe at the name. He'd started calling me Jenny in kindergarten just because he realized it made me mad. "What do you think I should have done about it? She was a grown woman. I couldn't stop her from doing whatever she wanted to do."

"About a month ago, she got fired from her best cleaning job. They accused her of stealing some jewelry from the master bedroom. A diamond ring from the lady's grandmother or some shit."

"Did she?"

He acts angry I would even suggest it, but then shrugs and lights another cigarette. "Hell, damned if I know. She swore she'd never stole anything from those houses, but I don't know where she was getting the money for those pills. After rehab, none of the doctors in town would prescribe anything stronger than ibuprofen."

I run my hand along my forehead and sigh. The hopelessness of my mother's life weighed me down, like a stone around my heart. "I should have come home," I say.

"Damn right you should have," Dylan says. "What kind of girl leaves her whole family and never even comes home for Christmas? Not once in four years did you come home. You have no idea how hard that was on her."

"I'm sorry," I whisper.

"Nobody here to apologize to anymore," he says. He gets up and tosses his cigarette into the almost empty bottle. "Now that Momma's gone, you can leave and never come back for all I care."

He leaves the room and goes back to the couch and starts flipping through channels.

I consider following him and telling him he's a real piece of shit, but take a deep breath and grab the keys to my truck instead. I pass through the living room, needing to get out of this place before it suffocates me.

"Where you going now?" he asks.

Daddy is still asleep in the recliner, and probably will be for another three or four hours.

"Someone has to make funeral arrangements," I say, not glancing back as I close the door behind me.

CHAPTER 38
JENNA

I somehow manage to survive until the funeral, but when the morning arrives, I have a hard time forcing myself out of bed. I want to pull the covers over my head and forget everything for a little while longer.

I have never felt so lonely in my life.

Instead of yelling at me, my father has spent the past two days in his recliner, staring at the television. My brother was gone when I got home from the funeral home, and I haven't seen him since. He's probably been off getting wasted with his friends. Do neither of them care that she's gone?

And what right do I have to care as much as I do?

I pull myself out of bed and go through the motions of getting ready. I pull my hair back into a messy bun and slide into my plain black dress. I feel numb, as if life has no meaning anymore.

Daddy is waiting for me in the living room. He's managed to squeeze himself into his one decent pair of slacks. His tie is crooked, but I can't bring myself to get close enough to him to fix it.

"Come on, then," he says. "Let's get this over with."

A tear rolls down my cheek as I follow him to his truck. I wipe the tear away, afraid that if I allow them to fall in earnest, they may never stop.

We don't speak on the ride to the funeral home, and I'm glad for the silence. I have nothing to say to him, anyway.

When we get there, the room is nearly empty except for a few of my mother's long-standing clients and a couple ladies I remember from her bowling team. My mother didn't have a lot of friends.

I walk to the front of the room and sit down in one of the brown folding chairs. There is no casket. My mother's wish was always to be cremated, and what remains of her lies encased in a brass urn sitting atop a table in the front of the room. My father sits next to me, and when his leg accidentally brushes mine, I move away as if he's burned me.

I want to tell him this is all his fault, not mine, but it feels useless to pass blame now.

After a few minutes of silence, Dylan walks in and sits beside us. He's wearing jeans and an old Metallica t-shirt. He's obviously hung over or high, and it takes everything in me not to tell him to leave. If he can't at least show a little respect for our mother now, then he shouldn't be here at all.

The funeral director comes in and expresses his deepest sympathies to the family, but there is no real emotion on his face. We are nothing more than a job to him. A duty that must be performed. My mother was no one in this community and no one has come to say goodbye.

But before the man begins the ceremony, the double

doors in the back open. I turn to see Preston, Knox, and Leigh Anne enter the room.

The tears I've been trying so desperately to hold inside all morning come rushing forth at the sight of them. A choked sob escapes my throat, and I stand on shaky legs as Preston throws his arms around me.

I thought it would be easier to do this alone, but I was wrong. I didn't realize how much I needed them here until they walked through those doors.

I lean against him, my tears soaking the black coat of his suit. Leigh Anne puts her hand on my back and whispers something to me. I'm crying too hard to hear her, but I feel her words in the deepest part of my heart.

The funeral director begins to speak, and I leave my father's side. I take a seat on the other side of the aisle, my friends gathered around me as I say goodbye to my mother one last time.

CHAPTER 39
PRESTON

A fter the ceremony, we walk out into the parking lot.

"Thank you for coming," Jenna says, wiping the tears from her cheeks. "I can't believe you drove all this way."

"Sorry we were late," I say. "We took a few wrong turns on the way in."

"It's okay," she says. "It's not like there were a ton of people here, anyway."

The only funeral I've ever been to was my grandfather's when I was seven. I remember the church being so full, there were people standing all along the back. I don't know what I was expecting today, but seeing only a handful of people there to pay their respects to Jenna's mom broke my heart.

"Do you want to get something to eat? Is there anything we can do for you?" Leigh Anne asks. She takes Jenna's hand.

"No, I don't feel like eating," she says. "I don't feel like doing much of anything, to be honest."

"That's understandable," Knox says. He lost his own

mother when he was younger, so out of all of us, he probably understands what she's going through the most. "It's going to take some time for things to feel normal again."

Jenna shakes her head and dabs a tissue at her eyes. "I thought I was done with this place," she says. "Like I'd moved on and moved past it, but the second I pulled into town, it all came rushing back."

Her brother and father walk out of the funeral home. Her brother barely glances our way, heading instead for an old worn out Dodge. He drives away without a second glance. Her father, though, heads right for us.

"Are these some of your fancy college friends?" her dad asks. He's bigger than I imagined him. Tall and fat. I try to picture him throwing a punch at Jenna, and wonder what kind of person beats up on his wife and children.

"Daddy, this is my friend Leigh Anne and her boyfriend Knox. And this is my other friend Preston."

I ignore the hurt of being introduced as a only a friend. "Nice to meet you, sir."

I hold my hand out to him, but he doesn't shake it. There's nothing about this man that's a gentleman, and the way he narrows his eyes at Jenna makes me worried. I feel the overwhelming urge to get her out of here as fast as possible, as if the air around us has turned rancid.

"So I guess you're too good to even sit with your own father during his time of need, huh?"

Jenna swallows, her jaw tensing. "This isn't about you, Daddy," she says.

"Oh, well, excuse me for thinking I had a right to mourn your mother," he says, his face turning red. "If I remember correctly, it wasn't you taking care of her the past few years, was it? No, you made it clear you didn't care about any of us when you left. You should have stayed gone."

I put my hand on Jenna's shoulder and try to walk her toward my car, but she pulls away.

"Taking care of her? Is that what you call it?" she shouts. "You let her drink herself to death, Daddy. That's on you, not me."

"Well, it certainly wasn't you staying up with her all hours of the night, making sure she was still breathing after going on one of her binges," he says.

"No, I got the hell out of your house," Jenna says. "The way Momma should have done years ago. If it wasn't for you, she'd have at least had a chance at happiness."

"You watch your tongue, little girl," he says through clenched teeth. "You always did think you were better than all of us, didn't you? Biding your time until you could leave us in the dust. But don't think I can't see straight through you. You might clean up nice, but underneath it all, you're a whore just like your mother."

Anger like I've never known rips through me, and I step in front of Jenna, shielding her from her father.

"Sir, I think maybe you ought to just head on home now," I say. "It's been an emotional day for everyone."

"I wasn't talking to you," he says, stepping forward until I can smell the sweat pouring off him. "But I bet you know better than anyone how much of a little whore she really is, don't you?"

Jenna puts a hand on my shoulder. "Preston, just walk away," she says. "He's not worth it."

But I can't walk away. Is this the trash Jenna's been dealing with her whole life?

"I feel sorry for you," I say, not backing down an inch. "I feel sorry that you're too blind to see the person she really is. The person she's become in spite of you."

"You have no idea who you're talking to, boy," her father says.

"Oh, I know exactly who you are."

"Preston, please," Jenna says. "Don't do this."

But I am so angry, I can hardly hear her. All I can think of is every mean word that must have come out of this man's mouth when he spoke to his little girl. How he taught her to never trust a man. The thought of him ever putting a hand to her makes me insane with rage.

"Is this how you've been putting yourself through school?" her father asks, his lips snarling up to show decaying teeth. "How many guys like this you got lined up, just waiting for a piece? Cause that's the only way I can figure you made it this far."

"You son of a bitch."

I can't help myself. My hand curls into a tight fist, and I slam it into his face. He's tougher than he looks, because I expect him to fall from a hit that hard. But he doesn't. Instead, he throws a punch straight at me, catching me off guard as my eye explodes in pain. I fall back two steps, my fists ready to fly again, when Knox grabs my arm.

Jenna steps in front of me, pushing me toward the car. "Just go," she says. "I can't believe you would do this, today of all days."

My stomach tightens into knots. "I couldn't stand the way he was talking about you," I say. I wrench my arm from Knox's grasp, but Jenna backs away when I move closer. "You don't deserve that and you know it."

"No, but I don't need you to fix my life for me, Preston," she says, her voice raised. "I don't need you to be some knight in shining armor, come to sweep me off my feet. And I certainly don't need you to go punching my father in the face on the day of my mother's funeral."

I struggle to catch my breath. I look over at her father, his fists still clenched and sweat pouring off his brow. "Jenna, I'm so sorry," I say. "I just—"

"You just need to leave," she says. Tears well up in her eyes and she shakes her head. "There's a McDonalds around the corner. Go get some lunch or something and wait for me there. I'll meet up with you in a little bit."

"Jenna—"

The cold disappointment in her eyes stops my words in my throat. Leigh Anne pats my shoulder and leads me back to the car.

"Just give her some time," she says. "It'll be okay."

But the light is missing from Jenna's eyes, and I'm terrified it will be never be okay again.

CHAPTER 40
JENNA

I ride back to the house with my father, Momma's ashes sitting between us on the seat.

He's furious and sweaty, and if I cared about him at all, I'd be concerned he was getting ready to have a heart attack. His neck is beet red and he can't seem to catch his breath.

There is so much I want to say to him, but I want to grab my things first. I want to be ready to go when I say what I have to say to this man who has taken so much from me over the years.

It only takes a moment to pack my bags. I'd had most of it organized before I drifted off to sleep last night. And as I carry my duffel bag into the living room, I also take the urn with Momma's ashes, cradling it in against my hip like a baby.

"What do you think you're doing with that?" he asks. He's already thrown his cheap tie to the floor and is reclined in his chair, feet up. I have a feeling I'll imagine him like this for the rest of my life, too worthless to even stand and say goodbye to his only daughter.

"I'm taking it with me," I say. "She never had a day of peace in this house, and I think she deserves some now."

He breathes out hard through his nose. "What do I care, right? I only dedicated my entire life to her."

I imagine what it would feel like to loop my hands around his neck and squeeze. "Yeah, you did real good by her. By all of us," I say. "Number one Dad."

"You are such a little piece of shit, you know that?" he says. He presses the bar that holds his feet up and attempts to stand. He's getting so big these days, it takes him a couple tries before he finally gives up and decides to lecture me from below. "You never did appreciate a single thing we sacrificed for you. Your mother, God rest her soul, worked two jobs just to put clothes on your back, and what did you ever do for her except leave?"

"She wouldn't have had to work two jobs if you would have been able to stay in one place for more than a month," I say. "But no, there was always some excuse with you, wasn't there? Always some reason you couldn't pick yourself up and help support your family. My whole life you've sat in that damn chair, telling all of us how worthless we are, but I think you know the truth. You had to keep knocking us down because you were terrified if we ever got out of here, we'd realize just how terrible you really are. Well, I did that Daddy, and I want you to know I see you. Say what you want about me, but I've made something of my life. I'm not going to let you destroy that."

"If you think that boy is going to stick by your side, you're crazier than I thought you were," he says. "He may seem all head-over-heels in love with you now, but there will come a day when he will see you as you truly are. He'll leave you in the dust so fast, it'll make your head spin."

"You're wrong," I say, swiping at the tears rolling down my cheeks. But as hard as I try to shut his words out, they soak into my skin, turning my heart to bitterness.

He cranes his neck around me to get a better view of the TV. I'm tempted to kick the damn thing in with my heels, but I don't. I stand and take one final look at him, realizing nothing I say will ever make a difference to him.

"I'm leaving," I say. "And this time I'm never coming back."

"Go on, then," he says. The first hint of tears well up in his eyes, but he can't seem to find it in him to look at me.

I'm grateful for those tears. For this one moment that shows he's at least still human inside there. That a part of him does love me, even if he has the worst ways of showing it.

I lean over and kiss his forehead. "Goodbye, Daddy."

He doesn't say anything as I turn and walk out the door.

PRESTON, LEIGH ANNE, AND KNOX ARE WAITING FOR ME back at the McDonalds in town. I wave to them through the window, but don't get out of my truck.

I know what's coming, and I don't want to pour my heart out in the middle of all those people.

Preston understands. He leaves the others inside and brings a hot coffee out to me in the truck. His eye is already turning purple from where my father hit him. I don't envy him for how that's going to feel in the morning.

We sit in silence for a moment, sipping our drinks. I feel so drained, I can hardly keep my head up. I want this day to be over. I want to go back to my apartment and sleep for a week.

"Jenna, I'm so sorry about what happened back there," he says. "I couldn't stand to hear him say those things about you."

"I know you were only trying to protect me, but you know to know that with my father, there's no winning. He will never back down, and he will never admit he's wrong," I say. "I kept telling you I wanted to just go. Why didn't you listen to me?"

"All I could hear were the words coming out of his mouth," he says. "Is that what you grew up with? I know you tried to explain it to me before, but Jenna—"

"Don't, okay?" My teeth grind together, and I breathe out through my nose, trying not to cry again. I'm so fed up with tears. I've cried so much the past few days, it feels as if they will carry me away like a wave. "This is why I didn't want you here in the first place. I didn't want you to see me here, because I was terrified you'd realize just how much I don't belong in your world. But maybe it's better you saw this for yourself."

"What are you saying?"

"I'm saying this is who I am, deep down. No matter how far I run, I'm never going to escape this, can't you see that?"

"Jenna, don't let him mess with your head," Preston says. "Why do you care what your father thinks of you? He's a piece of shit who has no idea who you are."

"He's right, though," I say. "I may not be a whore, but I'm not exactly daughter of the year, either. I left her, Preston. I knew she was in trouble. That she was drowning in her own addiction, and when things got too difficult for me, I abandoned her. I left her here with a man I knew was going to keep abusing her day after day. When I walked into my father's house a few days ago, it was so disgusting, I could barely walk through it without stepping on filth."

Tears fill my eyes, and I can no longer hold them back.

"That wasn't my mother. I didn't see a single sign of her left in that house," I say. "That's all my fault, Preston. I put my own life above hers, and now she's gone. She died unhappy and alone, thinking no one in the world cared for her."

"You did what you had to do to survive," he says. "If you had stayed here, what would have happened? You wouldn't have been able to save her, Jenna. She was going to make those same bad choices regardless of anything you said or did. All she would have done is drag you down with her."

"You don't know that," I say. "I could have helped her through rehab. I could have helped her find a good job afterward, encouraged her not to give up."

"You can't blame yourself for her death," he says. He places his hand on top of mine, but I pull away. "Parents are supposed to take care of their children, not the other way around. You got out of there. You survived. I'm sure that meant something to her."

The tears are falling in earnest now, coating my cheeks. My throat is sore from shouting. I just want this to be over.

"Even after four years, I still haven't escaped from this place. Not really," I say. I can hardly find the strength to speak the words, but I know this is the only way I can move on. "You're going to realize that eventually, Preston, even if you don't see it now. I think it's better for both of us if we just stopped pretending this was ever going to work out."

"What? Jenna, it's been a tough day," he says. "Let me drive you back to Fairhope. You're not thinking clearly."

"No, I think I'm finally seeing things the way they truly are for the first time we kissed," I say. "You and me are just not meant to be, Preston."

"I don't understand this," he says. "I know we had an agreement in the beginning. No pressure or expectations. But something changed along the way for me. I'm not willing to let you go this easily."

"You don't have a choice. Can't you see that? Despite what you think, you are not always in control. You don't always know what's best," I say. "Some day you're going to wake up and realize you dodged a bullet here, I promise you."

"Just like that?" he says. "After everything we've been through, you're just going to throw this all away? Why, Jenna? Because you're scared? I'm scared, too. I'm afraid I'm about to lose the best thing that's ever happened to me."

His words pierce through my heart. "I'm no good for you," I say.

"I love you, Jenna," he says.

I look over at him, and his dark brown eyes are filled with tears.

"I love you more than I ever dreamed I could love another person, and I am not going to let you walk away without a fight," he says.

"You don't have to," I say. "I'll walk away for both of us."

"I'm not giving up on us, Jenna," he says. "This can't be how it ends."

He runs a fingertip across my cheek, but I pull away, pressing my body against the door of the truck.

"You think everything's a fairy tale, don't you?" I say. "Not in my life, Preston. This was the only ending we could have ever had."

He sits there for a long moment, but when I don't turn back around, he gets out of the truck When he slams the door behind him, the sound is like a bullet to my heart.

I don't want to lose him, but I don't know how to be with him, either. This is better than waiting for six months or a year down the road when he realizes I'm not good enough for him. That something about me is rotten deep down inside.

After a few minutes, Leigh Anne knocks on the door of the truck and pulls me into her arms. She drives us back to Fairhope, never pushing me or asking me to explain. My head rests on her shoulder most of the way, and every once in a while, she reaches over to squeeze my hand.

CHAPTER 41
PRESTON

I feel as if the bottom of my entire world has fallen out and a deep chasm of nothingness has swallowed me whole.

How did things fall apart so quickly?

I knew our time together was coming to an end, but I had hoped for a miracle. I thought maybe we could outrun her past and build a real future together.

I never dreamed she would shut me out of her life as if our time together meant nothing.

Leigh Anne said to give her space, and she would come around. But I've given her weeks. She won't even pick up the phone. She avoids me on campus and when I've been desperate enough to knock on her door, she turns off the lights and refuses to talk to me.

I feel completely lost without her.

I can't concentrate on my work or my classes. The only thing that brings me any joy is spending time with Penny and little Rachel.

I hold the newborn in my arms and rock her back and forth. "She's beautiful, Penn."

"Isn't she?" she says. "I feel like I could just stare at her forever and never get tired of watching her."

"She's perfect."

"Almost perfect," Penny says with a laugh. "She looks like a complete angel right now, but wait until about seven o'clock tonight. She turns into a screaming monster and nothing I seem to do settles her down. The pediatrician says it's normal for babies to cry, especially in the afternoons, but I'm at my wits end. I'm hardly getting any sleep."

"Do you want to go take a nap for a little while? I can take care of Rachel for a little bit."

"Are you sure?" she asks. "I know you don't have a lot of experience with babies."

"I've got it," I say. "Just show me where the diapers and bottles and stuff are."

She stands and walks over to kiss my forehead. "You are the best brother in the world," she says. "Everything you need to change her is in this little basket here, and there are some bottles in the fridge. Just run some hot water in the sink and run the bottle under it for a few seconds to get it warm."

"Done," I say. "Get some rest."

"You're sure?"

I smile. "Yes, get out of here before I change my mind."

Penny kisses Rachel's head and goes into the back bedroom to sleep.

For the longest time, I sit and stare at this precious baby. I can't help that my thoughts turn to Jenna. If we hadn't broken up, she might have been here right now, helping me take care of her. For a little while, everything was more fun with Jenna around.

It strikes me again how incredible it is that Jenna managed to hold onto her joy after growing up in such a horrible household. My father is controlling, but at least he doesn't constantly put me down or belittle me. My father has always pushed us to succeed and be better. From the sound of it, Jenna's dad only ever told her she was worthless.

My heart aches for her. I want nothing more than to be there for her now, comforting her when she's going through so much. She blames herself for what happened to her mom, and it's not fair.

But if she won't even talk to me, how can I reach out to her?

The doorbell rings and the baby stirs. I gently lay her in the bassinet in the living room and answer the door. No one is there, but a small white box is sitting on the doorstep.

I look around, but see no sign of whoever rang the doorbell.

I don't mean to open it, sure that it was intended for either Penny or Mason, but the top isn't completely closed and something inside catches my eye. A purple butterfly made of delicate paper. I inhale and hold my breath as I open the box. More than a hundred hand made butterflies in various shades of gray and purple lie nestled in tissue paper.

Jenna had said she wanted to do something special for Penny, and I know without a doubt this is her gift to my sister.

I take one of the butterflies from the box and accidentally bend its wings. Tears sting the corners of my eyes.

It strikes me now that sometimes the harder you try to hold onto something, the more likely are to lose it forever.

I straighten the wing and set the paper butterfly back in the tissue paper.

I'll give her all the time she needs now and pray that someday she'll find her way back to me.

CHAPTER 42
JENNA

There are only a few weeks until graduation, but I can't seem to force any excitement through my veins. This is what I have been working for—the thing so many said I could never do—and yet I can't celebrate. Instead of a new beginning, it feels like a death sentence.

Everything I have built over the past four years is slipping through my fingertips. My friendships. My job. My identity as a student.

I keep my eyes open for jobs here in Fairhope, but the only things posted are with the Wright Corporation. There's no way I can to bring myself to apply for a job working for Preston's family. With him taking over more and more of the responsibilities of the office, I would be bound to run into him from time to time, and it would break my heart to see him so often.

I know my only real choice for a future is to leave

Fairhope. To start over and try to build something more stable for myself in a new city.

A week before graduation, my first real job offer comes in, and it's more than I could have hoped for. It's for a sales position in Nashville. It will mean long hours and a lot of travel, but the money is beyond good for a girl like me. And Nashville is supposed to be a fun city, right? I could learn to love it there, as long as I don't let anyone get too close.

The biggest catch is that the job starts June 1st. No exceptions.

June is only one month away, but the real issue is that the trial against Burke Redfield in Boston starts only two weeks before the beginning June. There's no way to know whether they'll be finished by then or not, and more importantly, how long it will take the jury to come to a decision.

I really want to be there for Leigh Anne when the verdict is read.

I make a call to the company and tell them about the trial, but the man on the phone apologizes. This is the last training session for six months. If I can't make it, I'll have to wait another six months and see if another position opens up.

"We value dedication, Ms. Lewis," Mr. Hanover says. "Prove to us you're one hundred percent dedicated to this position, and I can promise you, you'll be rewarded. Our company provides some of the best benefits around for entry-level sales reps. A company car, cell phone, and even a discount on rent in one of the most sought-after apartment properties in downtown Nashville. We only choose the best candidates possible, so we hope you'll be able to make it. We'd love to have an answer by the end of the week."

I thank him and hang up. There have been other job offers, but nothing has been as promising as this. The base salary alone is higher than many others, not to mention the potential for huge commissions.

I have never wanted to be a sales person, but after my mother's death, I realize now more than ever how important it is to be practical. Following your heart only leads to trouble.

But missing this trial is not an option. Leigh Anne has been there for me every step of the way over the past year. I want to see this through with her.

I'll just have to hope the trial is over in time for me to make the drive to Nashville. Somehow, it will work out.

And yet, I don't call the man back for five days. Every time I pick up the phone, something stops me. I don't know if it's the thought of having to start over or the thought of leaving everyone behind, but I feel like I'm waiting for some kind of sign that this is the right thing.

On my last day to decide, I run into Preston for the first time since we broke up.

It catches me so completely off guard, I don't even have time to turn and hide or pretend I didn't see him.

One minute I am heading to the coffee shop to grab my morning coffee, and the next I'm standing face to face with the first guy who ever said he loves me.

"Jenna. I've been trying to call," he says. He places his hands awkwardly in his pockets and shifts his weight. His skin is pale, as if he's been avoiding the sun lately.

"I know," I say. "I just think it's better if we don't argue about it when we both know nothing is going to change."

"It isn't?" he asks, his eyes so full of sorrow.

I shake my head and look away. "Not for me it isn't," I say. "I never meant to hurt you, Preston, but..."

My voice trails off and I shrug. I don't even know what to say to him anymore. I have to learn to let go of whatever it is I feel for him. Love. Lust. Friendship. If I'm truly going to start over, I have to move on from those emotions and focus on what's really important.

"I have to go," I say, and turn around.

"Wait." He grabs my arm and the touch of his skin against mine brings tears to my eyes. I miss him more than I'm willing to admit. "I just want you to know that I'm here for you," he says. "Not to try to fix anything or change you. Just to listen or whatever you need, okay? Even if you don't want to be with me, I haven't given up on you. If you need me, I'm here for you."

I nod and swipe at the gathering tears on my eyelid. "Thanks," I say. "I'll see you around."

I rush around the corner and press my head to the rough brick of the wall, letting the tears flow. When I've recovered enough to talk again, I make the call.

"Mr. Hanover? This is Jenna Lewis," I say. "I've decided to accept the sales position."

CHAPTER 43
JENNA

G raduation day comes and goes without any celebrations.

Penny is busy with the baby, and Leigh Anne and Knox have already left for Boston. I miss Preston, but I know reaching out to him will only make things worse.

I decide to spend the afternoon after the ceremony packing up my apartment instead.

I tape a new box together and start the process of sorting through my things. The artwork is the hardest to pack. I don't have the money to buy fancy packing materials, but I also don't want anything to be damaged on the trip. I do my best to wrap my books and sculptures in tissue paper before nestling them together in the box.

When the art is put away, I start on the kitchen. By the end of the evening, most of my apartment is packed and ready to go. The only things that sit out on the bar in the kitchen are my diploma and the urn that holds my mother's ashes.

I walk over and take the paper in my hands, running my fingertips across the raised letters.

My mother would have been so proud of me. She may not have admitted it, but I know she would have been. She'd always wanted me to go to college, saying I could make a better life for myself than she ever did. It's hard to believe I've actually done it. Summa Cum Laude. An honor graduate from a real university.

I suddenly feel very lonely, the thought of leaving wearing so heavy on my hard, I'm afraid it will kill me.

I decide to go to the one place that has been my constant since I moved here.

Brantley's is still busy with families and students celebrating the big day, and my spirit lifts when I walk in. Maria is standing by the hostess stand and gathers me up in her big arms.

"I was hoping you would stop by tonight," she says. "I missed seeing you today at graduation, but I was there, cheering you on when you crossed that stage. I'm so proud of you, girl."

"Thank you," I say, hugging her back. "Is it okay if I hang out at the bar for a little while?"

It's against restaurant policy for employees to drink at the bar, but I already had my last night of work this past week.

"Of course," she says. "You don't actually work here anymore. Might as well enjoy yourself."

"Thanks, Maria."

"I always knew I was going to lose you someday," she says, gently brushing my hair out of my eyes. It's the most tender move she's ever made toward me, and it touches my heart. "I'll be sad to see you go, but man, I loved having you for as long as I did."

"Don't get all sappy on me now," I tease.

She rolls her eyes and pushes me toward the bar.

I laugh and take a seat toward one end. Colton's busy, but I'm glad he's the one working tonight. He comes over as soon as he can and leans against the top of the bar.

"Well, well, if isn't our little graduate," he says, a slow smile spreading across his face. "Can I get you something to drink?"

"Champagne?"

"Champagne and strawberries," he says. "Coming right up."

He brings the drink over with a plate full of freshly cut strawberries dipped in chocolate. It's my favorite dessert on the menu.

"Thank you," I say.

"How come you aren't out celebrating?" he asks. "I thought you'd be living it up downtown by now."

I shrug and take a sip of the champagne. It's cold and sweet. The bubbles tickle my throat on the way down. "I haven't felt like celebrating much, lately, I guess."

"I never did tell you how sorry I was to hear about your mom," he says. "Were you close?"

"Sometimes," I say, and leave it at that.

"We're going to really miss you around here," he says.

"Have you given any more thought to that job over at Rob's?" I ask. "You'd do well there, I think."

"I don't know," he says. "I hate to walk out on Maria."

"She's seen a lot more employees walk in and out of those

doors than the two of us," I say. "She's survived this long. I think she'll be okay."

"I don't mean to pry, but what ever happened between you and Preston?" Colton asks, resting his chin on his hand. It's as if he read my mind. "I don't mean to pry, but I figured he'd be whisking you off to some exotic location right after graduation."

"He never belonged with a girl like me," I say. I down the champagne and he fills the glass again. I take a bite of strawberry and sigh.

"Any man would be lucky to have someone like you. I know it sounds weird coming from me, but I'm real sorry to hear things didn't work out between you two," he says. "There was just something about you that fit, you know? I would give anything to have a girl's eyes light up when she looked me the way yours did when you were together."

Did my eyes light up when I was with Preston?

I miss him so much, my heart hurts.

Colton excuses himself to wait on a pretty brunette who has taken the seat two down from mine.

I study her with her designer bag and perfectly manicured nails. Not a hair out of place. That's the kind of girl Preston belongs with, I think sadly.

I push the plate of strawberries away. I've suddenly lost my appetite.

CHAPTER 44
JENNA

Testimony in the trial against Burke Redfield begins on a Wednesday.

With five victims to testify, there is no way to know how long the trial might last, but I want to be up there for as long as I can to support my friend.

Penny and Preston's father arranged the rental of two houses in a gated neighborhood near the courthouse as a place for Leigh Anne's friends and family can stay. They even offered to fly us all up to Boston in their private jet, but I need to have my truck with me in case the trial runs long, and I have to leave to get to my job in time. All my things are already packed and loaded into the back.

With Leigh Anne scheduled to give her testimony third in line, I begin my drive on Wednesday afternoon, hoping they won't get to her testimony until at least Thursday. There are tears in my eyes as I drive away from Fairhope. My first time leaving the state I was born in, but I'm alone with no one to notice or care. It's as if all joy has been sucked from life, leaving only a withered shell of who I thought I had become since moving to Fairhope.

I arrive at the house Wednesday at nine in the evening.

"It's just hard to believe it's really here," Leigh Anne says. Everyone else has already had dinner, but Leigh Anne saved a plate for me. I eat as we sit at a table by the pool. "After all this preparation and media attention, it comes down to this."

"Are you nervous about tomorrow?" I ask. It's a stupid question, though. It would be impossible not to be nervous.

"I'm terrified," she says. "Sometimes having to go through the story over and over again is hard enough, but tomorrow, I have to talk about all those horrible things he did to me while he's sitting right there, denying it. I'm afraid it will feel like going through it all over again. I wish I didn't have to see him."

"How did things go today?"

"I wasn't allowed to be in there while the other testimonies were being given, but everyone said it went exactly as expected," she says. "The defense is trying to make a case that the five of us somehow planned our testimonies as a way to get media attention. It's ridiculous."

"It's all just part of the game," I say. "But the important thing is that the truth is finally coming out. After this, everyone will know the truth about him."

"I hope so," she says. She reaches over to take my hand. "Thank you for coming up here. It means a lot to me."

"I'm glad to be here," I say. "I just wish you didn't have to go through this at all."

In the morning, we all gather in the courtroom and listen to Leigh Anne's testimony. I am struck by her strength, not sure I'd be able to do what she's doing if this had happened to me. All those eyes on her, judging every word. Every choice.

And Burke Redfield in his expensive suit with his high-dollar attorneys, acting like this is all some big annoyance. Nothing to be taken seriously.

The courtroom is completely silent as she tells her story of the night she was raped. Her voice only wavers once, and somehow, she manages to get through it.

When she's finished and the cross examination is over, the judge calls for a break and all of us walk over to a little diner around the corner for lunch. I avoid Preston's eyes, and he seems to understand that this has nothing at all to do with us. We are all here for Leigh Anne, and nothing else matters.

The next full day of testimony passes quickly, and when the weekend comes, we take a break from the stress and worry of the trial by binge watching TV shows on Netflix. I'm thankful Preston keeps his distance, but there's a tension between us I can't deny.

I wish I could lean on him. Be with him and talk to him about how hard this is on all of us, but there's no use opening that door now, when I'll be leaving for Nashville in a week.

Leigh Anne is holding up amazingly well. She spends a lot of time alone in her room with Knox or snuggling with Penny's baby, but she never falls apart or loses her focus. I wish I could be more like her and find such strength in the hard times.

The following Wednesday morning, the state rests their case and the jury goes into deliberations.

In the house that evening, everything is quiet and tense, as if we're all holding our breath.

Penny, Leigh Anne, and I are sitting in Penny's bedroom. We try not to talk about the trial, doing everything we can to keep Leigh Anne's mind off the wait. It could be a day or a week, and there's no way to know what the result will be.

"You're really moving away from us?" Penny asks. She's nursing baby Rachel and the beauty of it makes my heart hurt.

I have never been one to think much about babies and having a family of my own, but my time with Preston awakened something inside me that I can't seem to shut off. What would it be like to love someone so much, you wanted to spend your whole life with them? What would it be like to someday hold a sweet newborn baby of my own?

Would I be a good mother? Or would I repeat her mistakes?

I swallow and look down at my hands. "It was the kind of offer I couldn't refuse," I say. "It's not too far away, though. I'll come visit all the time."

"Nashville is an eight hour drive from Fairhope," Leigh Anne says. "I wish you were staying a little closer. I want you to be happy, but I hate that you're moving away so quickly. You're starting next week?"

"Yep," I say, hardly believing it myself. "I've already moved out, so I'll be leaving from here. I still need to find a place in Nashville, but they said they'll have temporary housing set up for me for a few weeks until I get settled."

"I can't believe how fast this is all happening," Leigh Anne says. She brings her hand to her mouth and looks away. Her shoulders are shaking.

I move next to her on the bed and wrap my arms around

her. "I'm so sorry," I say. "I feel like I'm abandoning you when you need me the most."

It seems to be a theme in my life. Run away when things get hard.

She turns and throws her arms around me, and I hold her as she cries. Tears sting my eyes and fall down my cheeks. She's been such a rock throughout this whole process, but I think it's finally hitting her that it's all coming to an end.

When Leigh Anne pulls away, her eyes are red and puffy. "I'll be okay," she says. "It's just an emotional week. I'm happy for you, Jenna. I know this is a big opportunity for you."

Penny finishes nursing Rachel and comes to sit beside us on the bed, her sleeping baby swaddled tightly in a white blanket with dragonflies embroidered on it. "I don't want you to go, either," she says. "And I bet I know someone else who is going to miss you more than both of us combined."

I close my eyes and wipe the tears from my cheeks. "Preston and I were never going to end up together, and we all know it," I say. "It was better for both of us to part ways before things got too serious."

"Jenna." Penny's voice is soft and motherly. I look up to see her gently rocking the baby from side-to-side. Her eyes meet mine. "Things were already serious. At least for him. Why are you really leaving?"

I stand and run a hand through my hair. I don't know whether I'm angry or sad. Or both. Friends are supposed to be supportive about your decisions, right? Why are they giving me such a hard time about this? I already feel like I'm standing on such shaky ground, I could fall at any moment.

Leigh Anne stands and moves behind me. She puts a

hand on my shoulder. "If this is what you really want, we're one-hundred-percent behind you," she says softly. "But I think what Penny is trying to say is that we hope you're leaving for the right reasons, and not running away from something just because you're scared."

I shrug her hand from my shoulder and move away. "I love you guys, but this is so not what I need right now," I say. "I need to get some air."

"Jenna," Leigh Anne starts, but I'm already out the door.

By the time I make my way down two flights of stairs, down the hallway, and out the back door, tears are flowing freely down my face and stifled sobs are making knots in my stomach. I run over to the pool and collapse at the edge of the water, thankful the lights are turned off so no one can see me.

It's quiet out here except for the sound of the occasional car passing by in the neighborhood, so I hold my hand over my mouth as I cry. My breath comes in short bursts, as if someone is tightening a belt around my lungs. I try to calm myself, but an overwhelming sadness has taken over, and I can't control myself.

I thought I was at peace with my decision. I was certain this was the right thing for me, but when they started questioning me, it felt like my heart was being ripped out of my chest.

Not because they doubt me, but because they are right.

I do not want to spend the rest of my life working some sales job in Nashville, Tennessee. I know going into it that the hours for these first few years are going to be hell. Sixty to seventy hours a week, some of it on the road doing crappy cold call sales and boring business meetings. This isn't me. This isn't what I want out of life.

When I moved to Fairhope, I was running toward a new life. I was full of hope and determined to make something of myself.

Thinking I was leaving for the same reason was just be being blind to reality.

I decided to leave Fairhope because I'm afraid to let go and allow myself to be happy. I'm so scared of getting hurt that I pushed away the one person who would never hurt me.

EXHAUSTED, I GO TO SCRAPE MYSELF OFF THE CONCRETE when I hear footsteps behind me.

Leigh Anne is standing there, her face barely visible in the darkness. She has a light sweater wrapped around her in the unusually cool spring air. "Can I sit down?" she asks.

"Of course." I wipe my face on my t-shirt, snot and all. "Sorry, that was what they call an ugly cry."

She sits at the edge of the pool and dangles her feet in the water. "So glad this pool is heated," she says. "It's cool out here, but this feels perfect. You should try it."

I rearrange myself on the concrete and let my feet fall into the water. She's right. It's amazing, but the thought of a heated pool brings a rush of memories. Preston was nothing but patient and loving toward me, and I threw it all away like it meant nothing.

"Are you okay?" she asks.

"I can't even believe you're out here asking me that when you're the one going through so much right now," I say. "I'm so sorry I walked out. I came here to support you, not get into an argument. Especially tonight."

"We deserved it," she says. "I know we were pushing you too hard, but it's difficult to think about you leaving all of a sudden. It's so unexpected. We just want you to be sure it's what you really want."

"I know," I say. "I thought it was."

"And now?"

I shrug. "I don't know where I belong," I say. "I've never had friends who actually cared so much about what happens to me. I don't want to lose you guys, but at the same time, I'm so scared of what will happen if I stay."

"There are jobs in Fairhope, too."

"Working for the Wrights?" I say with a laugh. "I don't think that will work."

"There are plenty of other jobs," she says. "How many did you apply for in town?"

"None," I say. "I didn't see anything that made me feel excited."

"What about the job in Nashville? Are you excited about that?"

"Sales? Traveling and working seventy hours a week?" I say with a sigh. "It sounds like torture."

"I don't understand," she says. "Why take the job and leave everyone behind? I wish you'd open up and tell us what's really bothering you."

I kick my feet slowly in the water, letting the heat of it flow across my skin. I don't even know where to begin. I've kept so much from all of them. Preston's the only one who knows about my family and my past. "I'm terrified things won't work out for us, and that it will hurt so bad, I'll never get over it."

"So you'd rather leave and be miserable?" she laughs and bumps her shoulder against mine.

I smile. "It sounds dumb, doesn't it?"

"What's going on between you and Preston?" she asks. "I know you said you didn't want to talk about it, but if something happened between you guys and that's the reason you're leaving, it might help to get it out. Is this still about what happened with your dad?"

My stomach twists. "Is this really what you want to talk about right now?" I ask. "Talking about my small problems seems really selfish right now."

She shrugs. "It's good. I need something to take my mind off the trial now that the jury is out," she says. "We don't know if it will be tomorrow or next week before they come back with a decision. I'm afraid if I don't have something to focus on, I'll go insane."

I reach over and take her hand. "You've been such a good friend to me," I say. "I don't know what I'd do without you."

"I feel the same way," she says. She squeezes my hand and lays her head against my shoulder. "You helped me through some of my darkest times. If I can help you with whatever you're going through, even if it's just to talk through it and decide that leaving is the right thing, I want to be here for you."

"I'm in love with him," I say, feeling the tears constricting my throat again. "It feels like the least likely thing in the world to ever happen to someone like me, but I am."

"Have you told him that?"

I shake my head and silent tears fall down my cheeks. If I

keep crying like this, I'm going to be severely dehydrated in the morning. I feel like all I've done for weeks is cry. "No, I'm an idiot," I say. "I was too scared to tell him what I was really feeling, so I told him it was over between us. I thought if I ended things now, I would never have to deal with the pain of him rejecting me."

"Hiding your true feelings never makes it easier," she says.

"I think I know that now, but I have no idea how to untangle this mess," I say. "I've already accepted the job in Tennessee. They're expecting me in a few days. Besides, I can't stay in Fairhope for Preston. What if things don't work out between us? I mean, how could they possibly work out? Just look at his family. They don't want him to be with someone like me."

"It doesn't matter what his family wants," she says. "It matters what he wants. Look at me and Knox. I almost lost him because I was too afraid of what my mother thought. I would have regretted that for the rest of my life. I'm done with regrets."

Her voice is laced with sadness.

"How are you really holding up with all this?" I ask.

"Going back through what happened was the worst part," she says. "Having to sit in that courtroom full of people and talk about that night was like reliving it with an audience. And he just sat there with that smug look on his face the whole time."

"I hope they come back with a guilty verdict fast and wipe that smug look right off his face," I say.

"Even if they don't, I know I did the right thing for me," she says. "I have carried so much guilt about keeping it a secret for as long as I did. He was free to rape other women while I sat there, knowing what he was the whole time, and doing nothing about it. Telling the truth has been harder than I could ever have imagined, but at least the truth is out there now. No matter what happens with the verdict, people know what he is now and what he's capable of doing. That's enough for me."

"You are the bravest person I know," I say softly.

"I thought you said I was a marshmallow," she says, a slow smile spreading across her face.

"A brave marshmallow," I say. I pull her into my arms and hug her so hard.

"Don't stay in Fairhope for Preston," she says when we finally pull apart. "Stay for you, Jenna. Figure out what you want most and go for it, no matter how scary it may seem. You take it one day at a time and you build the life of your dreams. You're going to make mistakes and you're going to get your heart broken along the way, but that's what living is all about. Nothing is ever guaranteed in this life, but running away from something because you're afraid it might not end the way you want it to only leads to regrets. You have to learn to let go of that fear and take a risk. A leap of faith. What you find might surprise you."

I squeeze her hand again and we sit together for a long time, kicking our feet against the warm water, and wondering what tomorrow might bring.

CHAPTER 45
JENNA

The courtroom is freezing. They have the air conditioning turned up even though it's only eighty degrees outside. I am late getting here, because I overslept and almost missed the text from Penny that the verdict had come in overnight.

I have no idea whether a fast verdict is good news or bad news, but my stomach is tangled up in knots.

The seats are packed and people are standing in rows along the back, taking up every spare inch of this place. I see my friends sitting a few rows behind the victims and rush to join them right as the judge enters and everyone stands. Preston is at the end of the row and our eyes meet as I squeeze in next to him.

Fear and anticipation hangs thick in the air around us, and I shiver. My arm brushes against Preston's, and he leans toward me. I feel sick with worry, every muscle in my body tense.

At my side, Preston's hand touches mine. I link my

pinky with his and take a deep breath. It's the first time we've touched in weeks. Our first real connection. But he is my anchor against the waves of doubt and fear lapping at my heart. We are told to sit and the entire crowd of reporters, family, and friends sits down. Not a word is spoken.

I glance at Preston and he meets my gaze, fear reflected in each other's souls. He threads his fingers through mine, and we cling to each other as the jury files in.

I'm so nervous, I can barely hear. My ears are ringing and my heartbeat thunders through me.

"Has the jury reached a verdict?" the judge asks, his commanding voice confident and strong over the silence.

"We have, Your Honor."

The bailiff walks over to the foreman, who hands him a slip of folded paper. The judge glances at it, nods, and hands it back.

"Will the defendant please rise and face the jury?" the judge intones.

Burke Redfield stands. He straightens his collar and tugs on the bottom of his tailored suit jacket, the first sign of nerves he's shown since the trial began over a week ago.

All five victims sitting on the front row—including Leigh Anne—are huddled close, shoulder-to-shoulder.

I study the faces of the jurors as they look at him, trying to get some idea of their decision from the expressions on their faces, but I can't read them at all. I can hardly breathe, my lungs locked up and shallow, as if I'm sipping air through a tiny straw. I cling to Preston's hand like a lifeboat.

Time is moving in slow motion as the foreman unfolds the slip of paper and clears his throat.

"On the first charge of rape, we the jury find the defendant, Burke Redfield, guilty."

Tears sting my eyes at the word, and I exhale. Whispers shudder through the courtroom.

"On the second charge of rape, we the jury find the defendant guilty."

The foreman continues to read each individual charge—a total of seven counts of rape and indecent assault—and with each guilty verdict, a feeling of gratitude ripples through me. A few rows in front of us, Leigh Anne has her arm around one of the other women, their heads close together and their shoulders shaking with tears.

We wait as the judge and jury go through the rest of the procedure, and as soon as we are dismissed, Preston stands and pulls me into his arms. People begin filing out of the courtroom, some bumping against us as they race to leave, but all I can do is search for my friend in the crowd.

Leigh Anne comes to us, her face streaked with tears. There are no words strong enough to express what we are feeling. Instead, the group of friends who have come to stand at her side—Preston, Mason, Penny, Knox, Jo, and myself—surround her and pull her into a hug.

In that moment, I know in the deepest part of myself that this is what family is all about. Whether it's by blood or by choice, there are some people who leave a mark on your soul forever. You care about them enough to tell them when they're making bad decisions, and you stand beside them even when times get rough.

You love them, even when you're terrified that losing them will break your heart.

CHAPTER 46
PRESTON

I look for Jenna after everything settles down. Being there for the reading of the verdict today made me realize just how much I can't stand to lose her. I wanted to give her time, but I have to let her know how I feel before she leaves for her new job.

I go to her room at the house we've rented, but her things are gone. My heart plummets into my stomach. Please don't let her have left.

I race down the stairs to the garage where she's been parking her truck, but there's no sign of her.

Most of our group is gathered in the kitchen eating lunch. I pull Penny to the side.

"Have you seen Jenna?" I ask, my heart beating so fast. I'm so terrified she's left for her job in Nashville already, and that it's too late to make things right between us.

"Did you check her room?"

"Her things are gone," I say. "I don't see her truck, either."

"I think she parked out front," Knox says, overhearing our conversation. "I heard her say she was going to step outside to make a phone call."

I'm out of breath when I reach the pool and see her standing near the gazebo, her phone pressed to her ear.

When she sees me, she stops for a moment, her lips parted slightly. She turns away, and I wait for her to finish her conversation before walking over to her.

I have never been so nervous in my life. I know that she may tell me she doesn't feel the same way or that she's not willing to stay in Fairhope, but I have to at least tell her what's in my heart. I have to make sure she knows.

"I was afraid you'd already left," I say as I step onto the gazebo.

"I had planned to leave today," she says. "I had my bags already packed in the truck. I need to leave this afternoon to have any chance of making it to Nashville on time for my training."

"Don't go," I say. She opens her mouth to speak, but I stop her. "Before you say anything, please just hear me out."

Her eyes fill with tears, but she stays silent.

"I have been lost without you these past few weeks," I say. "I know that when we first started going out, we thought it was just for fun. Just for a while. But I never expected to fall so hard. Jenna, I know I can't even begin to understand what you've been through. I know losing your mother and having to face your past was difficult for you, but I can't let you go without telling you how much I love you. How much I need you. You still see yourself through their eyes, like you're worthless, but I know the truth. Jenna, I see you better than you see yourself. In the past few months, you have taught me more about strength and courage than anyone ever has.

"I know it won't always be easy, and it will mean facing the demons of your past, but I'm asking you to believe in me. To trust that sometimes love can heal, not destroy. To stop thinking about what happens when this ends, and finally open yourself up to the possibility that maybe what we have could last a lifetime."

She closes her eyes and tears run down her cheeks. My heart is pounding, and I'm so terrified she's going to walk away from me. That I'm going to lose her again.

"Jenna, I'll do anything—"

"I'm not going," she says, so softly I'm afraid I didn't hear her right.

"What?"

"I said I'm not going to Nashville," she says. She smiles through her tears. "That's what I was trying to tell you before you stopped me. I just got off the phone with them. I told them I'd changed my mind."

"You're staying in Fairhope?" I can hardly breathe. I'm afraid to let myself hope this could be true.

"I'm staying," she says. "Today in that courtroom, I realized my whole family is in Fairhope. Everyone and everything I love, Preston. Including you. You're right. I was so scared of how it would feel to lose you that I pushed you away before you got the chance to hurt me. I never expected to fall in love with you, either, but when it happened, it terrified me. I thought that once you realized the truth about my past and saw it with your own eyes, it would turn you against me. But what I realized today is that the being without you is more pain than I can bear, and the only thing

I would regret more than a broken heart is walking away from you."

I pull her into my arms, crushing her to me. My eyes fill with tears of relief and my heart overflows with love.

"There is already too much pain in this world without me bringing it upon myself," she says, her tears soaking into my shirt. "My whole life, I never learned to hope for anything more. I thought love was a fairy tale meant for princesses and storybook characters. I never dreamed it could happen to me."

"You deserve it more than anyone I know," I say. I draw her into a kiss. "If it takes me a hundred years to prove it to you, I'm going to show you that sometimes, people do get to live happily ever after."

EPILOGUE

JENNA

The whole crew is gathered at Rob's to celebrate Penny and Mason's wedding.

Much to her mother's horror, Penny chose a small poolside ceremony with only close friends and relatives. It was a breathtaking fall wedding with the kind of weather brides dream of. The brilliant golds and reds of the leaves on the maple trees behind their house were a perfect compliment to the shining bride, who held her five month old child in her arms as she exchanged her vows.

Knox closed down the bar for the reception, and we are all gathered around the small stage as Mason sings a song he wrote for his bride, a guitar cradled in his arms. It's a moment I will never forget, surrounded by the kind of family I thought I would never have.

Preston puts his arms around me and we sway together, our cheeks pressed tightly together as he whispers his love to me.

I remember our first dance on this floor last March, when every touch of his hands felt so dangerous, yet so right. I could never have dreamed that life would bring us to this moment, our hearts fully open to each other.

His parents have been more accepting of our relationship than I ever thought they would. Preston says that for all their pushing, they really do just want him to be happy.

His father has even agreed to give him a couple years off work for us to travel the world once he graduates in the spring. We've only just started planning where we want to go, but our first trip begins tomorrow. Two weeks in Tibet for Fall break.

I'm so nervous and excited about leaving the country for the first time, I'm sure I'll hardly be able to sleep tonight.

This has been a year of firsts for me. First love. First time leaving my home state. And at Penny's urging, first time opening my own store on Etsy. She's been helping me organize the business side while I've been working on fun and creative artwork to sell. Right now, it's mostly sculptures and small items for decorating nurseries, but the orders are already pouring in so fast I can hardly keep up with demand. With my friends beside me, cheering me on, the possibilities of what I can achieve seem endless.

When the song ends, Preston and I go to the bar for a glass of champagne. Colton winks and pours two glasses. He finally left Brantley's and took Jo up on her offer to work at Rob's. As the two of them work together behind the bar, I think I see the tiniest sparkle in Jo's eyes when she looks at him. I wonder if there's something brewing between them.

Preston squeezes my hand and kisses my cheek. "I'll be back in a second," he says.

He goes to the stage and holds up his glass. All around the room, our friends and family turn, their faces toward the happy couple beside Preston.

Leigh Anne comes to stand beside me, our matching lavender dresses shimmering in the light. She takes my hand, and I hold tightly to her. She's a new person since the trial. The fear in her eyes has been replaced with hope. Burke was sentenced to eight years in prison. It's not a harsh enough punishment for a guy like him, but at least the world knows what he did.

I know she will bear the scar of what happened to her for the rest of her life, but I hope now she has found some peace.

"As the best man and brother of the bride, I'd like to make a toast," Preston says. "To love. Sometimes, it can take years before you realize it's been standing right in front of you the whole time. Sometimes, it finds you when you least expect it. Love can be wonderful. Love can be terrifying. But when it's right, it's worth risking everything you have to hold onto it. Here's to Penny and Mason and baby Rachel. I wish you a lifetime of love beyond your wildest dreams."

"Here, here," Preston's father says, raising his glass.

We celebrate into the night, only getting a few hours of sleep until we board the plane. It has taken Preston weeks to obtain all the certificates and visas for me to bring my mother's ashes with me overseas, but the day is finally here.

We travel first to Shanghai, and then fly from there to Lhasa, Tibet. With only one night of rest, we dress warmly and trek into the Himalayan mountains until we find a spot that feels right.

The land here is so beautiful, it takes my breath away.

Snow-covered peaks surround us on every side. The architecture of the city itself is striking and so different from anything I've ever known. I want to drink it all in with my eyes and send it straight to my soul.

After a while, we find a quiet spot in the mountains beside a lake. Preston rests his arm across my shoulder as I say goodbye to my mother one last time.

"I know you made mistakes in your life, Momma. I blamed you for your choices and your decisions my whole life. It's only now that I see you were so afraid to leave my father and stand on your own that it paralyzed you. Your fear of just letting go and learning to trust yourself for a little while kept you from ever really finding happiness," I say. Cold wind stings my cheeks as a tear falls from my eye. "I hope that now, wherever you are, you have found peace."

I spread her ashes around the edge of the lake, watching as they settle on the water and the grass. I cannot imagine a more peaceful place to lay to her to rest.

I place the empty urn in my backpack and in time, we turn and walk further up the mountainside. My legs burn and the air becomes harder to breathe, but just when I think I can't take another step, the view opens up, revealing the entire city below us and the expanse of mountains behind.

I am struck by its beauty, unable to speak. I take Preston's hand and lean against him, feeling in this moment that the whole world has suddenly opened up to us.

I realize suddenly that our journey up the mountain is like life. Sometimes it is so difficult you think you can't possibly go on. Sometimes the fear of falling paralyzes you and makes you want to give up.

But if you never take those risks and you never learn to let go of your fear, you just might miss the moments that take your breath away.

ABOUT THE AUTHOR

Sarra Cannon is the author of several series featuring young adult and college-aged characters, including the bestselling Shadow Demons Saga. Her novels often stem from her own experiences growing up in the small town of Hawkinsville, Georgia, where she learned that being popular always comes at a price and relationships are rarely as simple as they seem.

Sarra owns her own publishing company and has sold three-quarters of a million copies of her books. She currently lives in Charleston, South Carolina with her programmer husband, her adorable redheaded son, and her beautiful daughter.

Love Sarra's books? Join Sarra's Mailing List to be notified of new releases and giveaways!

Also, please come hang out with me in my Facebook Fan Group: Sarra Cannon's Coven. We have a lot of fun in there, and I often share exclusive short stories and teasers in the group.

Want more? Come join us LIVE three times a week on my YouTube channel.

Connect With Sarra Online:

www.sarracannon.com